Love Finds You
in
HUMBLE
TEXAS

Lamentations 3:25 - 26 · 27

The LORD is good unto them that wait for Him, to the soul that seeketh Him.

It is good for a man that he bear the yoke in his youth. vs 27

It is good that a man should vs 26 both HOPE and QUIETLY wait for the Salvation of the LORD.

Love Finds You
in
HUMBLE
TEXAS

BY ANITA HIGMAN

summerside
PRESS

Cover and Interior Design by Müllerhaus Publishing Group
www.mullerhaus.net

Published by Summerside Press, Inc., 11024 Quebec Circle, Bloomington, Minnesota 55438 | **www.summersidepress.com**

Fall in love with Summerside.

Printed in the USA.

Dedication
....

To my agent,
Chip MacGregor.
Thank you for your expertise, your encouragement,
your prayers, and your friendship.
It has made all the difference.

Acknowledgements
....

Much gratitude goes to Pat Durham
for her help in understanding the life of an image coach.

Great appreciation is extended to Lilibeth Andre, who answered a
myriad of questions about the world of art.

And many thanks go to Carolyn McCarty for her hospitality in escorting
me around the fine city of Humble.

Any errors in the text are solely the fault of the author.

"Humility, that low, sweet root,
From which all heavenly virtues shoot."
Thomas More

HUMBLE, TEXAS, WAS NAMED FOR ONE OF ITS FOUNDERS, Pleasant Smith Humble (pronounced "umble"), who settled in the area with his family sometime before 1889. Pleasant was a prosperous wildcatter as well as a storekeeper and fisherman. He also became justice of the peace and started the first post office out of his own home. In the early 1900s Humble became an oil boomtown, and even though the yield has decreased since then, its oil fields are still producing. Today Humble has more than 14,000 residents and is a vibrant and growing city with friendly people, great restaurants, quaint antique stores, a downtown historic district, and the beautiful Mercer Arboretum and Botanic Gardens. Humble, Texas, reflects the qualities of its namesake, being not only a pleasant place to visit, but also a great place to call home.

Anita Higman

Chapter One

....

Trudie Abernathy always wondered about two things. First, how was it that some people could live charmed lives while others accumulated troubles like those beetles that spent their time rolling up balls of dung? And secondly, how could one person fall in love as effortlessly as a sneeze, while another hobbled along on love as if it were a twisted ankle?

I am the dung beetle. Trudie smiled over at her sister, who sat across from her in the limo. Lane Abernathy was the one who lived the breezy life. Lane was an image coach and always had a string of rich and handsome boyfriends while Trudie had never known the joys of having a steady anything—she was single, not-so-sexy, and somewhat sweaty.

Lane looked out the tinted window as she chatted about some new dress shop in town. Even though Trudie felt close to her sister, they invariably looked at life through different ends of the kaleidoscope. Lane always saw the pretty rainbow designs—the ever-changing wonder of being alive—while Trudie was busy turning the little contraption around to prove the whole thing was just an illusion created out of broken glass. *Yeah, that's so me.*

Lane fidgeted with her bridal pink suit—a color so fragile it looked breakable—while Trudie concerned herself with the impracticality of renting a limo. "I know it's my birthday, but you really didn't have to go to all this trouble. And you picked the priciest restaurant in town." Trudie ran her fingers along the butter-cream leather on the seat, thinking it looked good enough to melt over a bacon burger.

"But it's your favorite, and I can afford it." Lane got up and sat next to her sister. "Come on now. It's not just *any* birthday. It's your *thirtieth.*

13

And this year I've decided your gift will be a total makeover. All my sessions for free."

"Lane, that's way too much."

"No arguments. The works."

Trudie crossed her arms over her poly-blend maroon checkered jacket—a real find she'd managed to snatch up at a garage sale for fifty cents. Trudie rubbed elbows with her sister like she'd done in school. "Remember what our English teacher said about us? There's a certain beauty in being ugly."

"I remember well." Lane raised a shoulder. "We showed Mr. Belvedere, didn't we?"

"*You* showed Mr. Belvedere. If he could just see you now…all slender and blonde and graceful."

"Come on now, don't be so hard on yourself." Lane puckered her brow. "You just need a little polish."

"A little polish? I'd need a whole spa crew working around the clock."

"You can be so negative." Lane handed Trudie a mirror out of her Prada bag. "Just look at yourself and witness all the possibilities."

Trudie groaned. "Mirrors." What was it she hated about mirrors? *Let me count the ways.* Reluctantly, she looked into the glass at her somewhat straggly blonde hair, thinnish face, and pale skin. She was no longer sure what potential should look like. *Hmm. Mirrors.* They were like clocks—a reminder of time. Trudie didn't mind about the fine lines gathering around her blue eyes or her ivory plainness, but she did mind very much about the time. Each person would only be allotted so much of it. And now at thirty, the burning question was—had she fallen into the rhythm of her life yet? Was she using up the minutes and the decades wisely? "I don't think so."

"What did you say?" Lane shook her head. "You're always murmuring things."

Trudie handed the mirror back to her sister. Shame on Lane. She was going to force Trudie to be dissatisfied with her appearance and make her want to improve. "But you enjoy preening. For me, it's a waste of time."

Lane tugged on Trudie's sleeve while donning her puppy dog eyes. "You'll never guess what I did. I brought the tiara. It's in my purse. Why don't you take it home and wear it?"

Like the contents of a cistern suddenly being stirred, unnamed things deep inside Trudie rose to the surface. "I'm too old to wear that thing. Thanks, though." Mist stung Trudie's eyes, but she shook off the emotion. "Listen, I don't mean to downplay what you do as an image coach. You've helped a lot of people succeed in what they do. But wouldn't it be better for me to find a man who loves me this way than to remake myself into something I'm not? I mean, he might wake up the day after our honeymoon and ask for a refund."

"But you won't be somebody different. You'll be Trudie à la mode."

Trudie grinned, shaking her head at her sister. Then she leaned back, determined to enjoy the ride—something she had trouble doing in a limo *and* in life. The jazzy velvet luxury of their cocoon felt nice compared to her backfiring jalopy that had so many odd parts it could no longer claim a brand name. "Sometimes I think I was born on the wrong planet."

"That's what you always say when you're *wrong* and I'm right. Or when you want to change the subject. Come on now, give me a chance to help you. Pleeease."

It was always hard to say no to Lane. "Let me think about it."

Even though her logic was sometimes defective, there was something irresistible about it too.

"Well, here's my first tip. A little peachy lip gloss will light up the face instantly." Lane handed her a pink wand. "Try it. I bought it just for you."

Trudie swiped some of the slippery goop on her lips. She knew it was supposed to be silky and exotic, but why did it smell like dirty house shoes? "Thanks."

"By the way, I hope it's okay, but my financial advisor is meeting us for lunch. You remember me mentioning Mason Wimberley. I went out with him some months ago. He's a fine Christian man, and I think—"

"Yes, I remember you talking about him." Trudie lifted her hand. "But please tell me this isn't a blind date."

Lane pinked darker than her pumps.

"Oy. A blind date." Trudie rolled her eyes. Lane never could hide a secret from her.

"It was Mason's idea. You know, after I told him all about you."

"You either lied your head off about me, or he has issues you never told me about...like he uses one of those plastic toothpicks out of an army knife, or his hair has all migrated from his head to his ears." Trudie raised a big sister eyebrow.

Lane gave her a gentle slug on the arm. "None of the above."

"Then why did you stop dating him?"

"Oh, I just thought it seemed like a conflict to date my financial advisor." Her sister shrugged. "Kind of like dating your gynecologist."

Trudie laughed. "Well, not *quite* like that."

Lane chuckled and then stared at her sister long enough to catch her gaze. "I think it's time for your dreams to come true, Trudie."

See what I mean? As smart as Lane was, she was living proof that women who wore too much pink lost 20 percent of their reasoning abilities. That was how the male sex always got the edge in business. *They don't wear pink!* "Life's not a fairy tale, Lane. It's really just a cruel allegory with demented little gnomes who want to turn our happy coaches of merriment into pumpkin puree."

Lane pulled back, gaping at Trudie. "Where did you come up with that?"

Trudie blinked. "I have no idea."

"You used to say stuff like that all the time when we were kids."
Lane chuckled.

"I guess I did." Trudie dug her fingernail into the dimple on her chin. "But you know, life really isn't a bedtime story or a fun comic book. Those dreams you were talking about…they're gone."

Lane smoothed her already wrinkle-free skirt. "Remember on the farm when we'd climb up on the barn roof at night? We'd stare up at the stars as we talked about what we were going to do with our lives?"

Trudie looked at her sister. "Yeah, I do. I remember." Perhaps she could remember too well. She suddenly felt itchy and hot in her maroon jacket. "Why don't we talk about something else."

"I followed my dream, and I never gave up. I think that last part is the key."

She guessed that Lane wasn't going to give up easily. Trudie looked out the window at the pregnant blush of summer—like spring, it was another season for optimists. They were the two seasons she could never seem to catch up with. "Yes, you did make it, but God has been smiling down on you since the first day you showed your face."

"He's smiling on you, too."

Trudie patted her sister's hand. *Perhaps He had once.*

"You know, over the years you've done a lot of good at the children's hospital. Don't you think those kids would want you to do something for Trudie?"

Lane must feel desperate since she was playing the emotional card. "Okay. We'll see." Trudie cleared her throat. "So, is this Mason guy even a little bit handsome?"

Lane cocked her head as a smidgen of smugness lit her smile. "He dresses well, and he looks like Superman."

"Oh, really?" She couldn't imagine why her sister would give up Superman. Nobody would. *Unless, of course, you were Lex Luthor's girlfriend.* Trudie chuckled to herself. Then she lifted her foot and noticed a wad of green gum stuck to her shoe. She tried wiping it off without making a scene, but it persisted in becoming one with her sole. Oh, well. What could she say? Life was sticky.

The limo finished winding its way through the tree-lined streets and came to an elegant stop in front of Gaston's Bistro on Staitti Street.

Lane ran her tongue over her teeth and fluffed her hair. "Well, it's show time."

"Who's that man coming towards us?" Trudie ignored the chewing gum and instead scrubbed the perspiration off her hands.

"Oh, that's Mason. I guess he decided to come meet us out here. That's very sweet." Lane waved even though no one could see them through the tinted glass.

Before the chauffeur could get to their side, the well-dressed man called Mason opened the limo door for them. He held out his hand to Trudie, and she followed his arm all the way up to his face. *Nice.* She was so moved by his asymmetrical but compelling smile that her feet seemed to forget how to hold up her body. She bumbled outward as her mouth released a yelp that sounded remarkably like a newborn coyote. But the highlight of Trudie's descent into mortification was her hulking fall into the waiting arms of the man who really did look just like Superman.

Chapter Two

....

Mason latched onto Trudie with a firm grip and then lifted her upright. "Steady now."

"Thanks. I'm glad to have my feet back." Trudie took in a deep breath. Several people on the sidewalk stopped for a quick look. Embarrassment seemed too mild a word for the way she felt. She had become the color vermilion.

"Are you okay?" Mason still held her.

Being several inches taller, he looked down at her, but purely in a literal way, since there was no mockery in his eyes. "I just got discombobulated." Why had she said such a peculiar word? Maybe it was her brain that had become discombobulated. "I try to fall once a month. It keeps me humble."

Mason chuckled. "Well, let me know when you intend to fall again, and I'll make sure I'm there to catch you."

Mason hadn't quite let go of her, and for an instant, she felt a warm and dizzying surge of emotion. *Attraction.* It was a pleasant sensation— an unexpected delight—like a rainbow on a stormy day.

The chauffeur and Lane came around from the other side of the car, rushing toward them. "Trudie, are you all right?" Her sister reached out to her.

Trudie waved them off, since she'd never been prone to clumsiness in her life. "I'm fine. Really." Mason released her, and the warm rush faded. But since she'd also felt as graceful as a rodeo clown in a barrel, Trudie was glad for the moment to be over. She wiped her damp hands on her tan skirt and then noticed a tear in her pantyhose. *Great.*

Lane paid the driver and then turned back to Trudie. "Well, if you've recovered, are we ready for a birthday lunch?"

Mason offered himself as an escort, and Lane and Trudie each circled one of his arms. They ambled up the sidewalk, out of the searing Texas heat, and into the old-world atmosphere of Gaston's Bistro. The scents of fresh herbs and baked bread greeted them as well as the sounds of Josh Groban singing in French. *Nice.*

After they were seated, a waiter bustled over with his *bonjour*, his menus, and his enthusiasm. "I hear that today is your birthday, Ms. Abernathy."

Trudie nodded but hoped an oompah band wasn't going to appear out of the kitchen to help them celebrate. Or was that only in Germany? Who knew? Sometimes she felt as provincial as a jersey cow.

"Well, your birthday, July 14, has fallen on France's National Holiday." The waiter made a flourish with his hands. "Bastille Day. And that means complimentary desserts for your whole table."

"That's very kind." Trudie got a sudden urge for chocolate mousse and wondered if they'd have it.

"Thank you so much, Seymour." Lane smiled up at him, and he kissed her hand as if they were old friends.

Mason smiled and then busied himself with his menu.

Seymour draped the cloth napkins over their laps, and then another waiter scurried over with a basket of hot bread and butter.

When the menu had been perused and the queries answered, they all ordered Poulet aux Morilles. It was chicken, but Trudie thought the French made it sound so much more exotic.

Mason turned to Trudie. "Lane tells me you're an assistant manager in retail." He buttered a slice of bread.

Trudie ran her hand along the starched tablecloth. "Well, I suppose that's the elegant version. I just work in a lingerie shop over on Atascocita.

You know, nightgowns, bras, and panties and…well, you get the picture."
Trudie's face suddenly felt like an oven—warm enough to heat up a whole
basket of baguettes. Then she felt silly for blushing, since she rarely felt self-
conscious about the merchandise she sold.

Mason smiled. "It's a gracious calling."

She wasn't sure what to make of Mason's comment, but his sincere
expression told her he wasn't making fun. And yet the remark seemed
over-the-top to describe a salesclerk job. Trudie cleared her throat. "Well,
people who're trained professionals have a *calling*. People like me are the
servants to those professionals." *Oww. That sounded pathetic.* Her banter
was beginning to flop around like a flat tire.

Lane flinched.

Yeah. Guess that wasn't the best way to respond to Mason's genteel
compliment. And probably why she never had any dates. Way too honest.
Or rustic sounding. Or Jane Eyre-ish. Trudie dabbed the napkin on her
lips, even though she hadn't even eaten anything, and then realized she'd
wiped off the last of her magic lip gloss. Her face was now on its own. She
set the napkin back down on her lap and wondered if the thing would have
benefited her more if she had simply stuffed it in her mouth.

"I admire your candor, but I disagree." Mason tugged on the cuff of
his crisp white shirt. "All honest work is honorable."

Trudie studied him. She wanted to say, "Humph, how honorable is
selling panty girdles to women who really need a diet?" But for once, she
kept her thought to herself and took a piece of bread from the basket instead.

"And as far as servanthood," Mason went on to say, "Jesus had a
servant's heart. So if what you've said about your job *were* true, I'd say
you were in very good company."

Lane clapped her hands. "Bravo."

Mason glanced at Lane and then turned back to Trudie. "Were you
wanting to do something else with your life?"

Trudie felt an anxious need to lighten things up, especially since her sister was twitching all over, trying to get her attention. "Well, let me put it to you this way…it's a tedious and tiresome story, which I keep hidden in a secret box in my closet." She slathered a thick layer of butter on her bread and took a bite.

Mason picked up his glass of Perrier, paused with it in midair, and said, "Unfortunately, wording it that way only makes me more intrigued."

Trudie smiled. "I'm sorry to say your curiosity is wasted effort. I'm as interesting as a brown paper bag." She cringed. Even though her tone remained jovial, she felt like she was on the edge of social suicide. She was glad to see the waiter arriving with her sister's watercress soup. Lane would be busy eating instead of trying to coach her from the other side of the table.

Mason grinned at Trudie. "Usually people who think of themselves as the *most* remarkable are usually the least and vice versa."

Guess he wasn't going to let her off the hook that easily. "There is some truth to that."

He lifted his glass to her. "Thank you."

"It's just that I'd rather hear about *your* job." Trudie looked at him. "I'm sure it's more fascinating than peddling underwear."

"I doubt it, but since it is your birthday, I'll let you choose the topic of conversation…for now." He took another piece of bread from the basket. "As a financial consultant, I try to help people do more with the money they have. Advise them on their portfolios. Plan for their retirements. But it's not a glamorous job. And if it *is* a talent, it's shared by a lot of other people."

Now who sounded overly modest? Trudie looked into Mason's eyes, which seemed to be probing hers. She decided to reply, "Well, if what you do as a financial advisor works, which I'm sure it does, then it's sort of like turning water into wine. In fact, since that was a miracle performed by Jesus, I'd say *you're* in very good company."

Mason nodded and mouthed the word *touché*. "Well, people have recommended me to others."

Lane looked back and forth between them both and raised an eyebrow. "Mason is being modest as always. He has more clients than he knows what to do with." She winked. "Do you think you'll be expanding?"

"I'm not sure if I want to." Mason fingered the salt shaker. "I'd rather not feel any pressure to move my office to Houston. I like living and working in Humble."

Trudie had to admit that Mason wasn't at all what she'd expected from a blind date. Not even close. He appeared to be a gem found on a beach of ordinary pebbles.

At that moment a young woman walked up to their table, holding a bouquet of helium balloons, which was attached to a koala. "These are for a Ms. Abernathy."

Lane had an inquisitive brow. "We're both Ms. Abernathy, but since it's my sister's birthday, I think they must be for her." She gestured to Trudie.

The young woman handed the presents to Trudie. "These are for you, then. I hope your day is filled with all your favorite things. Happy birthday."

"Thank you. What a surprise." Trudie gave the cute little marsupial a hug and glanced over at her sister. "Thanks, Lane."

"I'm sorry. They're not from me." Lane's pursed her lips. "I wish I'd thought of sending balloons. Mason? Did you send them?"

He handed the delivery woman a large tip and then turned back to Lane. "Guilty as charged."

Lane lighted her finger just under her chin and gave her sister a smile. Trudie knew what the expression meant—that Lane had been right about Mason. And really, she *had* been so right. Trudie set the koala on the empty chair and gave his head a pat. "I think I'll call him Van Gogh. Thank you, Mason. It was a nice thing to do."

"You're very welcome."

Trudie tried not to stare at Mason. Who was he, anyway? Where had he been? *Right here in Humble.* But there had to be a flaw. Something huge. Maybe he really had an identity disorder, and he thought he was Da Vinci without the beard. Or he was a collector of Elvis paintings and still lived at home with his mamma. Or maybe he had a secret addiction to mac and cheese. Well, *she* had a secret addiction to mac and cheese, so maybe she'd better let that one pass.

Suddenly, the waiter whooshed over with a large tray of food. Amidst all the fidgeting at the table, Trudie gave Mason another subtle appraisal. Lane hadn't exaggerated about him being a Superman look-alike, and if he was without some major shortcoming, he appeared to be ideal.

But why get my hopes up? Trudie was well aware of the fact that guys like Mason could date anyone of their choosing. Actually, it was impossible not to notice that several women in Gaston's Bistro were giggling and gawking at Mason, probably checking him out for brightness levels in his plumage. As far as plumage, Mason was way off the charts. So, the chances of him asking her out on a real date—a plain woman of little education and no means—were slim. It would take a miracle. Now she sounded like a lowly character in a Jane Austen novel. But weren't miracles meant for everyone? Even for the square people who were never whittled smooth enough to fit into society's round hole? *Admit it, Trudie, you'd like to go out with the man.*

Mason and Lane dug into their plates of sautéed chicken, so Trudie did as well. Expect for the moans and raves over the cuisine, the conversation faded for a moment. When Lane started a new topic, Trudie just sat and listened for a while.

As her sister discussed business matters with Mason, Trudie saw something in Lane's eyes she'd never seen before—something curious when she gazed at Mason. She'd known that Lane had gone out with

Mason months earlier, but Lane had been the one to break off their budding relationship. Was her sister suddenly changing her mind about dating Mason? In fact, Lane seemed to light up in Mason's presence, and her laughter was like effervescent soda bubbles.

Trudie looked away and then back at them both, thinking her imagination was merely working overtime. She rested her neck on the palm of her hand, trying to decipher the situation.

As the banter and bursts of laughter between Mason and Lane intensified, somewhere deep in Trudie's heart, where dreams were secretly dreamed and hopes were secretly hoped, a little light flickered out.

Chapter Three

. . . .

Mason sat in his office, working at his computer. He'd made no progress on the spreadsheet he'd been fine-tuning for one his clients. His thoughts had tumbled around in his brain without order, like rocks in a tumbler, because of a woman named Trudie Abernathy. What a name. It didn't exactly inspire one to poetry, but that ivory face of hers and those piercing blue eyes—eyes that could bore through granite—well, they were an entirely different matter. And the woman didn't miss a thing. She was ready to praise, and yet she weighed and measured him as well as made him hope he didn't come up wanting!

He drummed his fingers on the desk, picked up a few macadamia nuts, and then popped them in his mouth. The buzz in his office startled him. The front door. Someone was in the reception area. He rose, wondering who could have dropped by. There were no morning appointments, so he hoped it wasn't a solicitor. With the daily interruptions from the phone and the door, he really needed to hire a secretary. He just wasn't excited about dealing with the interview process or the training. Before he'd made it out his office door, his friend Perry burst into the room along with his son, Zeek, who straggled in behind him.

"Hey, how ya doing, man?" Perry slapped Mason on the back. "We wanted to check in on you to make sure you were still breathing."

"I'm fine, just a little swamped." Mason shook his friend's hand while Zeek, ten years old and a handful, came around to give him a hug. "Hey, Zeek."

"Hi, Mr. Wimberley."

"You may call me Mason if you want."

Perry walked over to his son, smiling with pride. "Well, his mother has been teaching him manners."

Zeek rolled his eyes at his dad. "But manners are really for little girls."

Mason always enjoyed watching their father-son interactions. Reminded him that he needed to call his dad and catch up. "Oh, I don't know, Zeek. Manners are always good."

"Oh, yeah?" Zeek opened the candy jar on Mason's desk and stuck his hand inside. He wiggled his eyebrows as a look of expectancy lit his ebony face.

"Well, like right now, son, if you want some of that candy, maybe you'd better ask first." Perry gestured toward Mason.

"Sorry." Zeek groaned. "Mr. Wimberley, may I please have some candy?"

"Sure." Mason gave Zeek's shoulder a pat. "Well, and manners come in handy when you're grown up, too. They'll help you to impress women. And you won't sit at home alone without any dates."

Zeek scratched his head. "Is that what you do, Mr. Wimberley?"

Perry chuckled. "Hey now, son, I think you're getting a little personal."

"Yeah, but it's a reasonable question, considering my assertion." Mason leaned against his desk.

"What does *that* mean?" Zeek unwrapped several caramel candies and put them in his mouth all at once.

"It means you're right." Mason nodded, really thinking about it. "Maybe I need to go out and impress a woman with my manners."

Zeek laughed. He seemed satisfied enough with Mason's reply that he sat down in one of the chairs and promptly buried himself inside a car magazine.

"We should go. We're headed over to my in-laws' for some barbecue." Perry grinned. "Guess they're in the mood to *grill* things again, if you know what I mean." He pointed to himself.

Mason chuckled.

Zeek ran toward the door, stopped, and then made a big production out of swallowing his mouthful of caramel candy. "Mind if I borrow your car mag for a few days?"

Perry crossed his arms. "Now, son, I don't—"

"All the new magazines come this week, and I never know what to do with the old ones. So, please take all the magazines you want." Mason motioned toward the coffee table in the reception area, wondering why he even subscribed to magazines.

"Really? Thanks." Zeek ran to the coffee table and studied the pile.

Perry shook his head. "Don't let him bamboozle you like that. He does that same thing to his poor grandmother. Ten minutes after he's through the front door, he's got her cooking enough food to open a café."

Zeek stuffed a small pile of magazines under his arm. "Bye." He raced out the front door.

Mason smiled. "He's a nice kid. Feel fortunate to have a good family."

"I do. Every day of my life." Perry headed to the front door.

Mason followed behind him.

Perry reached for the door handle and then looked back at him. "Hey, you're looking kinda lonely, man. You want to come with us for some barbecue?"

"Thanks. Another time. I'd better just eat a quick lunch here."

"Okay." Perry waggled his finger. "But I've got one more thing to say."

"Yeah?"

"You know, I've been to your church, and I've seen the way the women look at you. Kind of like they're enjoying a big slice of my wife's ambrosia pie. You know what I'm saying? So, why haven't you gone out with any of them?"

Mason shrugged. "I have. But after awhile, they all start looking the same to me. Sounding the same. Dressing the same. You know."

"I hear ya. Well, sort of. Maybe, just maybe, you're being too picky." Perry stuck his hands in the back pockets of his jeans. "Naw, I take that back. I took my good ol' sweet time in looking for just the right woman, and I've never regretted it. Maybe all you need to do is—"

"I met someone." Mason wondered why he'd blurted out such a private thought. It hadn't really been a date—the poor woman had been railroaded into it by her sister.

"Oh, really?" Perry's eyes widened. "And so who is this lady we're talking about? I have got an inquiring mind here."

"Trudie Abernathy." Mason fingered the light switch without turning it on or off, and then he realized how goofy he looked. "We had lunch today."

Perry frowned. "But you dated her months ago. Wasn't she the one who called it quits after three dates?"

"No. That was her sister, Lane."

"So, what is that? You're dating Lane's sister?" Perry raised an eyebrow.

"No. I'm not dating her. Exactly." Mason massaged his neck, almost wishing he hadn't brought up the subject.

Perry jiggled his finger. "But you said you had lunch with her."

"I did, but her sister was there."

"Oh, wow." Perry chuckled. "Now, let me get this straight. You went on a date with Lane's sister, while Lane was there too? Boy, times are a-changin' since I dated."

Mason cocked his head. "Well, it didn't seem all that complicated at the time, ol' buddy."

Perry slapped Mason on the back. "I'm just messing with you. I get it. It was a blind date with no pressure. Women are pretty clever at figuring out how to do things like that. They talk a lot about us, you know. Men in general."

"Oh yeah? What are they saying?" Mason wasn't sure if he really wanted to know.

"Well, I found out all this stuff after I got married. Sheila says beyond faith…there's the lodestone factor." Perry nodded. "Makes all the difference."

Mason thought back to his geology 101 class in college. "That's a magnetic mineral. Right? I can tell your wife's a geologist."

Perry grinned. "She means something that attracts. The stuff you can't fool yourself about. For me, it blasted my heart to smithereens. I'm telling you, first time I met Sheila, I felt like that transformer in our neighborhood when it blew during our last thunderstorm. *Poom*." He thumped his fist over his heart. "Just like that. Right here."

Mason laughed. "Well, they say attraction is a mystery."

"Can't manufacture it or manipulate it. You can only appreciate it when it hits. Oh yeah." Perry arched his eyebrows. "*Poom*."

"You're a little bit unhinged. You know that, right?"

"Yeah, that's why Sheila loves me so much." Perry straightened his shoulders.

Zeek stuck his head in the door. "Dad? Are you coming, Dad?" He rolled his eyes. "Dad?"

Perry looked over his glasses at him. "You know, I really did hear you on the first 'Dad.'" Perry turned to Mason. "Well, keep the lodestone in mind. And let me know when she arrives. Later."

Mason wasn't sure, but he thought there was a chance, just a chance, the woman he was talking about had already arrived. He saluted his friend and Zeek as they headed out in pursuit of barbecue. Mason walked back into his office, sat down, and rolled his chair back up to his desk. Perry had been pretty funny—the whole transformer, lodestone thing, and yet that was some of what he'd felt when Trudie fell into his arms. The sensation had been unexpected, but certainly not unwelcome.

Maybe I should just call her. He'd been thinking about it on and off. He could just pick up the phone and see if she'd like to meet for coffee. No, that wasn't good enough. He should take her out to a nice restaurant. Then again, she'd probably like to keep a first date uncomplicated. On the other hand, he didn't really know Trudie well enough to know what she wanted. What to do? The more he thought about it, the more indecision he felt. *Good grief, man, get ahold of yourself.* Even though he hadn't dated in several months, he certainly knew the routine by heart—what to say and how to say it. He pulled out the top drawer of his desk and looked at Trudie's home number, the one Lane had scribbled on one of her business cards.

Mason picked up the phone, held it up as if it were a dead rodent, and then slammed it down. Why did he hesitate with Trudie? Was he intimidated by her? No. Was he scared she'd say no? He'd faced no before, but it wasn't usually at the very beginning. It was only after women found out more about his family. Found out about his family's business, the promise he'd made, and what that would mean for his future—their future as a couple.

He picked up the phone again, but at the same moment he heard another buzz. The front door again. *I have got to hire a secretary.*

When Mason looked up, he saw a stranger standing in his office doorway—a young woman with astonishing beauty. So astonishing that he blinked to make sure the woman was real.

The stranger fingered the collar of her white dress and smiled at him.

"Hi." Mason smiled back. The woman was no illusion, and as far as design, God had certainly outdone Himself. "May I help you?"

Chapter Four

....

Mason heard a shuffling noise behind the young woman and then saw his mother appear. He rose. "Mom, what a surprise. It's nice to see you."

"It's always a happy day to see you too." She put her palms together and smiled.

Mason came around the desk and gave her a hug.

When he eased away, his mother gestured toward the stranger. "Do you remember the lovely Lily Larson? She attended our church some months ago."

Mason scratched his chin. "Yes, now that you mention it...I do."

"It's so good to meet you." Lily reached out her hand to him. "Well... to see you again."

"Same here." He shook her hand. Lily's fingers were soft but also a bit clammy, like latching onto the legs of a frog.

Lily reached around the other side of the doorway and pulled out a picnic basket.

His mom fluttered her hands. "I know you barely stop to eat, so Lily here has been kind enough to whip up a little picnic lunch."

Mason crossed his arms. "But I've got—"

"Pish posh, now. I thought since it didn't feel muggy today we could eat outside under that live oak out there." His mother pointed toward the outdoors, her face suddenly brightening with a saintly glow. "'Twould be such a shame to miss something so lovely."

Uh-huh. Mason gave his mother an all-knowing smile as he raked his fingers through his hair. It was obvious what she was up to. Ever since he'd turned thirty-four, family members, especially his aunts, had gotten edgy, thinking he'd never marry. They'd become like a pack of overzealous cupids with a quiver full of arrows. But underneath their crafty ways, he also knew they meant well. And it was hard to be upset with any of them, especially his mother. That is, as long as she didn't make a habit out of setting up her grown son with dates. And besides, he'd have to eat eventually. Mason sniffed the air. Tempting aromas were already curling their way out of the picnic basket. It smelled like one of his favorites—fried chicken. Now there was some serious persuasion.

As they headed outside toward the picnic table, Mason wondered about Lily's secretarial skills and if she was in need of a job. Wouldn't hurt to ask. He made himself useful by spreading the tablecloth and setting out the food. And there was lots of it. Lily had made baked beans, potato salad, Southern fried chicken, and homemade apple pie. Not exactly a light picnic lunch. He felt officially buttered up. After they were all pleasantly munching, Mason asked, "Well, Lily, what do you do?"

"Well." Lily paused as she brushed some of the hair out of her face. "I *was* a secretary at one of the big realty offices in Houston, but I got laid off when they downsized."

Mason gave himself an extra helping of baked beans. "I'm sorry to hear that." So, Lily just happened to be out of work. *Hmm.*

His mother gave him a guileless shrug.

Okay, so his mother was wily on a massive scale, presenting him with a wife, the mother of his children, and a secretary all in one, but her scheming could certainly be used to his advantage. "Well, for some time now, I've needed a secretary."

"Really?" Lily's doe-like eyes got even bigger. "What a coincidence."

Uh-huh. Mason watched a jet pass overhead and poured himself something from the thermos. Pink lemonade. He didn't really like the stuff—reminded him of liquefied cotton candy—but he wasn't going to hurt anyone's feelings over it. He took a sip. Not as bad as he thought it'd be.

He turned to Lily. "I tell you what…if you come work for me, maybe we could give each other a two-week trial period. That way I can see if you can do the job, and *you* can find out if you can stand me. I'll pay you whatever salary you were getting before. So, Lily, what do you think?" Mason took a bite off the crispy drumstick.

Lily nodded. "I think that sounds perfect, Mr. Wimberley." Mist filled her eyes, and a single tear rolled down her cheek. "I can't thank you enough."

"Please call me Mason. And you're welcome. Do you think you can start on Monday?"

"I not only think I can, I know I can." Lily nodded again. "Oh, that's perfect. Just wonderful." She sniffled. "Wonderful and, well…perfect."

"Oh, this is a happy day when everyone gets just what they need." Mrs. Wimberley rocked her head back and forth as she took a big bite of potato salad.

Mason had to admit, if Lily's secretarial skills were as good as her fried chicken, she was going to do just fine. Maybe he should ask his new secretary a few questions to get to know her better. "So, I'm curious. Why did you want to become a secretary?"

"Well." Lily touched her fingers to her lips. "It was what my mother did. She was a secretary. And she told me I should be a secretary, so I became a secretary."

"Oh?" Mason shoveled a forkful of baked beans into his mouth. "By the way, I always have coffee in the morning. I'll make sure we stock your favorite kind too. What do you like?"

Lily shrugged. "I'll like whatever you like, Mr. Wimberley." When she took a sip from the straw, her lips came together in the shape of a kiss.

Hmm. Okay, downside to Lily being his secretary—her looks would be a mite distracting, and he got the feeling she wouldn't be very innovative. Maybe not too much fun either, but then a secretary shouldn't be expected to be fun. Upside—she would be obedient and hardworking. Mason determined not to nitpick her comments to death and just enjoy the fact that he would no longer have to deal with the front door or the phone.

"Oh, Lily," his mother said, "this potato salad is yummy. Like something Little Red Riding Hood would take to her grandmother. Tell me your secret."

"There's really no secret." Lily folded and unfolded her paper napkin. "I just follow the recipe. That's what my mother always says…'follow the recipe.' And that's what I do. Follow that recipe."

When Lily smiled again, Mason noticed it was a bit crooked. He cleared his throat. Well, perhaps there was more to Lily than he thought. Mason decided to go quiet for a bit so he could enjoy his mountain of food. His own cooking was passable, mostly macaroni and cheese, so home-cooked food was more than welcome. He suddenly wondered if Trudie was a great cook. Somehow it didn't really matter. Wouldn't change the equation.

He glanced at Lily. She was suddenly engrossed in a chat with his mother about paper towels and their absorbability. Even though Lily was not a philosopher, Mason was certain she was used to guys hovering like vultures and digesting her every word. She would always be the most beautiful woman at any party. Always the one sought after and photographed, perhaps pampered and indulged too often. No one could argue the main point—Lily was gorgeous. And her perfume wasn't bad, either. He wondered if it bothered her to be adored simply because she was lucky enough to be born with flesh and bone molded in all the right places—so splendidly that a glance from her would turn any sensible men into a blubbering puddinghead. Maybe it pleased her to be so admired. Strange thing to ponder over a mouthful of fried chicken.

His mother lifted the lid off the apple pie. "Well, you've gotten all hushed over there, Mason."

"Sorry. I'm just contemplating the beauty…of home cooking." He leaned on the picnic table. "So, Lily, what's your story? Tell me a little bit about yourself."

"I don't have much to tell, really. I'm just me. Little ol' Lily. I was born in Houston. I grew up in Houston. Went to college in Houston. And now here I am. You know, right here with you." Lily took a bird-sized bite of her chicken.

"Yes, here you are." Mason took in a deep breath, since he thought he might need the additional oxygen. Well, Lily didn't seem to be a very complex woman—all the better for what he needed at work. And even though she'd need some training, her help was looking more necessary by the minute. "By the way, if it's convenient, Lily, would you like to start work tomorrow morning at seven instead of Monday?"

"Oh, perf." She nodded. "I'll be there…I mean here. Thank you, sir. Thank you…Mr. Wimberley." Then Lily folded her hands in her lap.

His mother tried unsuccessfully to hide her grin as she handed everyone a slice of pie.

"Lily, it really is okay to call me Mason."

"Yes, sir…Mr. Mason." She smiled.

Lily would be a fine secretary. There certainly wouldn't be any disputes. She wouldn't hesitate to agree with him or do whatever he asked her to do. Mason took a big bite of the apple pie and groaned with pleasure. Then he bragged on Lily's baking until she was blushing and giggling. But in spite of all the beauty around him and all the fine cooking, his mind became engaged elsewhere, thinking of blue eyes laughing at him. Inquisitive eyes that belonged to a woman he could not get off his mind. *Trudie.*

"Mason?" Lily said to him in a distant voice.

"Hmm?"

"You've put your elbow in the baked beans."

Chapter Five

....

Trudie stood in her bathroom, fidgeting with her hair. It would be worth
the hassle, since she was celebrating her first date in six months. Or was it
the first date in ten months? *Oh, how time flies when you're not having fun.*

She chuckled as she wound another strand of hair on the curling
iron. But perhaps her last date didn't really count since it started as a
church group thing and dwindled to two, which left her with Stanley
Ledbetter at the local pizzeria. *What an odd recollection.* Trudie had
hung on to the bitter end, listening to Stanley's soliloquy on the brain
capacity of the local squirrels. To her credit, she didn't so much as grin
at Stanley's topic. But then she'd felt sorry for him since he had no good
hair days to speak of, and no one else in the crowd seemed to give a
flying squirrel about him.

Trudie combed all her curls, smoothing them together. Now, the fact
that Mason Wimberley had asked her out and was soon to arrive at her
apartment could be attributed to the benevolence of her sister. Yes, Lane's
relentless bragging and crowing must have worked on the poor man like
kryptonite. She laughed. So, her sister really hadn't revived her interest in
Mason. Apparently, she'd been quite wrong about that.

While holding her breath, she squirted some hairspray on top of
what looked like a passable hairdo. Normally she wore her shoulder-
length blonde hair flat and stuck behind her ears, but Lane had given her
some helpful as well as practical tips, and the whole process hadn't taken
as long as she thought it would.

She headed to the bedroom to get dressed. Her sister had taken her
shopping for a few "smart pieces" as she called them, so Trudie slipped

on one of those amazing *pieces,* which was a well-designed peach-colored dress made of linen. She opened the closet door and gave herself a look in the full-length mirror. *Nice.*

Trudie got closer and closer to the mirror until she could see all the lavender flecks in her blue eyes. "But I guess the real question is…am I really together? Who are you really, Trudie Marlow Abernathy?" *You've been a long time thrashing about inside there. When do you think you'll ever find the courage to unlock the door?* She had no idea. But she wished that just once she could stop by a mirror and look only at her hair.

Wanting to put herself into a more romantic mood, Trudie pulled out the smallest drawer on her armoire and lifted out a stack of Victorian Valentine cards. They were the only things she could afford to collect, but they were satisfying to look at—so lovely in design, each one so unique and ornate and full of romantic notions. She looked through the little pile and then tied them back up with a ribbon. She hadn't always allowed herself sentimental indulgences, since it usually led to disappointment, but the evening felt different. Tinged with hope.

Just as she put on her dangly pearl earrings, the doorbell rang. Trudie looked at her watch. 7:05. Mason was only five minutes late. Not bad. She put the cards back in their cubbyhole, ran to the door—pausing briefly to regain her composure—and then opened the door.

A bouquet of white daisies met her along with a man who was too handsome for his own safety. Mason was dressed in tailored slacks and a blue shirt. *Nice. Only in a fantasy could this be happening to me.*

"Look at you." Mason spread his hands out. "Lane told me what your birthday present was."

Trudie chuckled. "Well, I'm a work in progress."

"And a very lovely one."

"Thank you." Trudie shrugged, feeling warm from the sudden attention. Mason handed her the daisies.

"They're beautiful." Trudie held the flowers to her face, letting the petals tickle her cheek. "Did you know that daisies mean innocence and purity?" Of course, she wouldn't tell him that daisies also meant loyal love.

"I had no idea." Mason smiled. "Those certainly aren't words people use anymore."

"You're right." Trudie tried not to stare at him. "Would you like to come in for a minute? I'll put these in some water."

Mason entered her domain, and it was impossible for her not to wonder what he thought of her apartment. She didn't own anything expensive, but she hoped there was a bit of eclectic intrigue in every nook and cranny. At least that had been her intention. "Please make yourself at home."

"Thanks." Just before she stepped into the kitchen, she was happy to see Mason comfortable enough to look around at the many pictures on her walls. Trudie reached for a vase on top of her fridge, filled it with water, and then cut and arranged the daisies.

"This pencil sketch looks like an original," Mason said from the living room.

"It is."

"I'm familiar with Kitzman. My aunt bought one of his paintings."

Trudie set the flowers on her kitchen table and joined Mason in the living room. "His paintings have become more valuable...but unfortunately, *after* he passed away."

"I suppose that's happened too often over the years." Mason turned to look at her. "I do like this sketch. I assume it's Kitzman's view of life's crossroads."

Trudie stared at the drawing as she had so many times before. In one direction, a furrowed road led to a citadel on a hill, and the other path, lined with new grass and lit with sun, led toward the unknown. "It's what our lives are full of. Forks in the road. And sometimes it's that one choice…that one defining moment that makes all the difference. So simple a decision, and yet that choice can lead us to either joy or regret. Or—"

"Purgatory or paradise?" Mason finished.

"That was exactly what I was going to say. How did you know?"

Mason shook his head. "I have no idea." He took a step closer to her.

Trudie returned his gaze and thought that if color could be felt, she was suddenly swimming in a rich, cadmium blue. She'd never felt so alive.

Mason reached up as if he were going to touch her face, but then he lowered his hand. "My heart. It's pounding…really hard."

Chapter Six
....

Trudie smiled at him. "Please don't have a heart attack. I don't know CPR."

Mason laughed.

She stepped back out of their little whirl of emotions. She had such a pendulum swing of feelings when she was around Mason. Sometimes they were merely chatting, and it was an ordinary moment, and then there would be an unforeseen word or look from him that would alter everything. And then all things became suspended and memorable.

"Artwork is what keeps analytical people like me sane." Mason glanced back at the wall. "Kitzman. Did you know him?"

"Yes." She wasn't sure how much she should tell him about her past. "I knew him a long time ago."

Mason tilted his head. "A long time ago for you would have meant I was gazing at you in your crib."

Trudie chuckled. "In my youth, I had an interest in art. And Mr. Kitzman befriended me. He gave me that sketch."

"I read in an article that he was a recluse and that he disliked everyone. But I can see you being the one to charm him out of his world."

Trudie enjoyed the compliment, but for some reason it made her uncomfortable. "Well, I've never been much of a charmer. But there isn't a woman alive who wouldn't like to think that of herself." She grinned and then picked up her purse and a small overnight case. "By the way, after dinner this evening, do you mind dropping me off at Lane's house? We're going to have an old-fashioned sleepover."

"I don't mind at all. So, are you ready to go?"

Trudie nodded, and they walked to the front door together.

"You two are close, aren't you? You and Lane." Mason opened the door.

She looked up at him. "Yes, we are. Lane is a wonderful sister."

Mason seemed to ponder her words as Trudie locked up. She had to admit that even though she and her sister got along well together, there was still something that kept them from being as close as they had been in their early years.

"So, are you hungry?" Mason asked as he escorted her down the sidewalk.

Trudie turned her attention back to Mason. "I'm *always* hungry." She laughed at herself, knowing Lane would have rolled her eyes over that one. Not a very feminine thing to admit—that one had the appetite of a walrus.

"Glad to hear it. Women who just push bits of food around on their plates should never be allowed to dine out. Ever." He winked. "Do you like Italian cuisine?"

"It's never been my favorite, but I'm just happy to spend the evening with you."

Mason's eyes flashed with amusement. "Well, now I like honesty, especially when it has such a nice spin on it. So, where *would* you like to go?"

"Something casual would be fine. Maybe Banjo's Café."

"Good idea." Mason shook his finger. "They do have good fried chicken." He helped her into his car.

Trudie's face twitched into a smile as she looked around inside his vehicle and breathed in that marvelous old car smell. She'd expected a new Mercedes or Lexus, but it was a rattletrap just like hers.

After jimmying the driver's door open, he slid into the seat and patted the cracked dashboard. "Dear old Maggie. She got me through college, and now I can't seem to part with her."

Trudie chuckled. "I have a Maggie too. They're faithful. Ugly, but faithful."

"Oh, now don't let Maggie hear you talking about her that way. Beauty can be definable, but it can be equally unpredictable." Mason started the engine, which sputtered and coughed.

"'In the eye of the beholder.' Right?"

Mason looked at her. "Exactly."

He seemed to give Trudie that gaze again, the one that told her he was assessing her. For what, she couldn't imagine. She had her hopes, of course, but she knew reality would keep those dreams securely in check. Trudie drew away from his gaze before she did something silly like touch his hand—the hand that she couldn't help but notice was glued white-knuckled to the stick shift. Was he nervous? "Cars," she said absently.

"Yes, cars. Right." He looked forward again, put the car in gear, and pulled away from the curb. "Tell me about your Maggie."

They continued chatting about old vehicles until they were laughing so hard Mason nearly swerved off the road. They made it to Main Street—still in one piece—and he parked and helped her out.

After strolling past the museum, they crossed the street and stepped into Banjo's Café, which was named after the owner, Eddy "Banjo" Jones, who from time to time strummed a little for his guests. Trudie had always liked the atmosphere—photos of oil derricks and roughnecks and an array of pump jack paraphernalia—which celebrated the rich history of Humble.

A young woman seated them at a booth inside a small indoor gazebo. A canning jar sat in the middle of the table, overflowing with yellow roses and miniature Texas flags. Trudie had been seated there a few times before, but always alone. She scooted in across from Mason, looking forward to getting to know him better.

Trudie fingered the velvety petals. Just as she was about to comment on the folk song "Yellow Rose of Texas," she was interrupted by a chirpy waitress in overalls.

"Hi, I'm Cody." She handed them menus and then told them about the special for the day. "So, what would you folks like to drink?"

The waitress scribbled down their beverage orders, let out a little sigh over Mason, and then sashayed toward the kitchen.

Mason leaned over the table. "Trudie?"

"Yes?"

He cleared his throat. "I wanted to ask you if you'd like to—" His attention seemed diverted for a second.

Trudie followed his gaze over to a small crowd of people ambling into the café. She sensed a twinge of uneasiness rising in him.

The same group of people spotted him, waved, and then rushed right over to their gazebo. A woman, a remarkably attractive one, appeared to be leading the pack. She bounced on her toes. "I'm sorry to bother you, Mr. Wimberley. I mean, Mason. But I wanted you to meet some of my family."

Mason rose. "I would be honored. But first let me introduce you to Trudie Abernathy. Trudie, this is my newly hired secretary, Lily Larson."

Lily took hold of Trudie's hand and gave it an enthusiastic shake. "I'm so happy to meet you."

"Thank you. It's nice to meet you too." It was hard for Trudie not to notice how much Mason's male clients would enjoy being greeted by Lily. But she hoped it was only a good business move on Mason's part and nothing more.

Lily gathered her hands into a bouquet. "Well, and this is my mother, Dorothy Larson. And this is my older brother, Scotty Lee, and my little sister, Hillary Sue."

The little party beamed with good wishes, and everyone took turns shaking hands.

After all the introductions and chatting had ceased and the happy group had migrated to the other side of the café, Mason sat back down again. He looked exhausted. "Sorry for the interruption."

"It's no problem. They seemed like very nice people." But Trudie also had to admit it was the one time when she wished the beloved townspeople of Humble weren't so warm and friendly.

"Well, I don't really know them. I just met Lily and hired her this week." Mason fiddled with his napkin. "And well, Lily has been out of work. I think she's just grateful to have a job."

"I can tell." Trudie just hoped Lily wouldn't be *too* grateful. It was impossible not to notice the way she radiated glamour at every turn. She was shapely and resplendent and, well, beauty pageant material. Trudie felt a tug of envy and immediately dismissed it. She hated wasting her worries on such a useless emotion, and she didn't like to think of her fellow female sojourners as competition—even if they were. She supposed if anything were to blossom between Mason and herself, then it would just need to happen all on its own. With or without a ravishing beauty at work fetching him espresso and looking all pouty.

"Trudie?"

"Yes?"

"Are you okay?" Mason reached out to her but didn't touch her hand.

"Oh yeah. I'm fine. I just got a little lost inside my head there for a second."

"Is that anything like getting discombobulated?"

Trudie smiled. "A little."

Mason moved the cluster of roses to the side of the table. His jaw had a determined set to it. "Well, what I was trying to say earlier was, I wondered if you'd—"

Banjo music revved up so close to their gazebo, Trudie and Mason both startled. The owner of the café, Eddy "Banjo" Jones, had suddenly appeared, playing his instrument with an Earl Scruggs kind of sound.

As many times as she'd eaten there, she'd never heard Eddy's music before. His finger picking was skillful and fast, and Trudie wondered if he also played in some of the local live music places.

Eddy stopped right in front of their table, and for a few minutes he played a patriotic tune just for them. After he moseyed up to the stage area, Cody arrived with two steaming plates of fried chicken, mashed potatoes, and fried okra.

When the waitress had gone, Trudie grinned and once again turned to Mason. "I think you've been trying to ask me something." She stirred her creamy mashed potatoes around with her fork and took a bite.

Mason looked at her, the gold in his eyes sparkling. "If you want to hold off on coffee and dessert tonight, I have some at my house. I bought us some gourmet coffee beans straight from the verdant hills of Jamaica, and dessert straight from the frozen food section at the grocery store."

Trudie chuckled.

"No, I'm kidding, really." Mason lifted his chicken to his mouth and then set it back down. "But I did make us homemade cinnamon rolls, if you're interested."

She thought that prospect sounded wonderful as well as romantic, but she couldn't help but ask, "Were you that sure I'd say yes to dessert and coffee at your house?"

"No. But I was hoping. A lot. Sweated a little, too." Mason grinned.

Trudie paused, trying to absorb the moment. The fact that Mason had gone to so much trouble on her behalf was quite a surprise. Maybe she should say yes quickly to put him out of his misery.

Chapter Seven

. . . .

Mason slipped the house keys out of his pocket as he escorted Trudie up the cobblestone path toward his house. When they stepped out of the piney woods and the log cabin came into view, he heard Trudie gasp.

"Oh, wow, your house. It's somehow grand and charming all at the same time. You must love living in a place like this."

Mason smiled, pleased that she was so pleased. "I do."

"You know, I've driven on Will Clayton Parkway a hundred times and never knew this was back here. You own all this land?"

"No, just some of the acreage around the house." Mason let them in through the front door and then flipped on some lights.

"This is amazing." Trudie walked along the walls in the entry hall, gazing at the framed photography and the sculptures. "Did you take any of these photos?"

"I wish I had. But sadly no. I'm only a collector." Even though he had each piece of artwork memorized, he still studied them with her, grateful to see someone take an interest in the things he loved.

Trudie looked at him, surprise lighting her blue eyes. "You have some remarkable pieces here."

"Thank you." Mason looked down at his favorite statue, which was the figure of a woman carrying a basket of fruit and whose hands were folded in prayer. "Art helps to make life bearable."

"Yes, it does." Trudie reached out to the same statue and briefly touched the woman's face. "It expresses what's in our hearts when there are no words."

"Now that sounds like the reflection of a true artist."

"Oh?" A sadness washed over Trudie's face, but then it quickly faded.

Mason watched her, wondering what memory could have given her such an expression.

Trudie turned from the statue and faced the living room. "Did you have this house built?" She ran her hand along the polished railing.

"Yes, several years ago."

She stepped down into the sunken living room, her steps making tiny clattering noises on the wood floors. "It's like a rustic but elegant hunting lodge…only without the dead animals on the walls."

Mason chuckled. "Good description. That was kind of what I was going for. Only I'm afraid to say there are some dead animals on the walls in the den."

"Oh." She grinned.

He looked back at her, eating up her assortment of expressions. They held that pose, looking at each other for a second. "If you'll follow me into the kitchen, I'll turn on the coffeepot." Mason made his way through the living room and noticed his clothes were still strewn on the couch and the floor. When would he ever learn to pick up after himself instead of always relying on his housekeeper? Probably never.

Mason turned on the coffeemaker and then scooped two unburned buns out of the baking dish. He turned around to find Trudie folding the napkins.

"Where's your flatware?"

"Middle drawer." He grinned, thinking how much he enjoyed watching Trudie putter around in his kitchen. "Lane told me about your volunteer work at the children's hospital in Houston. And that you've worked there for years."

"I'm sure Lane bragged on me too much, but I have enjoyed working with the kids. They astonish me. I doubt I could ever give them as much love as they've showered on me." She placed the forks on the napkins.

"When do you go to the hospital?"

Trudie came over to him. "I'm on a summer break right now, but I'll be back there in the fall." She leaned on the counter. "By the way, I've been wanting to say how sorry I am for Lane's overzealousness…well, concerning us."

"What do you mean?"

"I love my sister, but just for the record, she was doing a little unauthorized matchmaking on my birthday."

"Oh, you mean the lunch. It wasn't a problem. Actually, I was concerned that you'd felt trapped that day."

"Well, maybe a little at first. But I got over the feeling pretty quickly."

Mason grinned. He loved Trudie's honesty. So few women said things straight out. To him, they always did so much beating around the bush that he wondered how they ever got anything said. He put the plate of sticky buns in the microwave, nuked them for a few seconds, and then set them out on the kitchen table.

Trudie looked around. "Did you design this kitchen?"

"No, but I did make quite a few adjustments to their plan. I also added the slate floors and the granite countertops." Mason poured them a couple of mugs of coffee and pulled out a chair for Trudie.

"Your house is well thought out. I can tell it came from an organized mind."

Mason sat down across from her. "I guess I have to be organized, since my business is chaotic at times. Oh, and unpredictable."

"Like a capricious woman?"

Mason raised an eyebrow. "That didn't come to mind." He caught himself staring at Trudie. Mason liked looking at her face. She didn't bother with a lot of makeup but always had a fresh-out-of-the-shower look. And besides enjoying her blue eyes, he especially liked her lips. They looked like the cherries he'd brought home from the grocery store.

Trudie took a bite of her cinnamon roll. "This is seriously good. You're not afraid to use extra butter and cinnamon."

"Glad you're enjoying it." He took a big bite as well, but it wasn't as much fun as watching Trudie dig into her roll with gusto. She really did love it. She wasn't just being polite. "You've got a little frosting on your mouth."

Trudie licked her lips.

Once again, Mason realized his gaze was drifting to her mouth. The chimes on his clock went off in the kitchen, startling him.

"And so do you have a recipe for these babies?"

"Yes, but I never follow it."

"I can't follow recipes either. I always like to see what might happen if I make some changes. You never know when there's a masterpiece waiting to happen." She took another bite.

Mason wondered if that was her philosophy in life. "My sentiments exactly." He took a sip of his coffee. It was strong but good. The caffeine would keep him up half the night, but then so would her beautiful eyes.

Trudie pointed to his guitar in the corner of the kitchen. "I assume you play."

"Yes, I do. With the dexterity and speed of a one-toed sloth."

She laughed. "I doubt that. I really would love to hear something."

"Maybe when you know me better." Mason rested his chin on his hands and looked at her. "Right now, I'm afraid I'll scare you off permanently."

Trudie smiled and took a sip of her coffee. Her long slender fingers wrapped themselves around the mug, embracing it. "Your Jamaican coffee was worth the money."

"Thanks." They continued to chat about light topics as they finished up their dessert and coffee. Mason was enjoying Trudie's company. So much so that he hoped nothing would go wrong—that she wouldn't ask too many questions about his family. At least not yet anyway.

"So, do you have an office in your home?"

"Office? I do." Mason stiffened. *Now why would she ask that?*

"I was wondering if you bring your work home a lot, or if this place is like a retreat."

"I do have a home office, but I only work here if I get really behind."

She took a casual sip from her cup. "And are you usually behind?"

"Sometimes." He smiled.

Trudie rested her neck on her palm as she gazed at him. "I'd love to see your office."

Mason nearly choked on his coffee. "Really? Why?" He doubted he could refuse Trudie anything, and yet he knew showing her his office on their first date would be a bad idea.

"Because for some reason I think someone's workplace might tell more about a person than where they relax."

Trudie's face looked so innocent. She meant well, but she was also a little too insightful. He felt himself squirm. It was too soon to let her into his life so profoundly. What if she disappeared as the other women had—the other women he'd grown to care about? "Well, I'd be happy to let you see it, but it's not really a place I show people...very often...anymore."

"I'm sorry." Trudie shook her head. "I'm way too nosy."

"No, you're not." He patted her hand, but the gesture felt awkward. There was a crease between her brows, and he was sorry to have been the one to put it there. The moment suddenly felt as uncomfortable as the one when his new secretary, Lily, had shown up at the café. Mason took a deep swig of his coffee and then another, hoping it would bolster his courage. "I'd like to show you my office right now. That is, if you're finished with your dessert and coffee."

"I'm all done, but are you sure? I don't want to impose."

"You're not imposing." Mason knew it was only a matter of time before he'd have to show Trudie all the facts of his life. He might as well know sooner rather than later how she would perceive them.

"Well, okay, if you're sure." Trudie set her napkin down on the table.

"All right then." Mason took one last sip of his coffee and then led Trudie through the kitchen, the dining room, and down the long hallway to his office. After a pause he opened the sliding oak doors, which revealed the other side of his world.

Chapter Eight

....

Mason followed Trudie into his office.

She walked over to the large aquarium and seemed transfixed on it, watching the array of saltwater fish dart and glide through the tank. "How wonderful to have this in your office."

He stood next to her. "I enjoy it…very much."

Trudie offered him another look of amazement as her attention was drawn to the opposite side of the room to his private atrium of tropical flowers and trees. "Oh, my. Palms and orchids." She pointed upward on the glass. "And you've got tree frogs in there too. I love tree frogs." An automatic mister came on and lightly sprayed the interior. Trudie turned back to him. "It's like a little paradise. No wonder you don't want to show this off. Your guests would never want to leave. It's the most incredible office I've ever seen. How could you ever get any work done here?"

"Fortunately, it's a secondary office." Mason smiled, wishing the moment could stop right where it was, so the inevitable wouldn't happen. But it did. He watched as Trudie strolled toward the wall of family photos.

"Your family?"

"Yes."

She smiled. "They all look so happy."

"They are. A little crazy sometimes, but I love them."

Trudie touched one of the pictures. "And this is your mother and father?"

Mason walked over to her. "Yes, that's Emily and Edward."

"Very handsome couple." She then pointed to an old photo of his parents at the dedication ceremony of their new business. "Oh." Trudie looked back at him. "So, it's your parents who own Wimberley Funeral Home here in Humble."

"Yes, that's right." He crossed his arms.

"I've driven by it a few times. It always looks so peaceful there nestled in the woods and the meadows. I like driving by it."

Mason felt a measure of relief wash over him. "My father would be pleased to hear you say it. Not everyone responds with enthusiasm."

"Really?"

"Well, as I'm sure you can imagine…people don't always like being reminded…you know…that this life comes to an end."

Trudie fingered the sleeve of her dress. "Dying is part of living."

Mason smiled at her.

She turned her attention back to the photo. "But the sign in front reads WIMBERLEY AND SONS. So, you have brothers?"

Mason knew the progression of queries. He knew them all too well. "I had one brother, Nate Wimberley." He stuffed his hands into the pockets of his slacks.

Trudie pointed at another family photo. "Is this your brother next to you here?"

Mason nodded. "It is. But that photo is an old one. He died ten years ago in a hiking accident."

"I'm so sorry." Trudie touched his arm. "I shouldn't have been so inquisitive and—"

"Trudie."

"Yes?"

"It's okay. I want you to feel free to ask me anything." Mason closed his hand over hers briefly.

"All right." Trudie wrapped her arms around herself, suddenly looking bashful. "Was your brother going to continue on with the family business?"

"Yes, he was. That was very much Nate's calling. Just like my father."

"But not *your* calling?"

"No."

Trudie touched the photo. "I think it's lovely that your father never changed the sign from 'and sons.' He must miss Nate very much."

"He does. We all do." Mason went over to his oak desk and sat on the edge of it. "But my father misses Nate in more ways than one."

"How do you mean?"

"Nate was going to eventually take over the business after my father retired. Now, well…my father hopes I'll run the funeral home someday." Mason waited for her response before he went on. He couldn't read her expression, but he wanted to. Desperately.

"Oh, I see." Trudie left the wall of photos and strolled over to him. "How do you feel about that?"

"I think being a funeral director is a very special vocation and, like I said, a calling. But I don't have it. Those are my honest beliefs. However, there is the family side to it. My father built the business out of one hundred dollars and a prayer. And he's proud of what he accomplished, since his own father was very poor. And part of my father's dream was to pass the business on to one or both of his sons. When Nate died…well, that changed everything."

"Your father sounds like a wonderful man. But what about *your* dreams?" Trudie lifted her hands. "I am so sorry. Forgive me. This is none of my business."

"There is nothing to forgive." Mason gripped the edge of the desk. "I've thought about that same thing many times. Countless times, to be honest. But I love my father, and I'd like to honor his wishes. To keep the business in the family." He looked at her. Trudie had such an angelic expression, but he wished he knew all that she was thinking. "My father's not planning on going to heaven right away, but unfortunately, he has a bad heart, and so I know he'd like an answer soon."

Trudie sat in the chair across from him. "It's hard not to admire you for your choice. To love your family so much. And it *is* a noble profession."

Mason wanted to hug her for her encouraging words, but he held back. "I can tell you, it's never been good material to discuss on a date. Not on the first date *or* even the tenth date. It doesn't set a very romantic mood."

"I understand now." She smiled. "Why you didn't want me to see this room. I'm not the only one who's asked about your family photos."

"That's right." Mason eased off the desk.

"And apparently other women have objected to your switching careers. They might not be certain they want to marry a man who runs a funeral home."

He looked at her. "Most women when they meet me, they see this successful guy in a regular job. All is well until I tell them about my possible career change. I keep hoping that if a woman gets to know me first, maybe it would change everything. But so far, it's never been enough."

Trudie rose from the chair and walked over to him. "I don't know you, Mason, although in this short time, somehow I feel as though I do." She reached up and touched his cheek. "And what I've discovered so far…well, what I think is…those women couldn't have been more wrong."

Mason rested his hand over hers. They both eased closer, hovering near each other. He lingered there next to Trudie, taking her in, studying every nuance of her face and enjoying every moment of it. She smelled of something delicate, like powder. All he could hear was the soft bubbling inside the aquarium and their breathing—which seemed to be a bit faster now. He'd never wanted to kiss a woman so much in his life, but he knew the time wasn't right. Yet. "The stars will be out tonight. Do you want to see them?"

"Yes. I'd love to."

Chapter Nine

....

Trudie backed away from Mason, feeling flushed and self-conscious. What had she been thinking? She'd taken a heartfelt moment and made it complicated. To reach out to him seemed like a natural response to his revelation, and yet it could have come off as too intimate. *Maybe I'd better lighten things up.* "I suppose you have a planetarium set up in your backyard."

Mason chuckled. "No, I don't even have a telescope, but that's what I've promised myself for Christmas."

Trudie followed Mason through the house and then out the back door, which led to a large wraparound porch. After a short walk up a flight of stairs, they were both standing on an open deck, looking at the sky. Mason had been right; the stars were out in their fullness, and they were already working their magic on the night. Incredible. "What was that like? To grow up in your family?"

Mason leaned against the railing. "Well, in many ways, it was like other families with their fathers going off to work in the morning. But when he came home, he didn't talk very much about what his day was like. My father had such a reverence for the grieving families that he was careful in choosing his words. Then, when he felt my brother and I were old enough, he gave us a tour of *all* the facilities. Afterward I remember thinking that I knew of no one else who was more suited to the job than my father. He'd been given a special gift."

"How did your brother respond to the tour?" Trudie sat down on one of the wooden benches.

Mason eased down next to her. "Nate had all the right questions.

The right attitude…great compassion without being overly emotional. My father could tell Nate had the gift too. Everyone knew."

Trudie thought of Nate and wondered what he'd been like as a brother. She took in a deep breath and gazed over at several willow branches that were swaying back and forth in the breeze. The night was warm and fragrant, and a chorus of bugs were busy singing their hearts out. It was a good night for heart-sharing. "I wish I could have known your brother."

"I wish you had too. He would have liked you. A lot. Which could have been a problem, especially since we were close."

Trudie smiled. "I'm curious. Did your family business affect your faith?"

Mason raised an eyebrow. "My, you really are the inquisitress, Miss Abernathy."

"That's true." Her face warmed. "Sorry."

"Actually, I love it that you've asked me." Mason rubbed his hands together. "I do think people try to sidestep thoughts of mortality. That is, until they're forced to think about it because of an abnormal test, or they experience the sudden death of a friend. But in the funeral business, my father is reminded daily that all of humanity faces a close to this side of eternity, whether rich or poor, young or old, beautiful or not so beautiful. But in answer to your question, I think the nature of my father's business has increased our faith, not lessened it." Mason looked at her again. "See why this doesn't make good date talk? Kinda heavy."

"I think it's one of the most interesting discussions I've ever had." Trudie looked up at the sky, marveling at the brightness and clarity of the moon. "What is that star near the moon?"

"It might be the planet Venus, but I'm not sure. That's why I'd like to take an astronomy class at one of the local colleges after I get a telescope. That way I can truly know and appreciate what I'm gazing at."

Trudie looked at him. He had such a fine smile—the color of sienna—

always warm and welcoming. She turned her attention back to the stars. "Do you think when we're born, God has our lives all set out for us, and our job is to fit ourselves into that groove? Or do you think there are many choices we could make and still live within His pleasure?"

"I'm not sure." Mason stroked his finger against his chin. "There have been times I thought I was sure about that answer, but the older I get, the muddier my views get on that subject." He rested his arm on the railing just behind her. "Now I have a question for you."

"Fair enough. I've certainly asked you plenty of questions."

"If there is one groove…I get the feeling you don't think you've found yours yet."

Trudie wasn't sure how best to answer. "Well, I've always tried to convince myself that I'm contented, but then maybe I've just been fooling myself."

Mason rubbed his hand over his slacks. "I've told you about my life growing up. I'd love to know more about yours." He raised a finger. "But first, not without some reinforcements. I'll go get us some fresh coffee."

"Thanks." Trudie watched Mason through the window as he retrieved some mugs from the cabinet and poured them fresh coffees. She had to admit, Mason was a remarkable man. She did wonder, however, about his change of professions. Managing a funeral home would be a much harder job than financial consulting, and it would no doubt be emotionally draining. If the wife chose to help her husband, she would need special gifts of her own—compassion in working with people who were grieving, not to mention diplomacy and sociability.

Trudie rose, stepped over to the railing, and looked upward. Clouds began rolling in, covering up the lunar display like a curtain on a grand stage. She sighed, thinking about Mason's possible career change. There really was no putting a soft focus on his choice. And yet if a woman's heart were truly captured by Mason—which could happen so easily—then nothing would hold her back. How could it? Wasn't love supposed to conquer all?

Mason walked back outside and handed her another mug of coffee. "I think you like it black."

"I do. Thanks." He was so attentive. So kind. She took another whiff of the brew and then several slow sips. Okay, at any moment he would expect her to tell him about her youth. What would she say? Was she ready to reveal her fears and dreams? He'd been so transparent—so giving of his feelings and views. She could do no less.

Trudie cleared her throat. "Okay, my childhood. I grew up on a farm in Oklahoma. My only sibling is Lane. My father was hardworking, but he was never too successful at farming. My mother was uncommonly beautiful. Like a delicate rose. In fact, she won a beauty pageant before she met my father. He was so proud of that, he kept her tiara on display in our house." She fingered her mug. "But unfortunately, both of my parents are dead now." Trudie turned to Mason, hoping he would be satisfied with her brief highlights.

"I'm very sorry for your loss. I'm sure they were fine people. But you failed to tell me much about Trudie."

"Oh. You noticed." She set her mug down on the railing.

"I did notice." He grinned. "Didn't you tell me earlier that you had an interest in art? Were you wanting to be an artist?"

"Well, I guess you could say that I was an artist early on. I'd sold some pieces through a gallery."

"Really? At what age?"

"Fifteen."

Mason's mouth came open. "My goodness. Please tell me more."

Trudie hesitated in continuing, but when she saw Mason's gentle expression, she said, "Well, it all began when my mother took me to a fine arts museum in Tulsa. Even though I was only seven at the time, I was blown away by that trip. Gradually, I took an interest in art, and my mother encouraged it. Years later I did well enough that my mother traveled to Oklahoma City to show my work to some of the galleries. Even though I was new and very young, people bought my work."

"That's amazing at such a young age." Mason took a drink from his cup. "I'm curious. Do mind if I ask how—"

"How much I sold them for?" Trudie grinned.

"Sorry." Mason shook his head. "That's kind of pushy of me to ask."

"I don't mind you knowing." Trudie knew Mason wasn't prying but was only asking out of genuine interest. "Sometimes I got paid several hundred dollars for a watercolor."

"Now that really is something, especially at such a young age." Mason set his mug down. "You must be very talented. Why aren't you painting now?"

"My mother's death stopped me. You see, her dying…it was my fault." Trudie looked away into the night, avoiding Mason's eyes.

Chapter Ten
....

Mason sat down on one of the benches. "I'm sure you just mean that you feel guilty somehow. I felt that way about Nate, too. Since I was his older brother, I always believed I should have done a better job of watching out for him."

Trudie kept silent for a moment, not knowing what to say. The last thing she wanted was to spoil a perfect evening with her confessions of guilt. But then she remembered the look on Mason's face when he'd told her about his choice to honor his father's wishes. She knew it had taken courage for him to tell her, especially since his news had brought rejection in the past.

"It's okay, Trudie. You don't have to say any more."

"No, I want to." She took in a deep breath and turned to face him. "I asked my mother to drive into the city that day. I demanded it, actually. A gallery was going to take several more of my paintings. My mother had become like an errand boy to me."

Trudie's eyes became misty. "I'm afraid the sudden ability for a kid to make that kind of money, coupled with all the recognition…well, it was pretty heady stuff. Over a rather short period of time, I became quite the diva." She sat down next to Mason. "A car ran a red light that day and killed my mother instantly." Trudie ground her fingernails into her palms. "But I will always believe it was my lack of humility that killed her. I doubt there's anything that will ever change my mind."

Mason covered her hand with his. "I'm so sorry. I wish there was something I could say that would convince you otherwise."

Trudie saw no judgment in his eyes, only compassion, so she

let her thoughts unwind a little. "Perhaps if someone would have reminded me of the Giver of my gift, it might have softened me. Made things turn out differently that day. I don't know, of course, but I do feel that acknowledging the Source of my talent might have refocused the limelight…changed my attitude…my demands. And, well, it might have lightened the emotional load too, since glory can be more of a burden than a blessing. At least it was for me."

Mason squeezed her hand. "So, you didn't continue your artwork after that?"

"I did on and off, but it gradually came to an end. I felt I didn't deserve to continue. And my father…well, he never blamed me for Mom's death, but he also didn't encouraged me in my art after that. So, I eventually let go of it."

"You could talk to your sister about it. Maybe she could help you find some closure." Mason released her.

"After so many years, silence has a way of becoming easier." Trudie circled her arms around her waist. "But I'll think about it." She smiled at him. "Since you suggested it."

Mason rested his arm behind Trudie. "I get the feeling that you've not shared this with other people. Never leaned on anyone."

It was true. She'd become like a rock, but it was fake all the way through. Tears came then, and she accepted his invitation to lean against him.

Mason reached into his pocket, pulled out a handkerchief, and handed it to her. "This is all my fault…that you're crying. Persuading you to tell me your story."

Trudie wiped her eyes. "Well, it's a good kind of tears, and it wasn't your fault. I was long overdue to talk about it. And you were the right person."

Mason wrapped his arms around her. "I'm glad you feel that way."

"In fact, it felt sort of…ordained." She looked into his eyes. There was so much compassion there, it tore at her heart.

He reached over and moved a strand of hair away from her face.

"What are you thinking?"

"How lovely you look."

"Especially in the *dim* moonlight?" Trudie fingered her earring and grinned.

Mason chuckled. "You're funny, too."

"I am?"

"Yes, and about as far from a diva as anyone I've ever known."

"Well, if one doesn't accept humility willingly, life tends to thrust it on you." As Mason stroked her cheek, for a moment Trudie forgot the point she was trying to make. She instead wondered what it would be like for a couple to be so compatible that they brought out each other's personal best. What would that feel like, and would that other person be someone like Mason Wimberley? She gazed into his eyes, searching them. "I wish I could read your mind."

"Are you sure about that?"

"I'm sure." She nodded.

"Well, I was thinking that you've had so much forced on you through the years, I wasn't sure if I wanted to coerce you into a kiss."

Without really thinking, Trudie reached up and touched his lips. She'd wondered what they would feel like against her fingers, and they were as soft as she imagined. "I don't think it's called coercion when the lady is more than ready."

Mason grinned and raised her chin.

She closed her eyes and, rising up to him, felt his lips cover hers. Somewhere deep in her mind's eyes, Trudie saw strokes of color and light, so much so that she thought a great work of art might be inspired by a single kiss from Mason.

When he released her, Trudie held her palm over his heart and leaned over to whisper in his ear. "I saw rainbows."

He chuckled. "I think I did too. It was a very good kiss."

They held that pose for a moment, a little out of breath, as they looked at each other. Then Trudie rested her head against him. Something was changing, and she knew she'd never be the same person again.

He brought her closer to him. "And to think I missed getting to know you in high school. I must have graduated as you were coming in as a freshman. And then as an adult I almost missed meeting you again even though you were only five minutes from my house." Mason kissed the top of her head.

And to think you were the blind date I didn't want to meet. Trudie smiled but hated to close her eyes again. Perhaps she'd wake up. It had become, after all, the perfect dream.

Chapter Eleven
....

Lane Abernathy paced in her kitchen, feeling nauseated. She'd already lost everything in her stomach even though she'd barely eaten all day. She had no virus. No food poisoning. Lane knew what was wrong—she was heartsick.

She eased herself down on a kitchen chair. How could she have done it? Forced Trudie into a blind date with Mason? And on her birthday? Her sister had gone along with it out of politeness, but in the midst of. her matchmaking, Lane realized what she'd really done. She driven away, given away the very man she loved. *Mason.*

How could love have happened so unexpectedly? Without warning? Lane had known the truth in her heart for several days, and yet it still surprised her to think of it. "What should I do? They'll be here any minute." Mason would drop Trudie off on her doorstep after their date. Her fingers trembled as they lighted underneath her chin. Lane thought she'd found a way to handle the whirling emotions, but all her pep talks had failed.

Her stomach cramped again, and she doubled over. When the pain let up a little, she reached for a ginger ale in the fridge, opened the bottle, and took a few tentative sips. It soothed her stomach a little and took the bitter taste from her mouth.

Lane let her mind filter back through the various scenes with Mason, the ones she'd tried to keep at bay for months. The feelings had come on so gradually, it had been easy to dismiss them, but when the full force of those emotions had arrived, there was no discarding them. Looking back, she could pinpoint the moment when her heart had been taken—

the day of Trudie's birthday lunch—when Mason had given her sister the balloons and the stuffed animal.

Lane folded her arms across the kitchen table. No man had ever done anything so charming for her. A few men had sent flowers over the years, but their gifts had always come off obligatory. Maybe even sterile of any real feeling. A bouquet of balloons with an adorable koala attached meant a man wasn't afraid to be intimate, wasn't worried about coming off whimsical and open. In that moment when the delivery was made, so much had been felt—so much had finally been acknowledged. Mason had revealed his spirit, and it was one she admired. And loved.

She took a few more sips of the soda, letting the sweet effervescence soothe her stomach, but another spasm hit her again the moment she thought of how she'd brushed Mason aside after only three dates. How could she have been so foolish? What did it really matter if they were dating at the same time they were doing business together? People did it all the time. Her reasoning had been as weak as skim milk. But what of it now? When it came to love and Mason, she no longer cared about decorum. She loved the man. If any conflict of interest arose, she could always fire him and then marry him!

Lane rested her head on the table. Maybe she was making herself sick with worry for nothing. What were the chances of Trudie and Mason falling in love on a first date? Virtually impossible. Although *she'd* fallen in love on a first date when she was in high school. Hayden Montgomery. It could happen. It *did* happen. But Hayden was long gone and married by now. Probably had two or three gorgeous kids, all growing up and happy.

She lifted her head, feeling a little better. Lane thought she saw a car light in the driveway. Ten thirty. It was them. Why had she promised her sister another session on Saturday morning after breakfast? And on top of that, it had to be the worst possible night for a slumber party.

A surge of panic swept through Lane. She would be forced to see them together, and then later she'd feel obligated to ask Trudie about every little detail of the evening. What would be the right thing to do? Tell her sister about her feelings for Mason? Or remain silent while Trudie dated him? In the meantime, she would be hoping and praying it would all come to nothing. *O God, what should I do? Speak out or leave my feelings unvoiced?*

Lane heard a car door slam, and her heart constricted.

Chapter Twelve
....

Lane ran into the bathroom to check her makeup. She certainly didn't want them to think she'd been crying. After dusting on a bit more blush and smoothing the wrinkles in her pants outfit, she felt she looked passable under the circumstances. Why hadn't they rung the doorbell? Lane made her way to the front door and looked through the peephole. Mason was kissing Trudie. And not just a good-night peck on the cheek. He was kissing with earnestness, and her sister was returning the kiss with equal dedication!

Before she could think through her actions, Lane flipped on the porch light. The area was suddenly illuminated with enough light to land an aircraft. *Well, that wasn't very polite of me.* Her shoulders sagged like a wilted flower.

Chuckles could be heard coming from the other side and then a soft knock. Lane sighed and opened the door. "Hello."

Mason smiled. "Hi, Lane."

Trudie picked up her overnight case and stepped inside the house. "Thanks, Mason. Take care."

He gave them both a little wave, glanced Trudie's way one more time with an expectant look, and then walked toward his car.

Lane winced, looking at his vehicle. She never could understand why such a wealthy man would drive such a wreck of a car. Not his style at all. If she were married to Mason, the first thing she'd do would be to sell that vehicle and get him something that would fit his dashing persona—a Beamer or a sporty Lexus.

"Hi." Trudie gave Lane a hug and then sort of floated into the living room. "You were right about everything, Lane. Mason is as wonderful as you said. Much more so, really."

"Yes." Lane was glad her sister wasn't angry for interrupting their kiss, but she felt a twinge of wooziness coming on again. The sight of Trudie so obviously swept away by Mason's charms was almost more than she could bear. "So, do you think you two will continue to go out?" It felt like a foolish question, since from the looks of their kiss, there seemed to be a mutual and genuine attraction between them.

Trudie appeared to be staring at nothing but the air. "He said he would call sometime tomorrow evening." She drifted to the couch and sat down.

"Oh?" Lane tried to add a lilt to her voice. She sat down on the love seat opposite her sister. The session she'd given Trudie on dress and hair had really paid off. She looked wonderful. Maybe a little too wonderful. Their date had obviously gone very well. Lane made the decision then not to tell her sister about her feelings. She wouldn't lie, but there was no need to bring up the subject.

Her sister looked into her eyes for the first time. Lane gave Trudie a warm smile, one she was certain would put Trudie at ease. She would take the high road, if indeed that *was* the high road. She had no idea. Maybe she would let the dates between Mason and Trudie play themselves out. Perhaps they would tire of each other.

Within seconds Trudie seemed to come out of a trance. "What's the matter?" She scooted to the edge of the couch. "Lane, have you been crying?"

"Crying?" Lane brightened her smile.

"There's something wrong." Trudie got up and eased down next to her on the love seat.

I won't tell Trudie the truth. I can't. But Lane knew she wouldn't really be able to pull off a lie. And besides, she knew God was listening. He was right there in their midst, and she didn't want to disappoint Him. Would the truth break her sister's heart? Then again, Trudie had never even said she would go out with Mason again. She'd only said he was going to call her. But considering the look of utter bliss she'd seen on her sister's face, it was a given how she felt. "It's not important tonight. Why don't you tell me about your evening?"

"I will…as soon as you tell me what's wrong."

Lane sat there silent, wishing she'd put on more makeup. Or perhaps she could have masked her feelings better. How had life gotten so messy? She'd always been able to label life's emotional clutter and either tidy it up or file it away, but this ordeal didn't feel like anything that could be labeled or filed or fixed.

Trudie touched her arm. "You can tell me anything. Remember, we're sisters. Haven't you always told me that sisters share everything?"

Lane swallowed the sour taste in her mouth. *Yes, but how can we share our love for the same man? It will tear us apart as easily as fabric.*

"Is it about Mason?"

She looked at Trudie then. Could she have already guessed? "I just want you to know that no matter what happens, I love you. I always will."

"What is it? Please."

Trudie's joy had been turned into such sadness Lane wanted to wipe it away, but she knew her words would only bring them both an even greater sorrow. "I'll say it straight out, since that may be the best way." Lane squeezed Trudie's hand. "I'm in love with Mason."

Chapter Thirteen

The second the words came out of Lane's mouth, she regretted them. *Why, God? Why couldn't I have lied...just this once?*

"Oh, I see." Trudie eased away from Lane and rested back on the love seat, her arms hugging her middle. "How long have you known?"

"I don't even fully understand my own emotions. I never intended for this to happen. But as I think more about it, I guess these feelings must have been coming on for a while, and I just didn't want to accept them. I told myself that I just had a very high regard for him. And too, I kept thinking I shouldn't date a man who was busy telling me what stocks to buy or how to plan my retirement. But really what did that matter? I should have acknowledged all that I felt."

"You love him," Trudie said softly as if she were still trying to absorb the news.

Lane wished more than anything that the words could be taken back. Not knowing what else to do with the strange quiet, she said, "Why don't I go in the kitchen and get us something cold to drink."

"Okay." Trudie rested her head against the back of the couch.

Lane went into the kitchen, but her sister didn't join her. She moved around from one spot to another, straightening things on the counter and putting things away, but feeling no more than a methodic numbness. What could be done now? There was no turning back on the truth—that door could never be closed again—and yet she longed to make things right.

Trudie appeared in the doorway.

Lane stopped and turned to face her sister.

"When we three had lunch together, I could see something in your eyes then, but I told myself it was only in my imagination." Trudie's fingers laced over her abdomen as if she were trying not to breathe. "You should have told me. Before Mason even asked me out. I could have told him no when he called. Why didn't you speak up that day?" Her sister's words carried no anger, only desperation.

"You're right. I should have told you right away." Lane lowered her gaze. "It was just so difficult, especially since I'd worked so hard at getting you two together. It would have come off capricious and unkind."

"I see." Trudie slowly nodded.

Lane knew what her sister had to be thinking—her belated confession could be described in terms far worse than capricious and unkind. "This isn't the conversation we were supposed to be having." She shook her head. "I want you to know that when I set up our sleepover I was still denying what I felt. I was still trying to figure things out, and I was hoping I was wrong. I really did want to be wrong."

Lane let out a long breath of air. "Oh, dear Trudie, this should have been your night. You should have told me what a wonderful evening you'd had with Mason. I was going to tell you how beautiful you looked. Which you do. We were going to stay up late and watch movies like when we were teenagers. Eat cookie dough, tell stories, and laugh a lot. And tomorrow I was going to give you a free session on makeup and poise." *How ridiculous that sounds now.*

"We still can do all of that if you'd like." Trudie's voice sounded encouraging but without its usual spirit.

"No, we shouldn't now. I won't make you do that. I think we're both too weary." Lane felt tears coming, so she turned toward the sink to avoid her sister's eyes. A moment later she could feel Trudie's arms wrapping around her and her chin resting on her shoulder as they used to do to each other when they were girls.

"Somehow in God's mercy, this will work out," Trudie whispered.

"Yes. Surely. Somehow."

Trudie released her, and they both puttered around in the kitchen, getting their favorite sodas on ice. But in spite of their casual appearance, a profound uneasiness still hung in the air.

When they'd gotten all settled, Trudie fidgeted with her glass of root beer. "I suppose we need to talk about the practicality of how this will work. Mason might get confused a little. And hurt."

"How will he be hurt? You will continue to date him. I can't ask you to stop. I won't. But I did need to be honest. To acknowledge how I felt." Lane took a reassuring sip of her ginger ale.

Trudie's mouth came open. "Surely you don't mean it. I can't date Mason as if nothing has been said. I could never go out with him knowing that you love him. I wouldn't enjoy his company. I would only be thinking of your suffering."

Lane sighed. "This is none of my business, but do you… ?"

"Yes?"

"Well, will my confession tonight merely put an end to some pleasant dates between you two? Or am I in the way of what could have turned into love?" Lane realized she was asking an impossible question, but she was anxious to know her sister's intentions. How she really felt about the evening and the future.

Trudie took a slow sip of her beverage. "It was a memorable evening. I've never met anyone like Mason. And as foolish as it seems, he took an interest in me." Her shoulders drooped a little. "And I think if we had continued dating, yes, there's a chance I would have fallen in love with him. But then Mason would be very easy to love."

"Yes. I see." Lane's concern about Trudie's burgeoning feelings had been real after all. She hadn't blown anything out of proportion. They were in the mire, and her familiar velvet rope of happy-speak and positive thinking wasn't going to pull them out. Only God could help them now.

"May I ask you a question?"

"Of course." Lane placed her hands in her lap, trying to remain calm.

"When I refuse Mason, what will happen then? Will you wait for him to ask you out? Or will you go to him right away to tell him how you feel?" Trudie's expression was neither angry nor full of anguish, but her chin lifted in what looked like resolve.

"I hadn't really made plans. I hadn't gotten that far." Lane released a mirthless chuckle. "I thought there was a chance you'd come back this evening uninterested in Mason. At least that's what I'd hoped for. I know that sounds awful. I'm just trying to be honest. But this…I didn't expect you to react this way to my announcement…that you wouldn't go out with him again." She gripped the edges of the chair. "And, well, when you walked in the door, I'd decided not to even tell you about my feelings." Lane hoped her ramblings weren't coming off disjointed or peevish.

Trudie smiled. "But you couldn't hide love. It's a feeling of epic proportion. It would only have been a matter of time before I figured it out."

"Yes, I suppose that's true." Lane placed her hands around her glass, embracing the coolness of it. "But I still can't get over it…that you'll decline another offer to go out with him because of me."

"There's no other choice."

Perhaps Lane didn't know her sister as well as she thought she did. "Trudie, are you absolutely sure about this?"

"I'm sure."

"Well…Mason and I have a meeting scheduled for next week. I could tell him I've changed my mind. That I would like to go out with him after all." In spite of her steady demeanor, the faintest tremor of panic trickled through Lane. *Am I doing the right thing?*

"Okay." Trudie stared into her glass of root beer. "When Mason calls me tomorrow, I will tell him no, but I won't give him an explanation. It will be easier that way, and there'll be no lies." She moved the glass away. "Mason will eventually stop asking me out, and then he'll turn his attentions back to you. Where they should have been all along."

Chapter Fourteen
....

Trudie woke up in the night, trembling and feverish. The pillow felt damp from a serious case of the night sweats. She'd dreamt she was falling into a boiling vat of liquid black. Awake, though, she felt miserable—like she was still cloaked in the colors of the night, and daylight would never come.

She fluffed her pillow and pulled her nightgown down, which had migrated up to her neck and was nearly strangling her. How did she think she deserved the attentions of someone like Mason anyway? He was a shining star while she was a meteorite, dull and inert. Trudie almost laughed, but it was wretchedly unfunny.

Humans are so flimsy, God. People were like willows branches, moved by any random breeze of feeling. But if her emotions were so sinuous, why did she feel her heart might snap in two? She'd had only one date with Mason. How could it be that she already cared for him? Trudie closed her eyes to shut out the world. And what would she say when he called? After her initial "no" Mason would certainly wonder why. When she refused to answer him, he might go off thinking he was being rejected because of his new career choice. The idea of hurting him as other women had before her was heartbreaking.

Trudie had always believed that God would work all things for good for those who loved Him. That verse was easy enough to live by in good times, but in rough times, did she really own all those words? Did she truly love God? Hard to tell for sure. Love on earth could be measured more easily by how much the heart ached when someone beloved was taken away. But to love the One who knit every gossamer tissue together and gave every breath, it was hard to know how that devotion should feel. She continued to ponder celestial themes, since they were intertwined with the earthly ones.

* * * * *

Some hours later, Trudie awakened again and looked at the bedside clock. 7:05. The memories of the previous evening swept through her mind, making her spirit groan with sadness.

Trudie sat up and massaged her neck. Work was what she needed, and lots of it. She was supposed to have the day off, but she also knew her boss, Rosalie, would have plenty of extra chores for her at Bloomers Boutique. She always did.

Feeling a need to get ready for the day, Trudie quickly showered and slipped on a fresh pair of slacks and a shirt. While her sister slept, she made enough coffee for them both and left a note on the kitchen table, saying she was going off to work and to have a good day. She added the last part so her sister wouldn't grieve too much. Trudie loved her sister and couldn't stand for her to mourn. Lane would surely feel the same way if the situation had been in reverse.

For a moment, Trudie paused. What *would* Lane have done if the circumstances were turned around? Would Lane continue to date Mason no matter what? Or would she bow out gracefully? And what about her own actions if all had been different? Trudie wasn't sure how she would have reacted or what she would have done, and the uncertainty bothered her.

She took her mug of coffee onto the patio and looked out on the golf course. There were some early risers already whacking balls down the fairway. The clouds above them hung in the sky like the fluffy behinds of Peter Rabbit and all his family. The sight was lovely and innocent, and it made Trudie think of the kids she'd read to and played with over the years at the children's hospital. They had suffered much harder times than anything she would ever know, and they had faced it with courage.

After a couple of slow sips from her cup, Trudie decided to look back at the summer morning through new eyes. It was indeed a remarkable day. And there was a sudden yearning inside her to make that dazzling sky come to life with watercolors. What would that feel like again? When she was a girl, she had always turned to art for pleasure, but she especially embraced it when life got hard. And she'd never in her life felt so close to God as when she was painting.

Her fingers stiffened around the handle of the mug as she remembered how her love for art and all her dreams had drifted away like the last fallen leaves of autumn. The very art that had brought her so much pleasure had brought her the worst kind of pain—the end to her dear mother's life. But she also had to acknowledge that it was never the art itself that had caused the accident. The fault had been hers, stemming from selfishness and pride.

Trudie strolled back inside the house, wondering if God had pardoned her yet or if she alone was the one who refused to give herself that freedom. She took another sip of her coffee, but it seemed to lose its warmth and flavor. No, maybe it was just bitter. She rinsed the mug, put it in the sink, and then headed toward the spare room to gather her things. She'd almost made it to the hallway when something shiny caught her eye. Trudie walked over to the curio cabinet in the far corner of the living room. Nestled on a bed of rich navy velvet was their mother's tiara. Lane had it beautifully presented under the halogen lights along with several antique vases and figurines.

She opened the door to the cabinet and let her fingers glide across the top of the crown. It was so radiant with its sapphires and diamonds. She could almost imagine her mother again, placing the tiara on her head. Then the way she'd cup her face and kiss her forehead. What would her mother say if she could whisper from heaven? Perhaps her mother would tell her that God was smiling on her still and that she shouldn't let go of the gift He'd given her.

No. Trudie shut the door to the cabinet. She quickly shook off the sentimental imaginings, since she believed it was a desperate attempt to assuage her guilt. She shut the lights off, and the glittering jewels on the crown went dim. Lane had hoped they'd trade off with the tiara so that it could be on display in Trudie's apartment half of the year, but she'd refused. It was in the right place. Right here.

Time to go to work. Trudie suddenly remembered that her car was still back at her apartment. So, how was she going to get to the shop? She didn't want to wake her sister, so she decided to borrow Lane's older car, the one she lent out from time to time. Trudie knew she wouldn't mind, so she added a P.S. to the note about borrowing her sedan, picked up the keys out of the entry table drawer, and headed to work.

After a short drive, Trudie turned the corner onto Atascocita and saw the familiar sign, BLOOMERS BOUTIQUE, which was painted in pink petunias and a pair of old-fashioned bloomers. She smiled. Rosalie had always been a girly-girl. Apparently the women in Humble loved all things feminine too, since business had been blooming for years, as Rosalie always said.

Trudie parked the sedan, strode up to the boutique, and opened the door. As always there was enough frothing female garb to boost one's estrogen levels just by breathing the air. And the place smelled of peppermint too. Guess Rosalie was still on her aromatherapy kick. But it was a nice scent, and the customers loved it.

"Ohhh, you're here, Trudie. Good, good. I needed you after all. At least for a few hours today."

I knew it.

Rosalie gave her a motherly hug. "How about you sort through the racks. I love my customers, but they get things sooo jumbled. We have the size eights in with the twenty-twos again."

"I'm on it, Rosalie."

"Oh, and you missed Suzette yesterday afternoon." Rosalie clicked her tongue. "Mm, mm."

"Did she buy her usual?" Trudie started organizing the rack of boudoir dresses.

"That dear woman. She keeps dreaming if she buys enough size sixes she'll *become* a size six. I hate to be the one to break it to her, but all that dreaming doesn't mix with grazing at the local pizza buffet." Rosalie shook her head. "Oh, well, hope springs eternal. Is that old saying about weight loss or love?" She chuckled.

Trudie didn't want to think too far down the road with that maxim, so she got busy with her work.

"Suzette brought us a batch of brownies. They're in the back next to the coffee machine. I've already eaten half of them, so you'd better dig in before they're gone. Oh, and Henry Bog dropped by this morning. He brought us some strawberries from his garden. He said they were loaded again this year. So, you've got a basket of fresh strawberries in the back."

Trudie shook her head. "What would we do without all our customers?"

"Mm, mm. Go out of business, I guess. Well, and I'd probably lose thirty pounds too." Rosalie shook with laughter.

Her boss could always change the tenor of a room in two minutes as she ferreted out the amusement in everything she encountered. It fit perfectly with her bright muumuus, her rosy cheeks, and that twinkle in her eye. "So, did our Mr. Bog buy another nightgown for his wife?"

"Yep. He says it's what keeps the pizzazz in their marriage." Rosalie made a little lasso with her finger. "Oh, and we had a customer today from out of state. I can always tell because they pronounce the *H* in

Humble." She winked. "Well, sweets, I've got to go in the back room for a bit. I'll catch the phone if it rings."

"Okay." The sudden quiet in the shop made Trudie's thoughts drift dangerously close to a topic she wanted to avoid—Mason. Correction. She didn't *really* want to avoid thoughts of him, but she felt it was the only way to retain her sanity. She would, however, need to come up with something to say to him when he called. Would Mason merely say good-bye when she refused another date, or would he be truly hurt? Amidst the queries filling her brain, she knew one thing was certain—she would miss Mason. Terribly.

The bell jingled above the door and the subject of her many queries stood in the doorway, smiling at her.

Chapter Fifteen

....

"Hello." Mason entered the shop, looking devastating in his suit. Kind of like Clark Kent without the glasses.

Maybe she should at least be polite. "Hi."

He looked around, raising a curious brow. "Are men actually allowed in here?"

Trudie laughed. "Of course." She knew he was kidding, but he did look intimidated as he stood amidst shelves and racks of female dainties.

Then in a sudden bold move, Mason strolled right up to Trudie.

"Were you needing bloomers?" was all Trudie could think to say.

"Uh, no." He leaned on a sale table full of long-legged panty girdles, winced, and then stood back up.

Trudie squelched another laugh.

Mason made a few odd maneuvers with his hands as if he suddenly didn't know where to put them.

"Are you looking for a kimono perhaps?" She raised her chin a bit.

Mason chuckled. "I came to see you. I thought you had the day off."

Trudie knew she was having way too much fun with Mason, so she reined in her enthusiasm. "I decided to work today after all."

"Well, I stopped by your sister's house, and—"

"What did Lane say?"

"I felt badly that I'd gotten her out of bed. She looked so...I don't know...tired. You two must have had a lot of fun last night."

Trudie went blank. How could she reply to that one?

"But Lane didn't say much. Just that she'd read your note and that you were here."

"Oh." Trudie nodded.

Mason fingered one of the boudoir dresses. "I came by to ask you to lunch."

"Lunch?" Here it was. The moment she'd dreaded. What could she say? What was right and good? She wouldn't tell him a lie, but to explain everything would ruin Lane's chances. She swallowed. "I'm sorry, Mason."

"What, you don't eat lunch?"

Trudie knew if she tried to talk, she might stammer. "No, I…I do eat lunch." There it was. The stammer.

"Well, maybe another time." He raked his fingers through his hair.

Stay calm. Answer slowly. "I don't think so." Okay, those had to be the hardest words she'd ever said.

"Oh." Surprise flashed across his face, then disappointment. "So you're saying *no* in general…about going out again. Is that it?" Mason said his words gently but looked her straight in the eyes.

Trudie wanted to hug him, to tell him what a wonderful man he was and how she'd miss him, but that was impossible now. Why hadn't Mason called her instead of just dropping by? She wouldn't have had to witness that look of distress. Suddenly her face felt prickly—a strange malady she sometimes suffered from when she got flustered. Trudie tapped her cheeks.

"Are you okay?"

"My cheeks just went a little tingly." Trudie tried to find something else to focus on.

"Tingly?"

"Uh-huh."

Mason moved closer to her. "Well, that doesn't sound too good."

Trudie shook her head. "No, that's okay."

He reached out, took the red peignoir she was holding, and set it back on the rack. "If this has to do with my family and any career changes, I want you to know I understand. But I believe we can work this—"

"No. It's not that." Trudie touched the sleeve of his cotton shirt and then pulled away. "I promise. It's not that." She would help Lane all she could, but she would not leave Mason to think his family's business was repugnant to her.

"Then what is it? Please tell me." He touched her arm.

Trudie removed the very same red peignoir from the rack Mason had just put away and said, "This is a size eight." Why she'd said those words she had no idea, except maybe to shift the focus away from her.

"Is that your size?"

She looked up at him, wanting so badly to slip her palm around his cheek the way she had only hours earlier. "Yes, it's my size, but I mean everything has gotten so messed up." Trudie bit her lip to keep the tears from coming.

Mason nodded. "Apparently."

Trudie held up the red peignoir. "I mean this needs to be put back. It's with the twenty-two plus-sizes."

He seemed to shake himself from a daze. "Well now, we can't have that, can we? I'd like to help you put things back in order." Mason gave her a weighty look and then took the skimpy piece of red froth out of her hands, walked over to the correct stand, and eased the peignoir smoothly into the right place.

Trudie put her hands on her hips. "You can't help me rearrange the whole store."

"Why not?"

She shook her head. "Because you're a customer. Well, not exactly."

"Good idea. I think I will be a customer."

Oh, no.

Mason looked through the selection a bit and then pulled out a size eight peignoir in lilac, one that was accented with a whisper of ivory lace. "Not bad." He held it up to the sunlight, allowing its translucent qualities to be fully revealed. "Very nice. What do you call this?"

Trudie cocked her head. "It's called *plumage*." She said it briskly so he might get the hint to stop torturing her with his charm. And leave.

"You don't say?" Mason didn't appear ruffled whatsoever.

"Women are just like birds in the jungle, always trying to impress." She sniffed the air.

Mason turned to her. "But isn't it usually the male birds that try to attract the female with *their* plumage?" He held up the delicate peignoir. "And I'll tell you exactly what this is. It's a work of art. And created by artists who love what they do."

Okay, so Rosalie would marry this guy on the spot. Trudie crossed her arms. "Yes. It is a work of art."

"And I'd like to buy it."

She grinned in spite of herself. He had, after all, picked her favorite color, but she kept that bit of news to herself. "Elegant choice." Trudie tilted her head at him and couldn't resist asking, "Now did you want a negligee to go with that peignoir?"

"Yes. Why not?"

"And what do you plan on doing with them?"

Mason gave her a teasing look of incredulity. "I'm buying them, of course."

Trudie chuckled and rolled her eyes. She knew it had been none of her business to ask, but he'd forced her into a funky mood. She certainly hadn't expected such a ridiculous reply. It was a side she had yet to see of Mason. But she liked it. A lot. That fact, though, only made her heart ache all the more. She handed him the matching nightgown.

He walked to the counter with his merchandise and handed her his platinum credit card.

Trudie rang him up while he went off, browsing for more nightwear.

Mason found another nightgown set in her size—this time in the softest rainbow colors—and handed them to her. "I'll take these as well. It's hard not to love rainbows."

She felt her face heat up. Trudie recovered herself and showed him the price tag. "This set is expensive. Two hundred ninety-nine dollars and ninety-nine cents."

Mason grinned. "And what a bargain it is at that price. Since one doesn't often see rainbows."

"Okay." Trudie nodded as she tried to swallow a myriad of emotions. She rang up his purchases again, folded each set into a gift box, and then tied them up with ribbons. Mason was being unbearably delightful, and it was about to do her in. The cologne he was wearing wasn't helping matters either. She wanted to selfishly forget about the promise she'd made to Lane, but that was equally impossible. Not when love was at stake. Love wasn't anything to be trifled with. And yet the gowns weren't for Lane. What would she do if he handed the gifts to her? Should she refuse his kindness?

When Mason had completed his transactions, he lifted the packages back over the counter. "Now, could you do me a favor and make sure that a Miss Trudie Abernathy gets these? Right away. Please." The gifts were poised just in front of her.

Hesitation became a living thing as Trudie tried to decide what to do. In the final seconds before vacillation meltdown, she reached out to Mason and accepted the packages. "I'll make sure that she gets them. Thank you." Trudie tried on a business-like smile, but it didn't fit. "Honestly, that was very generous and kind, but Mason, you didn't have—"

"No, I didn't have to. But I *wanted* to." He came around to the other side of the counter and said in a low voice, "I'm well aware of what passed between us yesterday evening. It was real. And you felt it too. So, something happened between the time I dropped you off last night and the time you arrived here this morning. And being a great lover of mysteries, I intend to find out what it is." He turned and strode to the door. "And in the meantime, prepare yourself, Miss Abernathy."

She blinked. "For what?"

Mason cocked an eyebrow. "To be romanced."

Trudie picked up a sheet of paper off the counter and fanned her face.

"Are your cheeks tingling again?" He opened the front door.

"Yes."

"Good." And on that note, Mason grinned and walked out the front door of Bloomers Boutique.

Chapter Sixteen
....

Trudie reached up to her mouth. It was open. She was still in a daze when Rosalie came in from the back room.

Rosalie—a woman who was a bit of a snoop and who hated to miss even the slightest hint of gossip or frivolity—looked around, sniffing. "Did I miss anything? I feel like I missed something."

Trudie clutched the packages. "A customer just bought me rainbows."

"The three-hundred dollar ones? Oww. Well, if it was a single man, you should run after him. And then wrestle him to the ground. He's a keeper, sweets." Rosalie started restacking bras on a display table as she hummed some country tune about love.

Rosalie was about as subtle as the Humble summer heat, but she was usually right. Trudie grinned to herself, wondering what Mason could have meant when he said to prepare herself. If it had been within the context of any other situation, she would have buckled under the influence of such romance. His brand of enchantment was heady enough to use in the dental chair instead of gas. A female patient could have a double root canal, and she would walk out grateful for the experience. There was no doubt about it—Mason was an intoxicating overload to the senses, and Lane would be the luckiest woman alive.

Trudie slipped her lingerie presents under the counter next to her purse. She would enjoy trying them on later at home. But as she went back to work, worries began to trickle into her thoughts. All in all, even though she'd been resolute in discouraging Mason, she'd done a lousy job of scaring him off. Now he was more single-minded than ever about going out with her. What could she do? Should she tell Lane that she might have a rougher road to walk in romancing Mason back? But that statement would only come off disappointing and egotistical.

She looked upward at the starry host even though it was only the glitter-enhanced ceiling of Bloomers. *God, it seems like I'm trapped now. What have I done? I'll have a life, but I won't really be living. Can somebody please let me out?*

* * * * *

At one thirty Trudie parked in front of her sister's house and headed to the front door. When she'd called Lane to see if she could give her a quick ride back home, Lane had not only agreed, but she'd seemed anxious to talk to her. Trudie leaned over to ring the bell, but Lane opened the front door before she could even press the button.

"Hi."

"Hello." Trudie handed her sister the keys. "Are you sure you don't mind taking me home?"

"Not at all." Lane locked up. "So, did you have a good day at work?"

"Tiring, but good." Trudie noticed Lane was fumbling with the key in the door, and the fabric on her suit was jiggling. She was used to seeing her sister excited but never nervous.

Lane finished up and glanced back at Trudie as they walked toward the car. "I guess Mason must have dropped by at work."

"Yes, he did." It was easy to see what Lane was hinting at. "He asked me out, and I said no."

"Oh." Lane scooted behind the driver's seat, looking somber. "Mason did call me later. He wanted to hire me as an image coach. I've never been more surprised in my life. I told him yes."

"Okay." Trudie could tell her sister was pleased, but for obvious reasons Lane was trying hard not to gush. She imagined Mason getting lessons on clothing and posture. *Did he think I wasn't going out with him because he needed improving?* How could he think that? But then maybe he really was toying with the idea of keeping his options open with Lane if Trudie kept saying no to his invitations. *Impossible.* Those strategies didn't seem to fit Mason's character. "Did you explain to him about your change of heart? That you were no longer worried about dating someone who you worked with?"

"No." Lane looked away. "I knew if I told Mason outright, he would suddenly realize why you're refusing to go out with him. Then it would all look like my fault."

Trudie could see some merit in her sister's assertion, but she remained silent.

"You know, I didn't sleep well last night. Which is why I didn't get up early. But I had a lot of time to think this over. You know, what you're doing for me." Lane gripped the steering wheel. "And here's what I decided...if you can give me just a little time to see if there's any hope for Mason and me, then if there isn't...I will walk away from him, no matter how I feel. I promise."

Trudie nodded. She wanted to know how much time Lane needed, but she felt that question might be too pushy. "Thank you."

"I forgot to ask you something."

"Yes?"

"Before I take you home, did you want to stop in for a session? It's still early." Lane donned that beseeching look she used to get when they were teenagers. The one that was so hard to say no to.

Trudie thought for a moment. "I'm pretty tired from work. Rosalie had me unpack a lot of boxes." She smiled. "Thanks, though. I'll look forward to it another time." And it was true. But at the moment, Trudie felt exhausted from work as well as disheartened about her sister's news concerning Mason.

* * * * *

As soon as Lane had dropped her off at her apartment and she'd shut the front door, Trudie slid to the floor and rested her head in her hands. "Okay, here are the crazy facts of my life. My sister is in love with a man who once liked her but didn't love her. Now I'm falling for the same man, and he appears to care for me too. But what we have isn't quite love. At least not yet. So, God, does one real love trump two maybe loves?" Okay, the angels had to be snickering over that prayer. She could almost hear them howling with laughter.

Trudie scrambled up off the hard floor. *I'll make tea.* Black currant—her mother's favorite. But when she reached up to the top shelf in the kitchen panty to retrieve the box, a tremor ran through her fingers. She'd purchased the black currant tea months earlier, but she'd never really had the courage to drink it—to dip into such an intimate part of the past. It had been more than a decade since her mother had died. Surely she could reminisce. But wasn't going over memories a meaningful act that should be enjoyed only by the innocent? She felt anything but innocent.

In spite of her reservations, though, Trudie lifted the box from the top shelf, opened it, and took out a bag. She heated a mug of water in the microwave and then set the bag inside. She watched as the color crimson curled its way through the water. The fruity aroma was so enticing, she could understand why it was her mother's favorite.

After taking a quick sip, Trudie burnt her tongue and jerked the cup away. The liquid spilled on her blouse. *Oh no.* She tried wiping it off, but it was too late; her blouse was soaked with stain. Shaking her head, she poured the tea into the sink. Trudie gripped the edge of the sink until her fingers ached. *God, I have lived with this shadow for too long. I know all those years ago, when I asked You to forgive me for any*

wrong I did in demanding that my mother make that drive into town,
I know You forgave me. But I have never once pardoned myself. And
I am so ready to do that.

Trudie released her hold on the sink, and like the untethering of a
string on a kite, she felt her heart begin to release some of the past, the
memories and guilt that had kept her spirit bound. She took in a deep
breath. *O Lord, I still miss her so much. Sometimes I can't remember the*
smile on her face, but I can still feel the empty place it left in my heart.
I've known pain that seems unbearable, unnaturally so. I learned how to
grieve for my father when he went to heaven, but I have yet to mourn my
mother's passing.

Memories she thought were long since buried began to trickle back.
Why had she accepted the strange notion that she didn't deserve to
grieve her mother's death? *Lord, my thinking was so faulty. I really need*
to... Before she'd even ended her prayer, tears came.

Trudie sat down at the table and let out all the pain—all the aching
sorrows she'd never allowed herself to feel. Images of her mother's
death—the news of the accident, the numbness of the funeral, the silent
stares—all flashed through her mind like the pages of a dark storybook.
Just when she thought her heart had fallen quiet, another round of tears
came. Finally she felt relief deep in her soul, felt freedom for the first
time in twelve years.

Trudie rose from the table, a little weak in her legs but strong in
spirit. She ran cool water over a washcloth, dabbed it on her face, and
sighed. *I feel sort of like an infant starting my life over. What should I do*
now? Maybe I need a sign.

The doorbell rang.

Chapter Seventeen

The door. *I must look like a puffy-eyed monster.* Trudie quickly checked the mirror, groaned, and then went to check the peephole. Two women with short red hair and freckles and big green eyes—obviously identical twins—stood just beyond her welcome mat, holding sets of colorful boxes. She wondered what was up with that. Trudie's curiosity overcame her apprehension, and she opened the door.

"Good afternoon. Are you Trudie Abernathy?" one of the young women asked.

"Yes. May I help you?"

"We have a delivery from Mr. Wimberley," they said in unison.

"Okay." Trudie wondered if she should refuse the present, since Mason had already spent way too much on all the gifts of nightwear. But to say no would come off rude and ungrateful. Especially since the two women probably wouldn't get paid if she shooed them away.

"These boxes are only part of the delivery," one of the red-haired gals said. "The rest of your present is in our van. We need your permission to set up."

"Set up for what?" *Prepare to be romanced,* Mason had said. Trudie's heart beat a little faster.

"Well, my sister Lucy here and I, Marietta, have an entire art studio for you."

"An art studio?" Trudie wasn't sure if she should jump up and down or spiral into a panic.

"Yes, I'm going to set it up in the room of your choice while Marietta sings to you." They beamed as brightly as their boxes.

"Really?"

The redheads nodded.

Then Trudie noticed a van on the street with the words SURPRISES UNLIMITED painted on the side. They were indeed serious.

"Whenever you're ready." Lucy wiggled her eyebrows.

Trudie guessed the sisters would like to get rolling. Perhaps their boxes were heavy. *Am I ready for this?* Then she remembered asking for a sign. *Maybe this is it.* "Please come in."

Before Trudie could even think through whether such a gift was appropriate under the circumstances, the two women stepped over her threshold. They smiled, ready to begin.

Where should she have them go? A little dazed, Trudie led them to the spare bedroom, and after several more trips from their van, Lucy began to set up an art studio. Then Marietta cleared her throat, blew into a harmonica, and began belting out "Starry, Starry Night."

Trudie watched and listened, stupefied. Finally, she just couldn't help herself and gave into a smile. Mason. He was at it again. What was she going to do with him? He would try to win her over, and at the same time his generosity and sweetness would break Lane's heart. It was an impossible choice. There had to be a better way.

When the twins were finished setting up and singing, Trudie handed both women large tips. "Thank you. The songs were lovely, and the studio looks incredible. I've never been given anything like it."

"You're very welcome." Lucy saluted her. "Surprises Unlimited...that's what we're here for." She chuckled.

Then they all strolled through the hallway into the living room.

"Your studio was our most fun request, by the way," Lucy said.

Marietta looked at her sister and then at Trudie. "But our most shocking request was when we delivered a jack-in-the-box...with a real Jack inside."

Trudie laughed. After another moment or two of chitchat the twins said their good-byes and Trudie shut the door. She went back into the spare bedroom and leaned against the doorframe to take it all in. An art studio. Just like that, Mason had made it appear. What a strange new reality.

She ran her hand along the worktable, the easel, the oak taboret, and then the canvas cart, which was filled with canvases. She pulled out some of the drawers on the oak taboret. *Oh my.* There in the neat dividers were brushes, charcoal sticks, and tubes of oil and watercolor paints, as well as sketchpads and watercolor paper.

Trudie sat down on the padded stool and swiveled around. Mason must have spent a fortune. Could he already care about her that much, or was this a random act of kindness for a new friend? Surely that was it. But then when he said to prepare herself to be romanced, he didn't appear to be referring to friendship.

She turned on the light over the worktable, thinking that even though she mostly painted in watercolors, Mason had prepared her for so much more. Perhaps someday she would expand her horizons. Then she noticed a small note taped along the side of the table. Trudie opened it and read:

God gave you the gift. Here are the tools to open it. Warmly, Mason.

Beautifully said. Then at the bottom was his home phone number. She leaned back in the chair. Who was this man? He seemed like an angel. No wonder Lane loved him. He was very loveable.

She fingered the dimple on her chin, still trying to get used to having an art studio in her apartment. It was perfect. Mason had thought of everything. But the space, as welcoming and inspiring as it was, seemed foreign to her. So many years before, her art had not only been an income, but an intimate expression of her inner life. It had been passionate, difficult, and pure joy. Would she ever feel those things again?

Trudie looked at her clean fingers. They used to get covered with charcoal, and she'd loved it. She really had forgotten what a blessing art could be. That door had been closed so tightly that even the people who'd known her over the years had barely remembered her interest in art. She hadn't even shared that part of herself with the kids at the hospital. What a shame. But God was the ultimate Healer, and just as He was the only One to atone for sins and set people free, He was the only One who could give her back the yearning to paint. It hadn't been God, after all, who'd kept her confined for twelve years; it had been the lies that had kept her caged—the belief that there could be no forgiveness for her.

She picked up a charcoal stick and a sketchpad out of one of the drawers. Just as she set them on the worktable under the light, the phone rang. *Mason.* What would she say? To refuse to go out with him now would seem ungrateful, and yet how could she? At the very least, she would thank him for his generous gift. She ran to the phone. To her relief, she saw that it was Lane calling.

Trudie picked up the portable phone in the hallway. "Hi, Sis."

"Sis? You haven't called me that since high school."

"Oh yeah?"

"You sound funny," Lane said. "Listen, I called with a surprise. It's a good one. I think you'll like it. At least you have to promise me you'll like it."

Now Lane had her worried. "Okay, I guess. What is it?" Trudie could hear the rumbling of thunder in the distance. They were due for some storm showers.

"I have never stopped thinking about you not going out with Mason, so I found someone else for you."

"You're kidding. Not another blind date?" Trudie groaned, and she didn't mind one bit that her sister heard her.

"Now, Trudie, let's keep an open mind. Think positive."

"I am. I'm thinking positively that this isn't going to work."

Lane chuckled. "You are so funny. Listen, this guy is an artist from my church. Around thirty. His name is Wiley Flat. You are really going to like him. I know you're a little tired from work, but I promise it'll be fun."

"I don't think so."

Lane cleared her throat. "Well, you'll have to forgive me then."

"Why do I have to forgive you?"

Hmm. Silence.

"Lane? Talk to me."

"Wiley is coming over this afternoon."

"Lane, how could you do this to me?" Trudie's hand slapped her forehead.

"You seemed more forlorn than tired when I dropped you off, and so I—"

"I know you're feeling guilty about Mason and all, but please don't think you have to do this."

"Listen, Wiley is just taking you out for coffee. That's it. No more. Then you both can decide if you like each other well enough to go out again."

I was born on the wrong planet. "But, but…" What could she do? "Oy."

Her sister sighed. "Are you mumbling again?"

"Yes, I'm mumbling." Lane had placed her in another precarious predicament. She certainly wasn't in the mood to go out with Wiley, and yet if she refused him at the door, it would seem cruel. What should she do, besides lock Lane up in a room where there were no phones or calendars? That option sounded tempting. Why was it so hard to say no to Lane? She knew she'd donned those puppy-dog eyes of hers. *Okay. Maybe coffee. This once.* "I will agree to this under one condition."

"You name it."

Trudie put her hand on her hip. "That you will never set me up with a blind date again."

"Wow, you haven't been so spunky since you were a teenager." Lane paused. "All right. I agree to your terms." She chuckled.

Trudie softened a bit. "I know you mean well, and I appreciate it. But I need to manage my life a bit differently now." *Or at least God does.*

"Hmm. I can appreciate that. Well, try to have some fun, and have an extra large cappuccino for me."

Maybe she could make the best of it. "Sure." Trudie sighed, looking into the hall mirror at her pale cheeks. "I guess I'm ready for that makeup session next week. I could use some color." She could tell Lane was smiling on the other end.

"Trudie?"

"Yeah?"

"I think we'd better hang up now."

"Why?"

"Because Wiley should be there in five minutes."

"Lane!"

"Love you."

Trudie sighed, shaking her head. "Love you too."

"Bye."

Chapter Eighteen
....

Trudie listened to the rain outside as she hurriedly readied herself in the bathroom. The whole time she treated herself to little grumbling speeches about her sister. Hopefully she had officially put an end to Lane's romantic manipulations. She knew her sister was just trying to help, but she was also aware that Lane was trying to assuage her guilt over Mason. It would be hard to stay angry with Lane, though, since Trudie had firsthand experience with the torturous ways of guilt.

Lane did have good taste in men—that was certain. So Wiley was bound to be a fine man, and she knew with even a little effort on her part, the date would go well. But for all the good qualities the man was certain to have, Wiley wouldn't be Mason. And no matter how hard he tried, there would be nothing the poor man could do about it.

She turned back and forth in front of the bathroom mirror, looking at herself. She'd tried dabbing on a little blue gray eye shadow from a little compact she'd found in a drawer, but she couldn't tell if the color made her look pretty or just bruised. And did that old perfume out of the same bottom drawer make her smell like baby powder or scouring powder? "Lane, I guess I do need your coaching," she whispered to the mirror. "But no more help with dates."

Trudie drummed her fingers on the marble counter. *There's a chance I look like a clown.* Why couldn't she tell? Certainly putting paint on one's face was very different from brushing it on a canvas.

The doorbell rang. *Oh, well. Good.* It was too late for any more fiddling. The way she looked would have to do. Trudie took in a deep breath, made her way to the entry, and opened the front door. "Hi. I'm Trudie Abernathy."

"Wiley Flat here."

Trudie reached out to him, and they shook hands.

"I promise you I'll try not to be as boring as my name implies." Wiley grinned.

She chuckled. Wiley fell into the cute but nonstandard category, with his neat ponytail, boyish features, and his Hawaiian shirt over his jeans. Okay, guess Lane was throwing her a curveball. "I'm going to have to be honest with you. My sister, Lane, whom I love, set this up between us without my permission. In fact, she just sprang it on me a few minutes ago."

"Oww." Wiley clicked his tongue. "Lane, you naughty girl."

Trudie smiled. "Yes, I guess she is. But in spite of my sister's finagling, I would love to have coffee with you."

"Are you sure? The ball and chain method of dating isn't exactly my style."

She chuckled. "I'm sure. But would it be okay if we just went out as new friends?"

"New friends it is."

Trudie glanced behind him, feeling glad that the rain had stopped. She grabbed her purse, locked up, and headed down the walkway with Wiley. "I heard you're an artist."

"Not quite, but close." Wiley glanced at her. "I am a great lover of art, and I co-own a gallery in Houston."

"Really." *Lane, dear Lane.* What was she up to now?

Wiley opened the passenger door of his BMW convertible, and Trudie tucked herself inside its leathery luxury.

They drove for a bit, past the town's artesian well and koi pond, and then parked in front of The Java Joint. "They have good lattes here if you like them."

"I do. And this is one of my favorite places. Did Lane mention it?"

"No, it was just a guess." Wiley opened her door and helped her out. Then he touched the small of her back as he escorted her up the sidewalk to the coffee house. After they'd gone inside, ordered, and picked up their beverages, they got snuggly situated in two overstuffed chairs.

Wiley stretched his arms over the side of the chair so that his hands dangled. He already looked very at ease in her company. "So, does your sister do this fulltime along with being an image coach?"

"Make sure I have plenty of dates? No, but it feels that way." Trudie picked up the wide-rimmed ceramic mug and took a swig of her latte. *Mmm.* Lots of creamy froth with cinnamon sprinkles. Just the way she liked it.

Wiley laughed. "I'm in the middle of a blind date marathon myself."

"Really. What number am I?"

Wiley fluttered his fingers near his temple. "Let's see. I think you're my twenty-ninth blind date if my calculations are accurate."

"And why hasn't one of the twenty-nine snatched you up?" She leaned toward him and lifted a brow. "Do you have a lot of quirks?"

"Oh, I hope so."

Trudie laughed. Wiley was different—refreshingly so. "And do you tell all your dates which number they are?"

"Only if the subject comes up. Most women have a great sense of humor, and so if the date doesn't work out she'll set me up with her best friend." Wiley took a sip of his latte, and when it left a mustache he just chuckled and dabbed it off. "I've adored every woman I've been out with. I just didn't love any of them enough to marry. But if nothing else, I am never without great company."

Trudie's muscles relaxed as she felt more comfortable in Wiley's presence. "I'll bet women are astonished by your candor."

"Yes, they usually are." Wiley grinned and pulled something out of his back pocket. "Would you like a protein bar?"

"No, thank you."

"I'm addicted to them." He ripped open the foil package. "And I find I can get twice as much done during the day if I have a few." Wiley took a bite of his bar and washed it down with a mouthful of latte.

"I'm curious about something." Trudie licked her lips. "But this is personal."

"I love personal questions. It makes instant friends. Or enemies." He winked.

"Has it ever happened that one of these women liked *you* very much, but you didn't want to continue dating her?"

"Oww. That *is* personal." Wiley pressed his forefinger over his lips as if in deep thought.

"Sorry. You don't have to answer that."

"No, no. I'm just thinking." Wiley held up his hand. "So far, I'm happy to say, that with the exception of a couple of slight misunderstandings, there have been no real disappointments or heartbreaks on either side. But what's a bit of heartbreak in pursuit of love? Love is everything. At least God certainly thought so." He set his cup down. "It's worth everything to find it. Don't you think?" He looked at her. "And if you ever do find it, never, ever let it go. It's a commodity that would drive Wall Street crazy if they could get their hands on it. It's the one thing everybody wants but not everyone can possess."

Trudie shivered.

"Are you cold?" Wiley leaned forward, looking concerned.

"No."

He looked at her intently over the top of his protein bar. "I see now."

"And what do you see?" Feeling bold, Trudie gazed back at him, taking in his startling hazel eyes.

"You're an artist." Wiley said the words as if whispered in a church sanctuary.

"Did Lane tell you that?"

He shook his head. "I can just tell."

Okay, now she was intrigued. "How in the world could you tell that?"

"In the way you talk. And there is a curiosity in the way you look at things. A subtle intensity that goes beyond normal."

"Well, thanks." Trudie cocked an eyebrow.

"I mean it as a compliment. You're gathering material, and you may not even know it."

Trudie leaned on the chair, resting her neck against her palm and thinking about his words. "I guess I'd never thought of my curiosity in that way."

"And it's in your eyes. The passion. And in your graceful hands. They're the hands of an artist."

Trudie glanced at her hands. "But couldn't an artist's hands be beefy and sandpapery?"

"They could. But I won't hold them." Wiley grinned and then took her hands in his, looking at them. "I get the feeling you're not working on your craft. Why not?"

"Well, it's a very long story." Trudie felt herself perspiring. She enjoyed Wiley's presence, but he was also making her feel prickly. And her cheeks were starting to tingle.

Wiley released her hand. "You hesitate in telling me, and that's fine. But I do want to say that when you're ready, I'd love to see what you do."

Trudie slowly nodded. "Fair enough."

"By the way, I don't think it's going to rain anymore, and the afternoon is far too scrumptious to waste inside. Should we go out onto the patio?"

"Good idea."

They resituated themselves outside on the patio under an umbrella of leafy bougainvillea. A dragonfly darted over to them, showing off its green shimmery beauty, and then it soared off in a frightful hurry. Fortunately, the storm had left the air cooler and smelling of rain. Trudie leaned back in her chair, trying not to take furtive glances at Wiley. The coffee date was certainly turning out differently than she'd imagined.

Wiley pulled something out of the back pocket of his jeans. He held up a tiny vial and chuckled. "I'd forgotten that thing was in there. It's a bottle of bubbles. I'd gotten it at a wedding, and I'd kept it to delight my niece. But maybe I really wanted it for myself. I've been fascinated with bubbles all my life."

"I have too. Since age five." Trudie smiled, remembering how she and Lane used to chase their bubbles until they doubled over in giggles.

"Five is a good age. It's when we play like we mean it." Wiley pulled the tiny wand from the bottle and blew through the ring. Bubbles exploded through the little halo and danced around them like tiny fairies. "You know, one of the many amusing things to know about bubbles is that as exquisite and colorful as they are, they have no hue of their own. They take on the colors that are all around them." Wiley handed Trudie the bottle and the wand.

Being a bubble lover herself, Trudie dipped the wand into the bath of liquid soap and blew into the ring. Several other customers stopped their chatting for a moment to watch the tiny show of iridescent orbs as they floated around them effortlessly. Then some of the bubbles popped while others whirled off in a breath of air.

"Artists are a little like that too," Wiley went on to say. "They've been given the job of reflecting all the color and life on this earth." He looked at her. "A rather sacred endeavor, I think."

Trudie sighed. Wiley was a surprise, and an unforeseen blessing. And Lane had been right about him. At that moment, Trudie wished she had a brother, and she wished his name was Wiley Flat.

"Are you a little hungry? They've got good sandwiches here."

Trudie grinned, wondering where he could put it all. "Sure. A sandwich sounds good."

* * * * *

An hour later when Wiley deposited her back home, Trudie remembered fondly that he'd downed two lattes and a protein bar, and that was all before their sandwiches, chips, fruit cup, and ice cream. Even with his overly enthusiastic eating habits, Wiley was a delightful man. He'd listened to her with genuine interest, and he was friendly and funny. Wiley would make some woman a playful and devoted husband. But even as fine a man as Wiley Flat was, he still wasn't Mason Wimberley.

Their date ended with a tender kiss on the cheek and the assurance of friendship. It had been a very full and freeing as well as a fascinating day.

Trudie wandered back into her art studio. She loved the fact that she really had an art studio. It was still a pleasant shock to see it. More than anything, she wanted to call Mason to thank him, but she wasn't sure it was wise. *However.* Not calling would be impolite. She stepped over to the phone in the hallway. She had Mason's number memorized from the bottom of his note card, so she pushed in the numbers with ease.

Trudie held her breath, realizing she had no plan. After she thanked Mason for the gift, what did she plan to do if he asked her out again? What would she say? To be kind to Lane meant being unkind to Mason. *Lord, please help me out of this strange and terrible circle.*

Chapter Nineteen

....

After several rings, when Trudie realized Mason wasn't going to pick up, she sighed with relief. She could simply leave a message on his machine. That would be so much easier. After hearing the beep, she said, "Hi, Mason. This is Trudie. I received your gift. It was the most amazing present I've ever gotten. Kind of like all my Christmases rolled into one. All that I need is here...to begin again. And you made that possible. How can I ever thank you enough?" *Trudie, hang up.* She gently put the phone back on its cradle. *Oh, dear.* She'd slipped and said too much. Her last words seemed like an invitation to call her. Or to drop by. Or to marry her!

Trudie was sweating again. She needed to get ahold of herself. *Breathe.* Maybe she could sit at her new art table for a while, just to get the feel of it. She eased down on the soft cushioned chair, hooked the heels of her shoes on the footrest, and swiveled back and forth. She switched on the light and then reached for the charcoal stick she'd gotten out hours before. *Hmm. Subject matter.* Bubbles came to mind, which made Trudie smile.

She began to sketch out a child blowing bubbles. The girl had on a jumper and a frilly blouse, and she was on her tiptoes in anticipation of the coming felicity. At first Trudie drew with broad strokes, and then she began to add more detail and some shading. After thirty minutes' work, she placed the sketchpad on the easel and stepped back for a better view. It was amateurish. The girl's feet didn't seem as if they even belonged under her ankles, and the girl appeared as animated as, well, paper.

Trudie tore off the page, crumpled it, and tossed it into the corner of the room. That was the one thing Mason had forgotten to purchase for her studio. A waste bin. Perhaps that was what she needed the most. She began again with a flower this time, an iris, up close, which always reminded her of the work of Georgia O'Keeffe. Irises were mysteries to her—so full of graceful lines, exotic interiors, and unfathomable delights. After working for half an hour, though, even the irises came out one-dimensional. "Flat" seemed to be the operative word for the day. She wondered if that bit of comedy would make Wiley laugh or cry. It was about to make *her* cry. She saw no humor whatsoever in the moment. There was no other way around it—she'd lost some of her skill from lack of practice.

Practice and patience. Those words appeared in her thoughts—and almost whispered in her ear. Then she remembered God's still, small voice. The clock on the wall read ten thirty. Maybe she needed some rest. Perhaps enough had happened in one day.

Trudie went to her bedroom and opened the closet door. On the top shelf was the little koala, her birthday present from Mason. And at the back of the closet, behind all her clothes, were the two nightgowns and peignoirs that he'd given her. She hadn't even tried them on, fearing what she would feel—that it would only make her speculate endlessly about the "what ifs." She shook her head. *Honestly, Mason, you have to stop buying me gifts.* But he hadn't been in the wrong; she was the one who needed to stop. No more. She made up her mind that whatever else he sent, she would refuse it. What else could she do? Whatever path she chose, her actions felt wrong.

She stared at the gowns in a fit of indecision. It seemed wasteful to never wear them. Finally, Trudie made a decision. She peeled off her clothes, slipped on the nightgown and peignoir with the delicate rainbows, and then gazed into the full-length mirror. Nice. Really nice.

Everything reminded her of him now. Maybe that was his secret ploy. And it worked better than he ever imagined. If Mason only knew the reason for her retreat. That part always hurt the most—the fact that Mason might think she was rejecting him outright. Nothing was farther from the truth. And yet she had to remain silent.

It was at least a blessing that she didn't attend the same church as Mason. Life would be that much harder. She padded into the bathroom to brush her teeth when she noticed an ivory envelope peeking out from behind the hamper. Must have fallen back there when she lifted the lid. Trudie picked it up and slid the invitation out of the envelope. Kelsey and Jerold. Friends from high school. And the wedding was Sunday afternoon at four. *That's tomorrow!*

She had at least remembered to mail the RSVP weeks earlier. What to do? She could pick up a wedding gift right after church, and then call Wiley to see if he could accompany her. It might come in handy to have a male friend who was pleased to escort her to events. It seemed like a good plan. Okay. Settled.

After a bit more bedtime preparation, Trudie slipped off the sheer robe and lowered herself onto the bed. Wearing the elegant gown made her feel less like torpedoing onto the bed. Instead, the nightwear made her want to stretch out and ponder. Actually, she became *so* occupied with ponderings surrounding the gown—the person who'd selected it for her, the hands that had touched it, the eyes that had given her such an intent look when he'd given it to her—that Trudie felt wild-eyed and completely unable to sleep. After an hour of tossing and turning and trying to get her mind off Mason, she gave up, changed nightgowns, and then plopped onto the bed.

* * * * *

The night fell softly on Trudie, and the morning came up in a bright crescendo of glory. Church had been bathed in a worshipful atmosphere—more than she ever remembered. She couldn't tell if the added reverence was in the service or in the sanctuary of her heart. But it had been real.

And then the inimitable and comical and courtly Wiley Flat had agreed to escort her to the wedding. He became particularly excited on the phone since he loved weddings even more than food. Wiley seemed to think weddings were all things beautiful and joyful and promise-filled, all collaged together in one sanctified portrait of love. Only hitch—there were no protein bars. Trudie smiled. *Wiley.* Sooner or later she'd find the perfect blind date for him. It appeared to be the custom, and she'd had plenty of lessons in setting up blind dates from watching Lane. *Hmm. Maybe Lily, Mason's secretary.*

Trudie took her time dressing in one of the new outfits Lane had purchased for her birthday. A red silk dress. She wished she'd made time for that makeup lesson, because just when she really wanted to look more polished, she was clueless. Hopefully her feeble attempts at makeup were more appealing than appalling.

The doorbell rang. No more time to fuss over her looks.

Wiley was at the door, looking both dashing and darling in his tan slacks and navy jacket. She tucked her arm through his, which suddenly seemed like a new habit, and they both headed out for what surely promised to be a wonderful evening. Also it was a chance to escape from Lane's inevitable inquisition about her first date with Wiley and her own ever-increasing pile of ponderings about Mason.

After a rather convoluted drive through some woodsy back roads, they entered a long private driveway, which then led to a clearing in the woods. Just beyond a pond and a three-tiered fountain stood an elegant Spanish-style mansion set amongst immaculately manicured grounds. "Now this is a romantic spot for a wedding." The word *palatial* came to mind.

"High school friends, you said?" Wiley looked over at her. "They have very good taste."

"Yes, they do."

"Very sumptuous." Wiley pulled up next to a Bentley and parked. "Are you still close friends with them?"

"No, not really." Trudie turned to him. "But Kelsey and Jerold...were both very kind to me when it would have been easy to ignore a new senior transferring in."

Wiley winced. "Not a good time to move...just before your senior year."

"You're right. It wasn't a good time."

"Why did your parents choose to move?" Wiley touched her arm. "You don't really have to answer all my queries."

"No, it's all right." Trudie fingered the latch on her purse. "Well, my family lived on a farm in Oklahoma. But after my mother passed away, my father wanted a totally new life. It was hard to blame him, really. The farm had too many memories. So, we moved from Oklahoma to a small house in Humble, and he went to work for an insurance company. It was a different world for us all." Trudie chuckled. "I'm sorry. I really didn't mean to say all that." Wiley was easy to talk to. Already such a good friend. "You listen too well. A dangerous trait when you're with a talkative female."

"I adore talkative females, especially when they have such interesting things to say. So, when you arrived at Humble High School, did you take them by storm?"

"No. But I was notorious." Trudie grinned at him.

He stroked his chin. "And what were you notorious for?"

"For being insufferably homely."

Wiley tossed his head back, laughing. "I won't let you say such things about yourself." Without hesitation, he lifted her hand to his lips and kissed it. Then he released her and came around to open her door.

Trudie thought nothing of the intimate gesture, since Wiley seemed like the kind of man who was generous with his affections. In fact, she fully expected him to find a way to kiss every woman at the wedding, including the bride! And Trudie would stand back and enjoy the show.

They climbed the concrete stairs to the entry and breezed through the double oak doors. Trudie was happily startled with the interior—with its multiple chandeliers, checkered marble floor, and two-story fireplace. Large sprays of white roses adorned the aisles, and linen-covered chairs sat neatly in rows waiting for their guests. She then turned her attention behind them to the winding staircase.

Wiley followed her gaze. "I'm guessing the bride will come down those stairs, looking luminous and very much like an angel." Wiley winked. "They always do."

Trudie smiled as she imagined the bride gliding down the staircase. In the midst of her reverie a flourish of chamber music started playing as several handsome young men dressed in tuxedoes began seating the guests.

Wiley and Trudie waited in line to be seated, and after a minute or two, one of the young men offered his arm to her. She looked down the walkway, and in that brief moment her heart fluttered, wondering what it would feel like to be the bride and not a guest. She took in a deep breath, circled her arm through the young man's, and allowed him to escort her toward their seats. Once they were both deposited comfortably, Trudie turned to Wiley. "What is it about weddings?" she whispered. "Such a mixture of solemnity and rapture."

Wiley leaned over to her. "No wonder our Lord's first miracle was at a wedding," he whispered back. ❜

Their heads touched gently, and Trudie thought their gesture may have looked a little too affectionate from behind. If anyone had been looking on, they would think they were in love. She placed her hands around her purse, opening and closing the latch. When she looked up again, Trudie saw a sight she could not have even imagined. Mason was walking up the aisle.

This time Trudie's heart didn't flutter—it nearly stopped.

Chapter Twenty

....

Mason looked at her, his expression riddled with a dozen shades of astonishment. Then he sat down on the other side of the aisle.

Trudie swallowed and then choked.

"Are you okay?" Wiley turned to her, attentive, patting her on the back. "Someone you know?"

She nodded. *Breathe. In and out. You've done it since you were born.* "Yes. Someone I know." She guessed Mason had just seen what surely looked like intimate behavior with another man. He must think her a fiend to go out with another man so soon after their date and after accepting such lavish gifts.

Trudie gripped the edges of the chair and glanced in Mason's direction, only to see another spectacle that was beyond her realm of belief. Lane was seated next to Mason, and she was making a thumbs-up sign, which was directed right at her. Trudie knew if she'd had a mouthful of punch she would have spewed it all over the guests. Someone once said—she had no idea who—that when life offered its most hilarious moments, it usually meant that someone else was being tortured. Well, this was comedy's finest hour, and her torture was complete.

Wiley leaned toward her. "Say, isn't that Lane sitting over there?"

"Yep. That's my sis."

"We could ask them to sit with us at dinner." He raised his shoulders and nodded, looking hopeful.

Perfect. Trudie smiled at Wiley but said nothing. *Why did Mason and Lane come?* She guessed that the bride and groom had not only befriended her but everyone else. Then she wondered what Lane could have meant by her gesture. Was Lane trying to give her the thumbs-up because of Wiley, or was she subtly saying that she was now with Mason? *With him,* meaning that Mason and Lane were a couple. But wasn't that the goal they'd both been working toward? She'd been consciously making a way for Mason to fall in love with Lane. And apparently it was working. Somehow seeing them together was more painful than she thought it would be.

The music changed and the bridesmaids began floating down the aisle. They were all adorned in Renaissance-style dresses with high waists and puffy sleeves. How different, but beautiful. Then Trudie immediately went back to the tragic comedy in her midst. She crossed her arms. Perhaps Mason had given up on her. Then when he was in the middle of a coaching session with Lane, he suddenly succumbed to her charisma. Lane was, after all, much prettier and more graceful and more business-like. And less sweaty. That counted for something during the long hot summers of Humble, Texas. And too, Lane Abernathy had made herself into a real lady. Pure class. What man wouldn't be enchanted by all her charms?

Then again! It had been only one day since Mason had stormed into Bloomers, bought up the store, and promised to rock her world. What happened with that? *I guess he only gives a woman twenty-four hours before he moves on to rock someone else's world.*

A pipe organ started to play Pachelbel's Canon, and the crowd rose. It was a majestic moment, one that always brought a joyful mist to Trudie's eyes. This time it brought tears along with a twinge of sadness. She hadn't wanted to be right about her life—that the colorful designs inside the kaleidoscope were really no more than broken pieces of glass.

The people turned toward the staircase behind them and watched as Kelsey Rayborn made her way down the grand staircase in all her luminous glory, just as Wiley had said.

Kelsey passed by them, her gown making a whispery rustling

sound. Trudie then refocused her attention on the groom. Jerold's eyes were glistening with wonder as he gazed down the aisle at his bride. In moments, they would be united in the sacrament of marriage. Such a holy thing that God had entrusted humans with. Remembering Kelsey and Jerold's steady faith in the Lord, Trudie's spirits rallied, reminding her once again that God was still in control—still working wonders that might at present be unseen.

The bride arrived at her destination, and the guests sat back down.

The minister smiled at them both and began, "Dearly Beloved, we are gathered here in the sight of God...."

As the familiar words flowed over the audience in a pleasant ebb and flow, Trudie tried with genuine willpower not to let her gaze drift over to Mason and Lane. Apparently self-control was lacking. She drifted anyway. The two of them sat quietly looking toward the bride and groom. Lane had a smile of bliss on her face.

When the vows had been exchanged and the prayers offered and the songs all sung, Trudie was certain people would say that it was a glorious wedding. Indeed the ceremony was beautiful in every way, and two dear people who loved each other were now man and wife. And on a purely practical side—but equally welcomed—not a single person had tripped, no candles caught anyone's hair on fire, and the flower girl didn't raise her dress over her head to show everyone her new ruffled underwear. The family and guests could breathe again. Life was good. At least it was for the bridal party. All that remained of the ceremony was the closing announcement.

"You may now kiss the bride," the minister said with reverent joy.

The maid of honor lifted Kelsey's veil, and Jerold went after his beloved with enthusiasm. It wasn't a kiss that shot up any eyebrows, but it did cause a few stray chuckles to ripple through the crowd.

Yes, it was a day of extravagant love and effervescent smiles, and Trudie decided that no matter what happened over the next several hours, she would smile along with everyone else. But she couldn't help but sneak another look over at Mason. He was busy grinning at the kissing couple while Lane was busy lifting her lacy wrap back over her shoulders. As she struggled with it, Mason came to her assistance.

Wiley leaned over to her. "I'm starving. How about you?" he murmured out the side of his mouth.

Trudie squelched a chuckle. She had thought he was going to say something reflective about the wedding or something witty about the kiss. "I'm afraid they may not have any protein bars."

"That's okay. I brought some." He lifted the flap on his jacket to reveal the tops of several treats.

Trudie rolled her eyes at him.

The couple turned their beaming faces to their friends and family. Then as the recessional music embraced them all, the couple strode down the aisle—hands clasped together while stealing glances at each other. They made their way under a set of stone arches and into a large banquet hall.

After the rest of the wedding party had made their way down the aisle and through the arches, guests began to rise and leave their seats. It was a moment Trudie had been dreading. "Wiley, I think—"

"Why don't we go over and visit with your sister and her boyfriend." Wiley rose from his seat.

Trudie put a smile on her face and joined him. "Good idea."

They both turned in the direction of Mason and Lane, and for a moment Mason appeared to be leaving without Lane. She caught up with him, though, and as they all converged in the middle of the aisle, Lane slipped her arm through Mason's. A flash of surprise crossed his face as he looked down at Lane's arm. But like a gentleman, he adjusted his arm to accommodate hers.

"Hi, Lane." Wiley kissed her on the cheek.

When Wiley eased back, Lane gave Trudie a sisterly twitch of the eye, but she didn't catch her meaning.

Lane turned to Mason. "I'd like to introduce you to Wiley Flat, who co-owns a wonderful art gallery in Houston. Wiley, this is Mason Wimberley. He's a financial consultant."

Mason reached out first. "I'm glad to meet you."

"Same here." Wiley took his hand with a firm shake.

Trudie felt like she ought to keep things looking casual, so she reached out to shake Mason's hand. "Hi."

He looked at Trudie. "Hello there." Mason's hand lingered over hers for a second or two longer than expected

Curious glances ignited within their little circle.

Mason and Trudie released each other.

"Wiley is a new *acquaintance*." Trudie put an emphasis on her last word and then looked at Mason, who now had an unreadable expression. "I didn't realize you two knew the bride and groom."

"Well, I really didn't know them all that well," Lane said in a low voice. "To be honest, I was surprised to receive the invitation."

Mason smiled. "I know them both well. I'm pleased to say that Kelsey and Jerold are two of the finest people I've ever known."

"Well, that's quite a recommendation. Trudie, you'll have to introduce me to them." Wiley made a little flourish with his hands. "By the way, I hope we can all sit together for dinner. Would that be acceptable to everyone?" He added some eager inflections to his voice.

"That would be fine." Mason adjusted the vest on his suit as he raised his chin.

Lane looked a bit disappointed. "Of course. Thank you, Wiley, for thinking of it."

Trudie nodded, her face already feeling tingly.

"I think they're seating everyone now." Mason motioned toward the banquet hall.

Their merry little band maneuvered through the archway and into the large dining room. Thousands of twinkly lights, urns of red gladiolas, and live mandolin music gave the hall an elegant and faraway ambiance. The lace-covered tables were adorned with gossamer ferns and crystal candelabras. Each woman was handed a garland of baby's breath with ivory ribbons. *Nice touch.* If all the women wore them it would certainly add to the Renaissance theme.

"Need some help with that?" Lane asked Trudie, pointing to her flowers.

"Sure." Trudie handed her sister the garland, and she gently nestled it in her hair.

"What a surprise," Lane whispered to her sister.

Trudie wasn't sure if she meant all the gifts of garlands or Wiley's presence or the fact that they were all put together as agreeably as pudding tossed into mixed greens. "Thanks."

Lane handed Trudie her wreath of flowers, and she pinned it to her hair, making sure it looked great on top of her up-do. The baby's breath went with her sister's moonlight pink dress as if it had all been coordinated that way.

Wiley grinned at them. "You two look like a couple of Shakespearean pixies. The flowers suit you both very well."

Mason didn't seem to know what to do with Wiley's comment, so he just grinned.

Lane touched the flowers on her head. "Well, it's a first at any wedding I've been to. I think the garlands are a unique idea. Although I'm wondering why the wedding planner didn't talk Kelsey out of it, since it won't work with all the women's hairstyles."

"What do you think, Trudie?" Mason looked at her. "About the bride's choice?"

Trudie joggled herself a bit. "You mean about the garlands? Well, this is more *their* dream than ours. We guests are just here to decorate and celebrate their day. So, the bride should do whatever her heart tells her, and we should follow her lead. And, well, since this wedding seems to have a bit of a Renaissance feel to it, that seems appropriate, since weddings are also about rebirth...you know, two people coming together as one."

"Nicely put." Wiley applauded.

Trudie felt her face warm.

Mason smiled at her while Lane looked rather self-conscious—a look that wasn't usually in her repertoire of expressions. *Oh, dear.* What had she said to get such a reaction? Had she disagreed with her sister too much?

"Perhaps we should sit down." Lane gestured to the tables before them like a game show hostess.

They all decided on a table, for a moment it seemed as though they were playing a game of musical chairs, with each person circling but not knowing where or when to sit.

Finally Mason pulled out a chair for Lane. He made sure she was seated and then he went to stand behind the chair opposite Lane.

Hmm. Trudie took quick note that there were only two possible seating situations remaining, and both of them meant sitting next to Mason all evening.

Wiley pulled out one of the two remaining chairs for Trudie, and then he sat opposite her.

When they were all settled at last, a collective sigh seemed to stir among them. Except perhaps for Wiley. He was happily oblivious to any stirrings of discontent. But Trudie felt the tension as if she were perched on a high wire without a net. *Well, here we all are.* Trudie took in a deep breath. *Let the circus begin.*

Chapter Twenty-one

....

After the bride and groom were seated at the head table, the waiters began serving everyone their salads.

"Well, isn't this cozy?" Wiley looked at each of them with contentedness, but he especially lit up when he spotted a basket of sweet breads and rolls. Following a declaration from Wiley that they were dwelling in a perpetual haven of rapture, a twitchy sort of quiet fell on them.

The squirmy situation made Trudie think of a basket full of snakes—silent, but tailor-made for trouble. Out of desperation for something to do besides fidget, she reached for her napkin, which was folded into a clever bird-of-paradise design. She tried memorizing its unique folds to recreate later, but it fell apart in her hands. *Hmm.* Sounded like her life.

Mason tugged on his collar.

Lane took a sip of her water. "Wiley, please tell me about your latest art show. I heard it was very successful."

"It was." Wiley took a slice of bread and passed the basket to Mason. "I'd like to take credit for it, but it was my partner, Kat, who found her. A brand new talent. Dauphine Marvel. And she is that. A marvel."

Lane leaned toward Wiley. "Tell me a little about Dauphine's work."

"Well, it's a bit is like Andy Warhol's. It radiates that same boldness with a connectivity to our lives, but Dauphine's work has several differences. I think you might..."

While Wiley and Lane chatted together like magpies about his latest art show, Mason leaned over to her. "Hello again."

"Hi there." Trudie looked into his eyes, which were so warm and welcoming, it made her wish they were the only ones at the table. But she squelched that thought just to keep her eyes from giving away any of her yearning. "I hope you got my phone message."

"I did."

"I'm really glad for this opportunity...you know, to thank you for recreating my spare bedroom into an art studio." Trudie laced her fingers together. "It's incredible. You should see it." *Oh, dear.* She'd gotten carried away. Her comment would make him want to come over to her apartment.

"I would love to sometime." He smiled at her. "And you're very welcome."

"It was far too generous. Honestly."

Mason shook his head.

"But I can't keep accepting gifts."

"I would ask you why, but I'll let it go...for now."

"Thank you." Trudie twiddled her thumbs on her lap and wondered what Lane would think if she had overhead some of their conversation. "I began to sketch last night for the first time in years."

"And what have you discovered?"

"That even if you don't forget how to ride a bike, after years without trying, you might fall down a few times."

Mason took a sip from his water glass. "I'm sorry if I caused you some bruises on your knees."

"There was no other way." Trudie shrugged. "Bruises seem to be part of life."

Mason looked like he was about to respond when a waiter whooshed over to their table, serving petite plates of garden greens. Everyone dug in, and suddenly the food seemed a priority over conversation.

Trudie was glad for the reprieve. Her muscles relaxed, but she had no idea how she would actually digest her meal. Her stomach felt like it was doing the rumba.

"Now, this table has become entirely too quiet," Wiley said as he buttered his roll. "Maybe we should rouse things a bit. I have a question, and I'd love for you each to answer it. Are you game?"

"I guess that depends on your question." Mason speared a tomato with his fork.

"Of course. I'll give you the question, and then you can decide." Wiley straightened his shoulders. "How do you think a person would know for sure...when they've fallen in love?"

Lane coughed.

Mason paused from buttering his roll but looked unruffled.

"That's quite a question you have there, Wiley," Trudie said, trying to come to everyone's aid.

Wiley raised his chin. "Come now. We're in the midst of love tonight. We should celebrate with the most succulent morsels of repartee. No talk of the weather or anything boring...like taxes and money."

Lane grinned. "Mason is a financial consultant."

Wiley put his hand up. "Oh, I'd forgotten. Please accept my apologies."

"No apology necessary," Mason said. "I get bored talking about money all the time, too."

"So, Mason, how would you respond to my query?" Wiley took a bite of his roll.

"All right. You have a reasonable question." Mason lowered his fork. "I think love can come from a thousand different places and in a thousand different ways. And...even if you only see the first glimpse of love...I think it might stand out as clearly as a rainbow in a black and white world. So, I don't think it's so much a matter of knowing love when it comes as it is what you're going to do with it when it arrives."

Wiley tapped his knuckles on the table. "Oh, excellent reply."

"Mason, that was beautiful." Lane lifted her glass to him.

Trudie looked into Mason's golden brown eyes, but he blurred a bit from the mist in her own eyes.

"Excuse me for a minute while I go powder my nose." Lane rose, smoothing her cameo pink suit.

Mason and Wiley both rose briefly until Lane had walked away.

Then Wiley's attention suddenly seemed elsewhere. "Oh, I've spotted someone I haven't seen in ages. I must go over and say hello. Please excuse me for a minute."

"That's fine." Mason went back to his salad.

Wiley left them and hurried off to another table.

Trudie wondered how it came to be that she'd wanted to go to the wedding to get away from all musings of Mason, only to be forced to sit next to him. Alone. "How do you like the salad?"

"It's not very filling, but then it's not supposed to be."

"Would you like another roll?" Trudie picked up the basket.

Mason looked at her. "That isn't what I want."

Trudie took a tissue from her purse and dabbed at her forehead and her cheeks. It was a good thing she'd made two applications of antiperspirant. She'd need it.

"You have a glow about you this evening."

"No, I'm sweating. I sweat a lot. It's one of my many imperfections."

Mason grinned. "Sweating is not an imperfection. All women do it. It's just that none of them will admit it but you. And I happen to be fond of honesty."

Trudie thought he was being wonderfully impossible. In fact, more wonderfully impossible by the minute. "So, what do you think of Wiley?"

He seemed to study her for a moment. "Well, that depends on his intentions toward you. If it's only in the friendship realm, then I would say he's a decent sort of man. But if he is more than a friend, then I would say he's a clown."

Trudie chuckled. "Wiley is a friend." Her heart ached, wishing she could sweep that look of perplexity off his face and wishing she could pick up with Mason just where they'd left off. It had been a breathtaking place to be.

"I want to explain something to you. I thought I could benefit from some of Lane's expertise, since I deal with people a lot, and when we were in her office yesterday, I noticed the wedding invitation on her desk. I made mention of it, and when she found out I was coming too, well, she asked if we could ride together. So, I don't want you to—"

Trudie gave Mason's arm a squeeze. "There's no need to explain anything."

They both stared at her hand—the one gently fastened to his arm. She quickly released him. "I think I'd better check on my sister. Make sure she didn't drown."

"Is that common in women's restrooms?"

"I heard of it once." Trudie grinned and took off toward an exit, any exit. Then as she meandered about, she wondered if Lane's overly Victorian remark about powdering her nose was really some sort of universal female code among women that really meant, "Meet me in the bathroom." Once she spotted the sign that read WOMEN, Trudie pushed through the door and entered the elegant world of black granite and pastel lights.

"Trudie. There you are. What took you so long?" Lane picked up one of the little individual towels and patted her hands with it.

"I wasn't sure if you wanted me to come in here or not."

Lane chuckled. "Of course I did. Even *I* don't say 'powder my nose.'"

"Sorry." Trudie looked at her sister more closely. "Have you been crying?"

"Just a little." Lane lowered her voice. "Why, do my eyes look red?" She looked in the mirror.

"No, not really. You look beautiful."

"Thank you. I was just so moved at what Mason said about me." Lane let her fingers loosen as if they were petals opening. "You know that I stood out as clearly as a rainbow in a black and white world. It was the most romantic thing a man has ever said about me."

Trudie pressed her finger against her chin. Her sister's words rendered her speechless for a moment.

Lane gave her head a little shake. "I mean, he wanted a couple of sessions from me right away, so instead of having him drive into Houston, he just came over to my home office yesterday. And he was friendly and amusing. I've never had such a good time. I had no idea he was having such amorous thoughts already. It's working, just as I'd hoped." Lane hugged Trudie. "And I have you to thank for that."

Trudie hugged her back. *O God, what should I do?* If she remained silent, Lane would believe a falsehood about their relationship. Trudie wondered if she should correct the mistake immediately. And yet if she spoke up, it would hurt her sister, and it would come off like sour grapes—as if she couldn't handle Mason's change of affections. Trudie ground her fingernails into her palms. *The truth will set you free.* And yet for a while it would be a miserable kind of freedom. "Lane, I need to tell you something. Right now."

Lane frowned. "I have to say, I was so surprised to see you and Wiley here. But why did you both just talk of friendship?"

"He's as wonderful as you said he was, but we've decided to be just friends." Trudie raised her finger to get her sister's attention. "But I need to tell—"

"Well, sometimes friendship can grow into more." Lane pulled a couple of hairpins from her purse. "Here, let me help you with your garland. I noticed it was sagging to one side." Lane straightened the wreath of flowers on Trudie's hair and pinned it in place. "There, that's better."

Trudie look in the mirror and touched the delicate flowers. "Thanks."

Lane looked at her in the mirror. "You haven't changed your mind? Have you?"

"About what?"

"About refusing Mason so that he could ask me out?"

Lane must have gotten a glimpse of her sadness before she'd put on a smile. What could she say in honesty? "It warms my heart to see you so happy."

"That's what I hoped you'd say." Lane gave her a hug, being careful not to tug on their satin streamers. "Thank you so much."

Trudie let out some pent-up air. "But there is still something I need to mention."

"Be sure and tell me at the table." Lane grinned. "Well, show time." Then she breezed through the doorway before Trudie could say another word.

The truth can set you free if you can ever manage to say it. Trudie sighed. The emotional mayhem humans were capable of in the name of love was almost comical. But not quite.

She sighed one more time for good measure and headed out of the ladies' room. Then Trudie paused, watching their dining table from a distance. Mason pulled out Lane's chair again, and within an instant they were laughing. Could Mason have meant what he said—only about Lane? Were his words really poking fun at her for refusing him? *Hmm.* Considering the rest of what Mason had said at the table, Trudie didn't think the idea was plausible, but in spite of her own common sense, she allowed a doubt to wriggle its way into her spirit like a weevil into a boll of cotton. And she knew well that it would keep her from mentioning anything to Lane on the subject of rainbows.

Trudie trudged forward. How would she survive the evening? She was suffocating. Wiley approached the table at the same time she did, but it was Mason who already stood behind Trudie's chair to pull it out for her.

"Thank you."

"You're more than welcome."

Before Mason sat back down, his fingers brushed along her back. Trudie hoped no one had noticed his subtle embrace as well as her sudden intake of air. She looked down at her plate of food. The main entrée had arrived—stuffed flounder. How apropos. Trudie took a bite. "Mmm. Just right."

"Isn't it though?" Wiley glanced around the table, first at Trudie and then at Mason, with a sudden look of understanding. "But perhaps a little fishy as well. Don't you think?"

"After they serve the wedding cake I hear there's dancing in the main ballroom." Mason grinned.

So, Mason is a dancer, and he's looking forward to showing off a bit. "I would love to dance, but I'm afraid I'm clueless." Trudie took a big bite of her fish.

"Well, that should be perfect then, since I haven't a clue either." Mason smiled and took a bigger bite of his fish.

Wiley dabbed his mouth with the corner of his napkin. "If you don't know how to dance, then you can simply move back and forth with elegance. No one knows the difference."

Lane chuckled. "Do you know how to dance, Wiley?"

"Of course, and do you, Lane, darling?"

"I do...some." She smiled at him.

"Well, then I expect at least one dance so you can prove it to me." Wiley tilted his head at her as if he meant it.

Lane looked at Trudie. "But you're with my sister this evening. That's not quite fair to her. I was—"

"No, no. It's all right." Trudie waved her off. "Wiley and I just came as friends. I would be happy to watch you two from the sidelines."

"We are indeed becoming good friends." Wiley lifted his glass to Trudie. "Thank you. By the way, Trudie, it's your turn. What was your answer to my question?"

"Question?" Trudie's throat suddenly felt as parched as if she'd eaten shredded cardboard—heavily salted. She picked up her glass and finished off the last drop of water.

"You know the question." Wiley shook his finger at her. "How do you know when you've found love?"

Perspiration made rivulets inside Trudie's dress as she tried to think of something safe to say—something that wouldn't encourage Mason, something that wouldn't upset Lane, and something that would entertain Wiley. Oh, dear. "I suddenly feel like a mouse who's stayed a little too long for the cheese dinner," was all that came out of Trudie's mouth.

* * * * *

After the meal had been consumed and the wedding cake sliced, Trudie groaned inside, realizing it was time to retire to the ballroom for another round of eye-twitching, tongue-tied torture.

The semi-merry band of four moved from the banquet hall, through a long colonnade, and into the grand ballroom. Yet another breathtaking room awaited them. The polished wooden floor shone under the lights of the chandeliers, and a small orchestra sat poised, ready to play.

The newlyweds whirled into the ballroom in a cloud of joy. They greeted a few people, then positioned themselves in the middle of the dance floor. A spotlight bathed them in a golden glow. Jerold placed his hand on Kelsey's waist, and she lifted her gloved hand to his shoulder. The conductor raised his baton, and then the music of "Some Enchanted Evening" filled the room. The happy couple began to dance as the crowd looked on. The tiny rhinestones on Kelsey's gown twinkled like starlight as they circled the room. Trudie felt certain Kelsey was living the fairytale wedding she'd always wanted—all things beautiful and filled with wonder. And she couldn't have been happier for the couple.

LOVE FINDS YOU IN HUMBLE, TEXAS

When the tune wound down, everyone applauded. Kelsey giggled and Jerold kissed her. Then the spotlight went out and the orchestra began to play "Unforgettable."

Wiley took Lane's hand, and they headed toward the middle of the floor.

Trudie watched as they moved gracefully to the music. "They're good. I had no idea my sister could dance like that."

"If you're not terrified of being mangled by my clumsy efforts, we might give it a try." Mason winked at her.

"But I thought you said—"

"Well, my parents taught me a little."

Trudie saw Lane having a wonderful time. There was no reason not to at least enjoy the evening. She held her hands up for him to sweep her away. And he did, slowly and steadily. "You're good." They stumbled a little, making Trudie laugh.

"Don't compliment me too soon. I said I could dance a little, and I meant it."

They swayed to the gentle rhythm of the music for a while without speaking. Trudie closed her eyes for a moment just to heighten the feel of his touch against her. She couldn't think of any place on earth she'd rather be than right there in his arms. Wasn't that a song?

Mason moved her a little closer to him, and she didn't pull away. "By the way," he whispered in her ear.

She opened her eyes. "Yes?"

"I don't quite have the mystery solved, but I'm getting there."

Trudie licked her lips. "What mystery?"

"I think you know what mystery I mean."

"Yes, I guess I do." She took in some extra air. "I'm sorry to be so much trouble."

Mason gently released her for a twirl, and while she still held his hand, Trudie managed to spin out and come back to him without faltering.

"I'm not usually a mysterious person," Trudie went on to say. "It's just that..." Her voice faded, since all she really wanted to do was enjoy the last few seconds she had with him. When the music came to a close, Mason gently dipped her backwards as he held her firmly in his grasp. For a moment, just a moment, she wondered if that was the fairy tale rapture Ginger Rogers must have felt in the arms of Fred Astaire.

When Trudie came back up, she chuckled at the surprise of the dance move, but the laughter disappeared when she looked into his eyes. She suddenly felt alone with him, as if no one else graced the dance floor and no time had passed since they were together in his house—when they'd shared their secrets and their laughter.

Mason smiled and touched her cheek.

Trudie's eyes filled with mist. He looked down at her lips, and for that moment the rainbows, which she'd put away with so many other impossible dreams, became real again. Then applause and chatter broke the spell. She eased out of his arms.

Wiley, who was red-faced and bent over, hobbled over to them. Lane followed behind him, looking worried.

"I'm afraid I've thrown my back out." Wiley shook his head. "Trudie, would you mind driving me to the minor emergency center?"

Chapter Twenty-two

....

Mason pulled into his garage, got out of his car, and slammed the car door shut. Then he got back in his car, turned off the motor, which was still running, and then slammed the door again. *I'm going to need to calm down.*

Once he'd lowered the garage door and gone inside the house, Mason loosened his tie and turned on the big screen TV. He thought watching a little baseball might help clear his head. But after a few minutes, he pushed the red button on the remote, turning off the TV. There was no escape.

Why was courting Trudie so much like chasing fireflies? He'd remembered how that went as a kid. No matter how stealthy he was, the insects would always vanish and then reappear just out of reach. He'd come close to wooing Trudie back. He could see it in her eyes, feel it in her touch. And then that Wiley character—a bit of a buffoon—had to go and wrench his back, all from acting as though he'd just entered a national ballroom competition.

Mason turned and noticed the lights of a car through one of the front windows. He glanced at his watch. Nine sixteen. He rarely got company so late. Trudie? Couldn't be. He looked through a front blind. Whoever it was shut off their lights and opened the car door. Looked like Perry. Good. He was the one friend who never minded what kind of mood he was in.

Mason opened the front door. Perry trudged up the walk, wearing a pair of old gray sweats and a look of frustration. When he'd made it partway up the walk Mason asked, "Hey, what brings you out so late?"

Perry rocked his head back and forth.

"So, you're in the doghouse again?"

"Yeah, I know." Perry raised his hands. "Remember this when you're married someday. Sometimes you just have to shut up."

"Sounds like good advice."

When Perry reached the porch he pulled Mason into a hug. "Hey, man, how ya doing?"

Mason groaned a little as he gave his friend a few slaps on the back.

"You in some kind of doghouse too?" Perry pulled back and looked at Mason.

"Not exactly. Come on in. We can watch TV with the sound off and talk awhile."

"Sounds like a plan." Perry stepped down into the living room, turned on the TV, and searched the channels for a baseball game.

Mason went into the kitchen, gathered up some chips and sodas, and headed back to the living room. "So, what did you say to upset Sheila this time? Or should I ask?" He tossed Perry a Coke.

"Well, as you know, Sheila's got a talent for decorating, but I think she spends too much money trying to prove it." Perry popped the top on his Coke. "So, I tell her that maybe we could talk about her purchases first, and she says that mindset stifles her creativity. Since she thinks that whatever I have to say will sound too negative."

"Will it?"

"Well, yeah." Perry took a sip of his soda. "Like for instance, she'll say we need new drapes to match the new couch, and I'll say what's wrong with the old drapes. *And* what was wrong with the old couch? Oh, and sometimes Sheila starts spewing decorator lingo about accents she needs to buy." He reached for the bowl of chips. "She'll use words like sconces and finials. I have no idea what either one of those things are."

"Well, I think sconces are those brackets on the wall that hold candles, and finials, well..." Mason pointed to a lamp. "See that ornamental thing on top? That's a finial."

Perry narrowed his eyes at Mason. "Now, how could you possibly know that stuff?"

Mason shrugged, dragged the bowl of chips back to his side of the coffee table, and took a handful.

"Anyway, after that the argument always starts sounding the same. Sheila says men are clueless, and I say it's hard not to be clueless when you're dealing with the fickle brain of a woman."

"Oww." Mason winced. "You said that?"

"I was pretty heated. So, I figured I'd better come over here and get myself calmed down." Perry hooked his finger on the edge of the bowl of chips and pulled it back his way.

Mason looked at his friend. "Well, I know you two love each other."

"Got that right. She's the love of my life." Perry horsed down a few chips. "So, how was the wedding? You don't look so good, old buddy."

Mason set his Coke down on the coffee table. The downside to giving Perry an update about Trudie was that he would probably admonish him for doing everything wrong, but the upside was that he might have some helpful tips. "To be honest, I'm not sure what happened at the wedding."

"So, this must be about that new woman you like. Trudie. So, what's the problem?"

"Well, let's put it this way...she's declined another opportunity to go out with me." Mason gave Perry a dry smile.

"Hmm. And you both had that lodestone, magnetic field thing going, right?"

"Something like that." Mason leaned back on the couch. "I just can't figure it out. It was going so well, and then something or somebody changed her mind. She's really close to her sister, Lane, so I thought maybe she'd said something—"

"So, you think Trudie's sister could have told her not to go out with you again. Now why would she do that?" Perry leaned forward, weaving his fingers together.

"I don't know. But she has been acting different lately."

"Yeah?"

"Uh-huh. Lane's been acting...friendlier." Mason let a few of the recent scenes with Lane play through his head. "*Real* friendly, come to think of it." He rubbed his chin, realizing he'd been a fool not to notice what was going on. "Maybe men really *are* clueless."

Perry looked at him. "How do you mean?"

"That's it. Lane changed her mind. She wants to go out now, and Trudie is getting out of the way for her."

"You think that's it?"

Mason nodded. "Yeah. That's it."

"So what are you going to do about it?"

"I have no idea. I mean, I like Lane. She's nice...beautiful and charming, but she's..."

"But she's not *the* one." Perry nodded. "I hear ya."

"It's a mystery. You just never know who you're going to hit it off with." Mason crossed his arms, remembering how warm Trudie felt next to him as they'd danced. Soft as his down comforter. No, softer. "Or who you'll start caring about."

Perry shook his head. "The way I see it, you're really in some pretty bad mess here."

"Thanks." Mason grinned.

"Hey, I mean it. If you tell Lane you're not interested, she'll be upset. Then Trudie might not want to go out with you. Then again, Trudie might go out with you anyway, but you'll be breaking that sacred bond between the sisters. And that's really not good. Especially if you end up wanting to marry Trudie someday. You gotta keep that sisterhood thing going."

Mason pulled back, staring at this friend. "Sounds sort of reasonable."

"It's the truth, I'm telling you." Perry cocked his head. "Like for instance, Sheila has a sister, and I've learned *never* to say anything bad about her. *Ever*. Even if Sheila says bad stuff about her sister. Doesn't matter. If I say something bad, *I'd* be the one breaking that bond. Not fair, but these are the rules, man. I don't know who made them, but I can tell you, I think they've been written in stone tablets somewhere and have been passed down since the Pharaohs." He rolled his eyes. "So, *now* what are you gonna do?"

"I think the only way not to upset Lane is to let her see that I'm not the right one. Once she realizes that all on her own, she'll walk away."

Perry pointed his finger at Mason as he narrowed his eyes. "Smart move, man. If women think that something is their idea, then the whole universe comes back into order. Beauty out of chaos. That's the way God set it up."

Mason shook his head at his friend. "You're full of it."

"Don't I know it?" Perry chuckled. "Now can we stop talking and watch some of the game?"

"Sure." Mason put his feet on the coffee table and turned up the volume on the TV.

* * * * *

An hour later, after watching the last half of a baseball game, Perry decided he'd calmed down enough to apologize to Sheila properly.

Mason walked him to the door.

"Thanks, man."

"Anytime."

Perry shook his hand. "Later."

Mason shut the door and headed toward the master bedroom for the night. He knew Perry's marital problems were real, but not serious. Their marriage had always been an inspiration to him. Love was worth the effort, Perry had always said. And pursuing Trudie would be worth the effort too, even if it meant holding back—just for a little while.

Mason rounded the corner to the bathroom a little too fast and bumped his head on the edge of one of the French doors. He let out a yelp. After rubbing his throbbing head an idea began to form. Maybe it was time to tell Lane about the family business and his father's hopes for his future. That news might allow Lane to see another angle on his life, and there was a good chance she wasn't going to like the view. Come to think of it, Lane had an appointment with him the next morning— something about trying some riskier investments.

Perfect timing.

Chapter Twenty-three

········

As bits of the previous evening came back to Lane, she squeezed the steering wheel even harder. The wedding had been enjoyable but equally disconcerting. Wiley's sudden injury had certainly been cause for concern, but over the course of the festivities, she'd sensed some unsettling reactions from Mason. Sometimes she could feel his budding affections toward her, and then in the next breath she noticed glimmers of what looked like attraction toward Trudie. *How perplexing.*

Lane's fingers began to throb, so she loosened her grip on the wheel. She turned left off Will Clayton Parkway and pulled in front of Wimberley Financial Services. After parking and easing out of her Lexus, she smoothed her melon pink suit and made her entrance into the reception area of Mason's office suite. *Show time.*

A young woman greeted her at the front desk—a beautiful woman with incredible bone structure. *Hmm.* But that dirt-colored dress she had on made her look like a mummy. *Ghastly.* With some image coaching, though, the woman could be a model. Guess she'd rather work for Mason. She could certainly understand the woman's reasoning.

"I'm Lily Larson." The young woman rose from her desk.

"Hi. I'm Lane Abernathy." She shook the woman's hand.

"It so good to meet you. Mr. Wimberley said you'd be coming in this morning. Would you like something to drink? Coffee, hot tea, or Pellegrino?"

"Pellegrino would be nice. Thank you." Lane had just started to sit down when Mason opened the door to his inner office. "Come on in, Lane."

"Thanks." She walked up to him expecting a light hug, but he shook her hand instead. *That was different.*

Lane sat down and studied him a bit. Mason seemed rested and well-groomed as always, but there was something in the way he avoided her eyes that unsettled her. Like a locked door that had always been previously open.

"Are you comfortable?" Mason looked at her then.

Now that you mention it, not really. Lane wondered where he'd hidden the sociable Mason Wimberley she'd always loved. "I'm fine. Thank you."

Mason sat down at his desk and glanced over several pages of paperwork. "You said you wanted to adjust your portfolio to include more growth stocks, and you wanted to check out some international markets. I have to warn you, though, even though these investments can generate a much higher rate of return, they are far riskier, and they may not perform as you're hoping."

Lane tried to take in the new, more serious Mason. She grinned, thinking he was about to burst out laughing, but he didn't. "Are you all right?"

Mason shrugged. "Yes."

Where was the small talk? "Did you enjoy the wedding yesterday evening?"

"I did. Kelsey and Jerold couldn't be happier." He glanced at his watch. "They should be on their way to Hawaii about now."

"Ahh, honeymoons." Lane sighed. "What could be more satisfying?"

"Well, you might find some heavy returns on these growth stocks pretty satisfying."

She chuckled. "Now you're just being silly."

"Ms. Abernathy? Here's your drink." Lily handed Lane her sparkling beverage with ice.

"Thank you."

When Lily had gone, Mason got up and shut the door. "Before we go into the details here, I wanted to tell you something else today."

Lane leaned forward. "What is it?"

"It's about my father."

"I've never had the pleasure of meeting him. I hope he's well."

"Well, I'm sorry to say that he isn't well." Mason didn't go back to his chair but leaned against his desk.

"Oh, I'm sorry to hear that." Lane suddenly realized that even though Mason had talked about his parents a little since she'd known him, he was never very specific about anything. Now she wondered why.

"My father has been suffering from a bad heart for some years."

"There's nothing that can be done?" Lane took in a deep breath.

"I'm afraid not. And he has seen some very fine specialists." Mason laced his fingers together. "But I needed to tell you something else."

"Yes?"

"Well." Mason coughed. "I may not always be your financial advisor."

"Really? Why is that?" She took a sip of her beverage.

"My family owns Wimberley and Sons Funeral Home here in Humble. I'm assuming you've seen the sign and you knew they were my parents."

"Yes, I guess I've seen the sign a few times. I probably thought it was an uncle of yours." Lane wondered where Mason was taking the conversation.

He went back to his chair and sat down. "My brother was to take over the business someday, but he passed away some years ago. My father left the sign as is. He didn't have the heart to change it. But I've been asked numerous times...by my father...to take over his business if, well, if something should happen to him. And I have considered it seriously for some time now. I feel certain I'll say yes to him soon."

Lane tried to keep her shoulders from sagging. What unexpected news. She wasn't quite sure how to respond. "I'm so sorry. This must be hard on everyone." She wanted to reach out and hug him, hold him, but he appeared more distant than ever.

Mason gave her a solemn nod. "It isn't easy."

"But it would also be a shame to walk away from all that you've built. I mean you have a gift for helping people with their money. And you'd lose everything."

"Yes, I've considered all that. But I think it's the right thing to do. Eventually I'll have to tell all of my clients, but I thought you should know first." Mason shuffled some of his papers. "Now, I guess we'd better get on with what you came for."

But she didn't really care about growth stocks; she cared about him. Lane had hoped for a moment to tell him about her change of heart. She'd hesitated before, but now she needed to know for sure how he felt. *And I'll never know unless I ask.* "Mason, I want to talk to you about something."

He seemed distracted with a spreadsheet but looked up at her. "Yes?"

Lane searched his eyes and found nothing to persuade her to follow through with her queries, so she let them go. For now. "Never mind. Let me hear what you have to say about those growth stocks."

* * * * *

Thirty minutes later Lane was back on the road and speeding south on 59 toward her office in Houston. As she thought more about their conversation, she began to understand why Mason had told her about his plans before anyone else. It was obvious. He wanted to see if she could consider a different kind of life.

She glanced at her empty ring finger. If she could marry Mason, she would be willing to accept his career change in a heartbeat. And besides, when it came to funeral directorship, wives weren't really expected to help out with the business. Were they? Perhaps sometime later she could encourage Mason to let someone else run the day-today operation so he could continue with his own profession. He was, after all, too talented to give up his own promising career.

But Mason still needs to know how I feel about him. If she didn't tell him, they would continue to function in a state of misunderstanding. Lane determined then that she would make herself vulnerable before him as he had done with her. At the very next opportunity, she would not only tell him she'd changed her mind about going out with him, but that she'd grown to love him with her whole heart.

Lane looked at the clock on the dashboard. If she hurried a little faster she might have enough time to drop by the nail salon before her first client appointment.

She opened her cell phone. Maybe she'd give Trudie a quick call to see how Wiley fared at the minor emergency room. Just as she speed-dialed her sister's home number, she saw flashing red lights in her rearview mirror. *No, please, no. Not another speeding ticket.*

Chapter Twenty-four

....

After a long day at Bloomers, Trudie dropped her car keys on the entry table and collapsed on the couch, feeling as animated as a sack of dirt. What a day. The summer sale on padded bras had been hugely successful. In fact, they'd been swamped with female customers, all eager to enhance nature's endowments, as Rosalie called them.

Trudie rolled her head back and forth on the cushion and rested her arm over her forehead. In the quiet, she could hear the ticking of the wall clock. The seconds always marched on, relentlessly turning into minutes, and those would eventually accumulate into a decade like a pile of rocks. So far she'd been blessed with three piles of rocks. But with each tick and with each pile, she always sensed the same nagging questions. Was she using her time wisely? Was she becoming who she was meant to be?

The doorbell rang. Having company was the last thing Trudie was in the mood for, but she headed to the door anyway and opened it. "Cyrus. Hi."

"Hey." Cyrus shrugged.

"Is your mom working late again?"

"Naw. She lost her job." He looked at her with his big brown eyes, which were always searching hers.

"I'm sorry to hear that."

"Yeah, me too. So, Mom's out there looking for another job." Cyrus kicked at the concrete with his Nikes. "She wanted me to ask if I could stay for a little while till she gets home."

"Sure." Trudie opened the door wider. "Come on in." They did their usual funky handshake as Cyrus lumbered inside.

Trudie noticed his dark skin was glistening with perspiration. "You look like you've been running." She gave him a hug even though he didn't look like he was in the mood for one. She always enjoyed having Cyrus over but was never quite sure how to talk to a preteen boy.

"Naw." He looked around her apartment. "I was playing basketball in the courtyard with some of my friends."

"And are you good at it?"

"Not really." Cyrus plunked himself down on the couch and looked at her. "You know, I'm old enough that I don't need a babysitter."

"I'm sure that's true." Trudie sat down next to him. "But it'd be a shame if your mom couldn't focus on getting a good job because she was too busy worrying about you."

Cyrus seemed to think that through. "Maybe." He sniffed the air. "Something smells different in here."

"Could be my paints."

"Paints?" Cyrus wiped his forehead on his Houston Rockets T-shirt. "You mean like you're painting the apartment?"

"No, I mean like an artist's paints."

Cyrus lit up. "Really?"

"You want something to drink?"

"Naw." He leaned forward, his hands on his knees. "But I'd like to see the art stuff."

Trudie grinned. "Okay. Let's go." She headed back to the studio, and he followed right behind her.

Cyrus gasped when he entered the room. "Ohh. Wow."

"A friend of mine bought it for me."

"That must be some friend, huh?" Cyrus ran his hand along the easel.

Trudie smiled. "He is special."

"You should marry that guy. He must love you a lot to buy you all this."

She chuckled. "His name is Mason. He was trying to encourage me. I started painting when I was a little younger than you."

"Were you good at it?" Cyrus looked at her.

"People said so. But I think I've lost it. I can't figure out what's missing."

Cyrus walked over to the trash bin. "It's full. You throw everything away?"

"They're not good enough to sell."

Cyrus shrugged. "But who cares?"

"What do you mean?"

"Isn't art supposed to be fun?"

"Yeah."

"Well, can we have some fun?" He placed his folded hands in front of him. "Please?"

"Okay." Trudie pulled out some tubes of paint from the taboret and taped two fresh pieces of watercolor paper to the worktable. She let him sit down and get comfortable. "So, how does that chair feel? Pretty good?"

"Yeah." He swiveled around and then looked down at the paper. "So, is it okay if I give it a try?"

Trudie nodded. "Wet your brush, load it with paint, and go for it."

Cyrus did as she said and began swirling cerulean blue at the top of his paper like waves in the ocean. He appeared to be enjoying himself, wriggling his tongue back and forth—a quirky habit Trudie remembered doing as a young artist. "You can use the palette there in the middle to mix the colors."

"I've got an idea." Cyrus grinned. "My mom's on that new fish diet. Why don't we both paint fish that are on a human diet?"

Trudie laughed. "Okay." She wet a brush and decided to paint a puffer fish with a guilty smile and some diver's flippers coming out of its mouth.

After a few minutes, Cyrus looked over at Trudie's work. "Okay, now that's demented."

"Thanks." She looked at his whale, which had round spectacles and was staring hungrily at a tiny boat just above him. "I like yours too."

Cyrus rose from the stool. "Now let's switch paintings and keep going."

"Switch?" Trudie chuckled. "Okay." She sat down on the chair, and Cyrus began working on her painting.

Trudie looked at what Cyrus was doing to her work. He was adding a handlebar mustache to its mouth and painting an oversized umbrella in its propeller fins.

Cyrus took a look at what Trudie was doing to his blue fish. She was busy adding pink lips and a dainty ballerina tutu. He doubled over with laughter.

After a few more flights of their imagination they traded paintings again for the finishing touches. Twenty minutes later they stood back and gazed at their shared masterpieces.

Cyrus laced his hands on top of his head. "Okay, now that was cool."

"Yeah, it was." Trudie looked over at him. "Well, you can either take your painting home, or these can be the first works of art hung in this studio."

"Really? They're good enough to put on the walls?"

"Yep."

Cyrus nodded slowly. "I'd like mine right over there." He pointed to the wall in front of the worktable.

"Done. I'll let them dry, but the next time you come, they'll be matted and framed and on that wall right in front of us."

"All right." They gave each other a high five.

"So, they still do high fives at school?"

"Naw." He shrugged. "It's just something my mom likes to do."

"Oh, okay."

Cyrus looked at Trudie. "Hey, maybe I'd like to be an artist someday.

Only maybe I could be one of those guys who does the magazine ads and stuff."

"A graphic artist?"

"Yeah, maybe."

"You can do anything you set your mind to."

He rocked his head up and down. "Yeah, that's what my mom always says."

Trudie grinned. *Thanks, Cyrus.* Watching him express himself with paint was not only satisfying, but liberating. She would always need a daily reminder that art was about fun too—not just about seeking to satisfy the marketplace.

The phone rang and Trudie went into the hallway, saw it was her sister, and picked up. "Hi, Lane. What's up?"

"Well, you said you wanted a session this week. Are you ready at seven o'clock this evening?"

Trudie hated to keep putting her sister off. "Sure. I'll be there at seven o'clock. Thanks."

"See you then."

After Trudie hung up, she called to Cyrus, who'd shambled off into the living room. "Hey, are you hungry?"

"I'm *always* hungry."

She chuckled. *That's what I thought.* "How about a grilled cheese sandwich?"

"Got jalapeños?"

"I believe I do."

Trudie and Cyrus fried up some sandwiches, laughed some more, and then ate their little feast. Just when Cyrus had finished off the last of his milk, the doorbell rang.

"Must be your mom." Trudie wiped her hands on a dishtowel and went to the door.

When she opened it, Cyrus's mom, Kesha, was standing on the welcome mat, looking tired but pleased. "Hey there. Thanks for helping me out."

"No problem."

When Cyrus joined his mom, Kesha placed her palm on the top of his head and leaned his face up for a kiss on his forehead as if he were the greatest joy of her life. "I missed you."

He rolled his eyes but grinned.

Trudie smiled, enjoying the mother-son exchange. "I was sorry to hear you'd lost your job."

"You and me both." Kesha shook her head. "But I had some good interviews today. So, I'm pleased about that." She turned to her son. "Cyrus, I guess we'd better go."

He looked up at his mom. "So, what are we having for supper?"

"Meatloaf, mashed potatoes, and fried squash." Kesha chuckled. "You are one finely tuned eating apparatus. Do you know that, Cyrus?"

He gave his mother a toothy grin.

Kesha looked back at Trudie. "And tomorrow I'm going to make you a batch of peanut butter cookies you will never forget. That is, if I can keep Cyrus out of the cookie dough. Bye now."

Trudie waved as they left. Just before she shut the door, she could hear Cyrus say to his mom, "Hey, I think maybe I'd like to be a graphic artist someday." It was a moment that reminded Trudie that she wouldn't want to miss the joy of having kids. But she was thirty, and now any hopes for marriage and a family seemed to be slipping away.

Fifteen minutes later she was driving down Will Clayton Parkway toward her sister's home on the golf course, but her mind was still thinking of marriage and a family. Of course, the only person connected to that dream was Mason. She barely knew him, and yet that hope of falling in love and marrying and starting a family had never been tied so closely to any other man. What could she do?

A lone tear slipped down Trudie's cheek. She swiped it away.
At the wedding Mason had still shown some interest in her, but how
long would it last? Could it be that without realizing it, Lane was
destroying the only chance she had for happiness? When would it be
the right time to share those concerns with Lane? Maybe she had a
good opportunity. *Right now.*

Chapter Twenty-five

....

Lane swung open the front door before Trudie could ring the bell. "Hi."

"Hey, Sis."

"I'm so glad you could do a session this evening. Come on in." Lane gave her a hug. "I've got the master bath set up for us."

Trudie followed her sister through the living room toward the hallway that led to the bedrooms. She'd always loved the way her sister had decorated her home—Tucson style with a luxuriant number of original oil paintings.

Lane took a pumpful of hand cream as they passed by the powder room. "You really are doing much better with your hair, by the way."

"Thanks."

Lane smoothed the lotion on her hands and arms. "And that beige silk top is the right color for your skin tone. Good purchase."

"Thanks."

When they reached her master bedroom, Lane turned to face her. "Let's stay in here for now. It'll give us more moving room to work on your posture. Then we'll go over makeup in the bathroom."

Trudie took in a deep breath. "What do you want me to do?"

"Okay, first of all..." Lane raised her hands in a swanlike gesture. "Think royalty. We want to move with grace and style. We want to have our shoulders straight and our head held high."

Trudie obeyed, but at first it felt uncomfortable—like someone trying to bend a stick to its breaking point. "Okay, how's that?"

"Not too bad. Tuck in those buttocks."

"Really?" Once again, Trudie tried to follow her sister's instructions.

"Be sure and keep your feet firmly on the floor."

Trudie flattened her feet.

"You have a tendency to lower your chin. But you'll want to keep it even with the floor." Lane smiled. "And I think you've stopped breathing."

"How can you possibly remember to do all of this stuff, just to stand still?" Trudie took in some air, trying not to get flustered.

"It's easy when you've practiced. Now let's try moving a little. As you walk, you'll want your arms to move like this." Lane began to float across the room, elegantly as always. "And the tips of your fingers should brush the sides of your legs. Okay, let's give that a try."

Trudie sashayed across the room as she tried to remember her sister's every move.

"All right." Lane grinned. "That was an attention-getting start."

"I guess our goal isn't to frighten people." Trudie laughed.

"You'll want to glide rather than bounce. And don't sway your hips."

Trudie thought it might be easier for a chicken to learn how to climb a tree than for her to learn how to glide. "Okay, got it. Sort of." No, she didn't really have it. She felt like a bumbler. Was there such a thing as a female bumbler? Guess she'd be the first.

After Trudie had managed to learn to walk without looking like the Incredible Hulk and after she'd learned a host of other secrets to proper posture, she was more than ready to move on to makeup selection and application. She was then escorted into the beautiful world of Lane's master bath—plush towels, white marble, and even a tiny crystal chandelier. It always brought a sigh. The bathroom counter was covered with more facial products and makeup items than she knew existed. "Do you use all of these products?"

"Well, not all at once." Lane laughed. "Now, when you think of makeup, think balance. We want to try to create the illusion of an oval face, since that shape is the most appealing."

"Okay." Trudie sat down on the vanity stool and stared at herself in the mirror, something she still didn't like doing. *I'm so pale.* "Color would do me some good. I'd at least look like I was walking among the living."

Lane grinned. "Now, you have just enough red tones in your blonde hair that you're considered a spring, and so that will determine what colors we choose. For instance, some of the best eye colors for you will be in the browns, taupes, and peachy colors."

After Lane had brushed on her foundation and had applied all the rest of the magical cosmetics from her bathroom counter, Trudie was amazed that her eyes shone brighter and bluer. She not only looked alive, but pretty. "Lane, this really does look good."

"You were always lovely. But this just shows it off a bit more." Lane began gathering up some of the products. "Now when you take this makeup home, I want you to remember to blend. A lot. That's what keeps us from looking—"

"From looking like a gargoyle?"

Her sister chuckled. "Well, not quite a gargoyle. But blending is important."

"But, Lane." Trudie winced. "I can't possibly accept all this makeup from you. I know this is the good stuff. The *really* good stuff. And you've spent way too much money on me already."

"It's the least I can do." Lane touched her shoulder then, not like a professional image coach but as her sister.

Trudie wasn't sure what Lane meant. Could she be referring to Mason? Perhaps Lane felt Trudie deserved some consolation prizes since she was willing to walk away from Mason. *That's a pretty terrible thought.* Her sister couldn't help loving Mason, and she'd given of herself in so many ways. But Trudie knew she would trade all of Lane's generosity for one more date with Mason.

"I know just what you need." Lane clapped her hands together. "I'll be right back." Her sister rushed out of the bathroom.

Trudie stood back, looking at herself in the mirror. There was no doubt about it; Lane had indeed transformed her into a more pleasing-looking woman. But whether she could keep up the new look was another issue.

Moments later Lane came back into the bathroom flushed and excited as she placed their mother's tiara on Trudie's head.

"Lane, I can't wear this." She wanted to remove the tiara at once, but she also didn't want to hurt her sister's feeling or ruin the happy moment.

"But we always did that growing up. Remember? Whenever either of us did something remarkable, Mother would let us wear the tiara for the day." Lane seemed to drift away with her happy memories.

"I remember all too well." Trudie lowered her gaze.

Lane stroked her back. "Surely you're not still blaming yourself for Mom's accident after all these years. You needed to let that go a long time ago."

"Actually, I did begin that process recently...of letting go."

Lane crossed her arms and looked at Trudie in the mirror. "You know, I never really understood why you blamed yourself in the first place. Surely you remember that Mom was a terrible driver."

"I didn't remember that part." *Why had I forgotten?* Had she blocked that from her memory?

"Oh, Daddy used to joke all the time that someday Mom would kill us all with her driving. None of us were in the car that day, or that would have become true." Lane stood behind Trudie and placed her hands on her shoulders. "So, it doesn't matter whose errand she was on. Mom was always distracted when she was driving."

"Why do you think she was such a bad driver? What was so diverting?"

"Even as loving as Mom was, she had flaws too. We all do." Lane gave Trudie a little shoulder rub. "But if you want to, you're welcome to ponder that question. And knowing your melancholy temperament, I'm sure you will...for years. But there's really no need to now. Mom is happy in heaven, and all is well."

All is well.

Lane raised her chin and folded her hands in front of her. "And that tiara does belong on your head, especially today. You look beautiful. You should celebrate that fact. Look at the way it sparkles."

"I'm sure you know why it sparkles like that." Trudie licked her lips. "It's not filled with rhinestones."

"Yes, I know. They're real diamonds and sapphires."

Trudie looked at Lane in the mirror. "And did you ever know where the money came from...to buy all those jewels?"

Lane shrugged. "I just assumed it was Daddy's nest egg. I didn't think he should spend his retirement money that way, but who was I to question him. I was still in high school."

Trudie removed the tiara. "It wasn't Dad's retirement money, Lane."

"It wasn't?"

She turned away from the mirror and set the crown on the counter. "It was all the money I'd made selling my paintings to the galleries. It was my college savings. All of it."

"No." Lane's hand covered her mouth. "You shouldn't have let him. Why didn't you stop him?"

Trudie looked at her sister through tears. "Because Dad's grief was so terrible. And because it brought him so much comfort to honor Mom in that way. I couldn't say no. I just couldn't do it."

Lane sat down on the edge of the bathtub. "Why didn't you ever tell me?"

"I don't know." Trudie sighed. "No, that's not true. I do know. In my young mind I mistakenly thought the sacrifice would somehow atone for my sin."

Lane took hold of Trudie's hand. "But you didn't really *do* anything."

"I was guilty of more than just insisting Mom drive into Oklahoma City that day. Because of my success at such a young age, I'd become full of myself...belligerent and prideful. No one could stand me."

"I did."

Trudie chuckled. "That's because you were expected to. You were my little sister."

"Well, it was just a phase you went through, just like I went through my fat phase. And besides, I'm certain you no longer have a prideful bone in your body."

"But I wish I could have been a different person before Mom died. I wish I could have..."

Lane patted Trudie's hand. "We all have regrets. I have mine too."

"Really?"

"I just try not to dwell on them, since there's nothing I can do about it." Lane clasped her hands together. "The day of the accident, just as Mom was walking out the door, she told me that she loved me. And I didn't say it back. I'd been upset with her because she'd refused to buy me a pair of shoes I'd wanted, which I didn't really need, but at the time I thought I had to have them. Anyway, I was upset, and I didn't say 'I love you' back to her."

Lane sighed. "I saw all the joy fade from Mom's eyes as she walked away toward the car. It was as if someone had turned off a light. Ever since then I've never forgotten that expression on her face and what she would have looked like had I said those words. Now I'd give anything to be able to tell her that I love her. But it's too late."

"I never knew." Trudie shook her head. "I'm so sorry."

"Well, none of us live forever, so I'm sure someday I'll get the opportunity to tell Mom that I love her. And so will you." Lane smiled.

"You turned out pretty wise for a baby sister."

Her sister arched an eyebrow. "Who's calling me a baby? We were only two years apart. I mean, you were barely dry out of the womb when I came along."

They both laughed.

"By the way, about the money and college. I'd always thought you wanted an art degree, but when the time came and you didn't go, I was never sure what happened. But I should have asked you why you'd stopped painting." Tears filled Lane's eyes. "So many things should have been said and done. So many things."

"When Mom died, we all became sort of tilted like those rides at the carnival. It changed all our lives."

"Yeah, and me starving myself." Lane shook her head.

"Yes, but at least you became gorgeous in the process."

Lane chuckled. "Well, losing all that weight didn't come from any discipline." She picked at the ruffles on her blouse. "I was just too sad about Mom to eat."

Trudie sat on the tub next to her sister and pulled her into a hug.

"I guess it's pretty important that we tell the people we love how we feel about them. And I do love you, Trudie."

"I love you too, Sis." Trudie felt the moment was so healing that the last thing she wanted to do was to bring up a sensitive topic, so whatever she intended to say about Mason—she let it go.

Lane hugged her back.

Their faces touched and more tears fell, mingling on their cheeks.

Chapter Twenty-six

....

A few days later, Trudie stood staring into the cold and barren abyss of her refrigerator. She had nothing in there but a half-carton of goat's milk, which she couldn't continue to drink since it made her smell like a goat, and some green bean casserole with all the onion rings eaten off the top. *Hmm*. Oh, and a crew of condiments gone very bad. She hated seeing an empty fridge. It meant she'd have to make a trip to the grocery store. Not her favorite place in the world.

In between little fits of bemoaning her inevitable quest for supplies, Trudie changed into a jean dress, drove to her local grocery store, and grabbed a petite shopping cart. A single person only needed a small cart since there was no need to buy a lot—and certainly no one else to please. There were positives about being single. She had trouble making a list of all the good things at the moment, but Trudie was certain there was an impressive list. Somewhere.

She strolled down the processed "dinner-in-a-box" aisle—the place all heart-smart people were supposed to avoid. But since running out of mac and cheese constituted a pantry crisis, she would forgo the health tips. Apparently everyone else had done the same thing, since there was quite a herd of people in that same ominous prepackaged aisle.

Just as Trudie reached for the deluxe style mac and cheese in her favorite brand, she saw a hand reaching for the same product on the shelf. She looked up and saw Mason.

Surprise flickered on his handsome face and then was replaced with a look of pleasure.

Trudie gave him a big grin before she could filter her expressions.

He was clad in denim too, just like her. Only she had on a denim dress, and he had on denim jeans and a denim shirt. They were like a cornucopia of denim, and apparently she was getting downright silly in her head.

"So, I see you're a macaroni and cheese fan, too?" Mason lifted two boxes off the shelf and handed her one.

"Uh-huh. I am a fan." *Boy, that was deep, Trudie.* "It's a good comfort food."

"Perhaps we both need some comforting." He gave her an earnest smile.

Then they stood grinning at each other until it became obvious that someone would have to break up their little fest.

Mason looked in Trudie's cart and then cleared his throat. "You don't have any perishables yet, so do you want to have a quick cup of coffee in the café here?"

Suddenly their sweet reunion took on a more serious quality. She probably shouldn't. But what if she treated it like coffee with an old friend? Surely Lane wouldn't deny her that? But she and her sister's bond had grown so much stronger with the recent heart-sharing that she hesitated in doing anything that might weaken it.

"I'll even let you buy my coffee."

Trudie chuckled. She could feel her resistance fading so fast she felt like a charlatan. No, she was a charlatan. "Okay. But just for a little while." So much for hesitation. *Lane, forgive me. But just for a few minutes I'm going to give myself this gift.*

They wheeled their carts toward the open café area. Trudie tried not to steal glances at him but failed. Every time they were together, she sensed a rightness, a wholeness she couldn't even begin to explain or understand. She just loved being with him and talking to him. And, well, kissing him wasn't bad, either. Kind of like reaching a great summit. Or watching a live birth. Or seeing a rainbow after a storm.

ANITA HIGMAN

But if they were to have a "friendship coffee," she'd have to hide all her similes in her pocket.

After they made their cappuccino orders, Mason made no move to pay for his coffee.

Trudie laughed, but it came out as a giggle. "You really *are* going to let me pay for your coffee. Aren't you?"

Mason nodded. "Of course I am."

"I'm glad." Trudie grinned. He was a man of his word and a teensy bit smart-alecky about it, too. And she liked it. Way too much. And besides, considering the purchase of her art studio, she probably owed him about a thousand cappuccinos.

When they'd picked up their beverages on the counter, Trudie found a table in the front. He followed her and eased down across from her. She certainly didn't want to sit in the corner and give the impression that they were a couple.

"So, is Wiley okay after throwing his back out?" Mason appeared genuinely concerned rather than just making chitchat.

"He's fine. They gave him some powerful pain pills that night, and he seemed to be in excellent spirits when I dropped him off. In fact, he thought he was singing in the rain...even though there wasn't any rain."

Mason laughed.

Trudie blew on her drink to cool it off. "I wanted to thank you again for the art studio. I'm using it more and more. It's...well, it's not an exaggeration to say that it's changing my life."

"I'm glad. Very glad." He reached out to her, almost touched her hand, but didn't quite. "I hope you will invite me to your first art show."

"Well, I'm far from ready to have my work hung in a gallery again, but if it happens, you'll be at the top of my invitation list." Trudie thought it might be best to keep the conversation light. "Is your father doing any better...with his heart?"

193

Mason sighed. "No, I'm afraid not. He's the same. But thank you for asking."

Oh, dear. So much for keeping it light. Trudie took a swig of her cappuccino, but since the liquid was still too hot, it burned her tongue. She tried not to wince.

"Thanks for buying the coffee."

"You're welcome."

Oh, no. Silence again. It was obvious they were stepping carefully on what felt like thin ice. But they were still in danger of sinking.

Mason looked away. "There's that song again...from the wedding."

Trudie turned her focus to the music playing over the speakers. "Unforgettable." They just weren't going to get a break. Everything around them seemed to be a reminder of what had passed between them. "It makes me think of a radio station I listen to sometimes. In the evening they play a lot of romantic tunes like that. I could listen to a CD, but hearing people talk about their favorite song adds such a human touch. You get to hear a bit of their stories. It's nice."

"I know what station you're talking about."

"You do?"

"I do."

She shivered.

"Are you cold?"

Trudie took a cautious sip of her coffee. "No, not at all. I'm very warm." *Oh, brother.* Why had she said it like that? She needed a quick conversational diversion. "So, how is your work?"

"Busy...as always."

"Well, people love to invest in the future." Why was everything coming out loaded with innuendo?

"Yes, they do." Mason caressed the handle on his cup but didn't drink any of his coffee. "Funny thing about investments. Sometimes when stocks are going down the wise investor stays with it even during the downturn. And in the end, they're usually the winners. The ones who didn't give up." He looked at her then with those brown eyes of his.

Trudie felt her face flush as she touched her cheeks. Every bit of her wanted to speak up and say what was in her heart, but the respect she had for her sister's feelings kept her silent.

He took on a more serious air. "At some point my clients have to ask themselves what kind of investors they really are. The skittish kind...or the ones who hang in there." Mason rose from his chair.

Instead of looking astonished and asking Mason if he were leaving, Trudie looked up at him and said, "So, what kind of investor are you?"

"I think you already know." Mason leaned down and gave her a tender kiss on the cheek. Then, just like that, he walked out of the grocery store, leaving his coffee, his shopping cart, and her in a state of mystification and skin-tingling euphoria.

Chapter Twenty-seven
....

Two weeks had passed since he'd kissed Trudie's cheek in the grocery store. Mason hadn't forgotten the surprised look in her eyes or the pleasure he'd felt in putting it there. But in spite of that one fine moment, he felt no closer to the object of his affections.

Mason got out of his car and turned his attention to his father. He saw him in the cemetery a good distance away and began walking toward him. His father had on a three-piece suit even though the temperature was in the nineties. But that was just like him. He had so much respect for the people who were grieving that he felt a hot suit in the summertime was an acceptable burden if it would add to the dignity of their day.

As Mason approached, he could tell his father was standing over the grave of an old veteran friend of his—Leon Atkinson.

His father looked up. "Hi, son. What brings you here today?"

"Well, Mom said you were in the hospital this morning."

His father chuckled. "Yeah, much ado about nothing, as Shakespeare would say."

Mason stuffed his fists in his pockets just like he used to when he was young. "What did the doctors say?"

"They said I'd live. But I know what you're really asking. How long do they think I have?" His father shrugged. "They still don't really know. One doctor thought a few months. Maybe a year or two."

"I see." Mason took in a deep breath.

"It's all right, son." He smiled and pointed at a newly planted tree not far from them. "Who's that gardener fellow of ours? Oh, yes, Simon

Mueller. Anyway, he likes to plant live oak trees. Funny tree to plant in a cemetery. I always thought so anyway. Why don't we walk for a bit? It's a good day."

Mason wondered how it could be a good day when his father had such dire medical news, but he was pleased to spend some time with him. As much time as he could get. As they walked through the cemetery, his father pointed out the graves of people he'd known through the years—people who'd changed his life in one way or another.

"I have had a good life. I've loved and lived and through it all I have known the Lord. I had two wonderful sons, whom I loved with a whole heart, and I am blessed with a fine wife." He smiled. "How can I be caught complaining?"

"I guess asking God for a few more years wouldn't be complaining." When Mason saw his father stumble a bit he reached out to him.

"I'm fine, son, but thank you." He sat down on a concrete bench under a loblolly pine.

Mason stood next to his father, knowing that the subject of his health was officially closed for the moment. "I know you'd like a decision from me about taking over the business."

"Well, I didn't want to push, son, but I'm sure you've felt pressure. Especially after Nate died. He wanted the business. But I know your gifts lie elsewhere." He coughed and cleared his throat. "But I will say this... one of the blessings in this vocation is the opportunity to tell people about our faith in the Lord. When people are bustling around with their schedules, it's hard for them to hear the truth. But when everything stops, when they suddenly see the end to someone's life, someone dear to them, it changes them. They suddenly listen."

"It's a fine calling, Dad."

His father seemed to study him. "And a calling you feel you never received?"

Mason rolled up his sleeves and sat down on the bench next to his father. He'd chosen to accept his father's offer, but it broke his heart that when the moment came to give him an answer, he was still hesitating. "I've prayed about it. But I just don't know for sure."

His father slapped his hands on his legs. "Well, that's an honest answer if ever I heard one. Perhaps this ministry was meant for another man, and I can't see it yet. Why God still hides things from me I have no idea, since we've been such close friends and all, but in His sovereignty, He knows best. Through a glass darkly, I suppose, until we're on the other side." He started to whistle a hymn, and then rose from the bench. "I'm rested. Let's walk some more."

Mason strolled alongside him, grateful for some quiet time with his father.

"We're a heartbeat away from August now. A transition time and one of my favorite times of the year. You see?" He pointed to the sun. "You can tell it looks different in the sky now, rather misplaced and not so zealous. Like a weary traveler." He stumbled again and Mason reached out to help him.

His father touched one of the headstones to right himself. He took a handkerchief out of his pocket and dusted the stone. "There, that's better. They get so old and dusty, don't they?" He shook his head and put his handkerchief back in his pocket.

Mason swallowed back the emotion that was building inside him. To watch his father grow thin and pale had been one of the most agonizing things he'd ever known. *God, give me strength.*

His father lifted his hands toward the sky. "Ah yes, we're headed toward autumn, the season of jewels. My only regret is that we don't have lots of those pretty colored leaves. But we have everything else in Humble, so I'm not complaining. No, don't want to be caught complaining. No use for it."

Mason had noticed his father talked more about simple things and less about business—more about the past and less about the future. It bothered him, but talking about it would sadden them both and inspire no one. "I've probably become pretty proficient at complaining." He'd suddenly blurted out those words, but he wasn't sure where they'd come from.

"So how's love, my boy? Has it found you yet?"

"I'm not sure about that, either." Mason paused to look at a statue of two cherubs locked in an embrace, their faces frozen in rhapsodic contentment. He hadn't remembered seeing that one before.

His father stopped. "Not sure about love? Or not sure about a particular woman?"

Mason was glad he didn't have to tiptoe around the facts with his father. "I'm sure about love in general. I'd like to marry someday. I've just never met the right woman...until recently."

"Oh?"

"But I'm afraid it's gotten complicated."

"It was that way with your mother and me. Love can get messy."

"Oh yeah? How so?"

"Well, her parents didn't like me at the time. I was a pauper, and she came from money, as you know. I came off looking like an opportunist. But it wasn't that way at all. I loved your mother. But I faltered...waited too long. Their wealth intimidated me. Or I should say I let it paralyze me. So, I nearly lost your mother to another man because I was too afraid to speak up. Too timid to say what needed to be said."

"I don't think I'd heard those particular details to that story."

"Well, I always hated to grow old and start repeating myself." His father grinned. "So, whoever this woman is you're talking about, if you think she might be the one, don't hesitate too long, son. Work things out. I'd like to go off to heaven someday knowing love found you."

Mason and his father strolled off together, surrounded by hundreds of headstones and a lifetime of memories. He wondered if his father was right about waiting too long to speak up. The original plan had been to allow Lane ample time to see that they weren't compatible. The idea seemed practical in theory, but it wasn't working very well. *Perhaps the time has come to make things right.*

Chapter Twenty-eight
....

Trudie finished up her sketch of a porch swing, which was encircled by a monstrous bush of lilacs. She tore the paper off the pad to study it. Her drawings had steadily improved. The perspective on the swing and porch were right, and it had enough dimension with light and shadow. But even though the picture was technically correct and she was enjoying her work again, something else was missing.

She looked at her fingers and the side of her right hand, which were tinged with charcoal. It felt good to be in the midst of doing something she truly loved. That part felt just right. But she still wasn't sure she wanted to go back to the same style she'd grown accustomed to. A lot had happened over the years. She'd grown up, and as an adult artist perhaps she felt like stretching her creative muscles a bit. *But how?*

Trudie remembered the playful atmosphere Cyrus had brought into her studio. Maybe she could create something for Cyrus—something that would make him laugh. She began again, this time drawing a flower that was unknown, a blooming plant that might be found on the planet Glopiral. At first she made sweeping motions to create the stem and triangular leaves, and then she gave more detail to the marbleized petals. *Hmm. Not bad.* Maybe the flower would be called "butterdils" by the locals on Glopiral. She grinned.

An hour later when Trudie was finished with the rough version, she had a good long look. She liked it. The sketch was very different from what she was used to, but it had been satisfying to draw. More so than she imagined. She signed her name at the bottom of the picture for the first time since her reentry into the world of art. This one she would give to Cyrus.

Then she thought about Mason and how much he deserved a roomful of drawings and watercolors for all his help. But giving him anything might look like an invitation to ask her out, and that would only complicate matters.

She touched her cheek, remembering the kiss that had come so unexpectedly in the grocery store. Mason had meant his kiss as a reminder—a promise that he hadn't given up on her. Then a twinge of guilt seized her. Perhaps Lane needed to know. Trudie wanted to do the right thing, but she wasn't sure how to confront her sister. She didn't want to upset their new sisterly joy, and yet maybe she'd done her a greater disservice by being silent. Perhaps she wasn't really giving Lane an opportunity to find love, but was instead setting her up for the greatest heartbreak of her life. Trudie looked around the room. She wouldn't have to say much about Mason and his feelings if Lane were to simply see the studio he'd purchased for her. Maybe that was the answer.

The phone rang, and Trudie was glad to see that it was her sister on the line. "Hey there."

"Hi. I thought it might be fun to shop at a couple of the antique stores, and then have lunch at the tearoom. How does that sound?"

Trudie looked at the clock. It was already ten forty. She'd truly lost track of time. "That's perfect."

"Good. I'll pick you up in fifteen minutes."

"Okay."

After hanging up, Trudie checked her hair and makeup in the hall mirror. Not bad. She'd begun to include makeup in her morning routine, and she was amazed that it wasn't taking up as much time as she thought it would.

A few minutes later, the doorbell rang. Trudie straightened her shoulders and tried to remember all her sister's tips on posture.

On opening the door, her sister said, "Ohh my. You look good, Sis. Really good."

"Thank you." Trudie wigged her eyebrows.

"So, are you ready to go?"

"Well, there is something I want to show you."

Lane looked at her watch. "Well, can it wait until I bring you back? If we're too late at the tearoom, there'll be a line."

"Oh, okay." Trudie locked up but was determined to show her the art studio when they returned.

They headed out in Lane's Lexus, and within a few minutes they were parked near the Historic Downtown sign of Humble. They walked for a bit, crossed the street, and then entered the mystique of Hobbart's Antique Emporium.

Lane always liked to mill around while Trudie immediately started touching objects and considering their design. She noticed a lone vase sitting on a small end table. The ceramic piece was decorated with Indian paintbrush and Mexican primrose, all hand-painted in exquisite detail. Trudie looked at the price tag. Ninety-nine dollars. Not within her budget, but it was pretty.

She saw her sister stroll into a separate part of the store, so after sighing over several more vases and their price tags, Trudie followed Lane into the next room. The space was filled with antique furniture and knickknacks with a Texas theme—wrought iron lone stars, oil paintings of bluebonnets, and an array of cowboy paraphernalia. In the corner were several grandfather clocks, all standing together in a row as if they were soldiers guarding the passing of time. When she approached Lane, she had her hand resting against the face of a mantel clock. She seemed to be peering inside. "Are you okay?"

Lane nodded. "Of course."

But Trudie noticed that her sister wasn't quite herself—friendly but with a pensive, faraway look. She wondered what was wrong.

"I suddenly remembered something you always used to say in high school."

"I doubt it was anything worth repeating."

Lane turned to her then. "Oh, but it *was* worth repeating. Worth remembering."

"What was it?" Trudie took a step closer to her.

"You called them the pickles and the posers." Lane touched her sleeve. "Now do you remember?"

Trudie chuckled. "No."

"Well, the pickles were the hard places we found ourselves caught between, and the posers were the hard questions of life. Those questions that adults couldn't answer easily. So you called them the pickles and the posers."

"Humph. Sounds like something goofy I'd come up with."

"Not so." Lane shook her head. "I used to think it was just the melancholy in you that made you see things so differently than I did. But now I see it was clarity. And I wish I had more of it."

Trudie had never seen her sister so introspective and so sad, and it troubled her to see it. "I think you're suddenly looking at my youth through rose-colored glasses."

"You don't give yourself enough credit." Lane's expression sagged. "No, *I* didn't give *you* enough credit over the years."

Trudie crossed her arms. "That's not true."

"I was the worst possible sister."

"Please don't think that." Trudie took her sister into her arms and held her for a moment.

"You once said that if we didn't humble ourselves, life would find a way to do it for us." Lane eased away. "I guess you could say that I've had an epiphany."

"Do you want to tell me about it?" Trudie sat down in a chair and Lane sat across from her.

"Well, as Daddy used to say, 'There are fences that need mending.' I have something for you. It's in the car. I'd planned on giving it to you in the tearoom, but I want to give it to you right now. If it's okay."

"Of course." Suddenly they were surrounded by the sounds of dinging and bonging and cuckooing all coming from the clocks around them, announcing the passing of the hour.

Lane brightened a little. "See? It's time."

"Time for what?"

"Let's go. I have to do this now." She squeezed Trudie's hand.

"Okay."

They walked out of the shop toward Lane's SUV. When they were both inside the car, Lane reached behind the seat, brought out an elegant hat box, and handed it to Trudie. "This is for you. You should have had this years ago."

Somehow Trudie knew. It was the tiara. She opened the box gingerly, and nestled inside the black velvet was their mother's crown. "But you know I've—"

"There's more." Lane touched her arm. "The stones...I had them all removed. The tiara is now the way it was meant to be...with rhinestones. I sold all of the sapphires and diamonds. Got a very good price." Lane handed Trudie a check. "And this is yours. It's all the money from the sale, and the rest is from me. It's so you can get that art degree you wanted. You deserve to have that dream. You deserved it all along."

Trudie stared at the check and the large amount. "But you can't do this with your own money. I won't let you. I know those stones were valuable, but they couldn't possibly have been worth this much."

"It doesn't matter."

"You just can't." Trudie held the check out to her. "It's too much. I won't let you."

"I've already given it to you, and I'm not taking it back." Lane pulled her hands away and smiled. "And why shouldn't I? You're my sister, and I love you."

Trudie shook her head, trying to take it all in. She felt so much emotion build up she wasn't sure what to say. How would she ever be able to pay Lane back for her generosity? Certainly not by showing her the art studio. The idea no longer felt appropriate. Instead, tears streamed down Trudie's face as she took in a few gulping breaths of air.

Chapter Twenty-nine
....

Lane turned over in bed and wiped the tears off her face with her pillowcase. She'd never been in the habit of going to bed in the middle of the day. What was the matter with her? Her clothes were getting all wrinkled, and she didn't even care. Giving Trudie the tiara and the check had brought her great joy, but her emotions were jumbled with grief.

She scooted up in bed and looked out the window. Clouds had rolled in, and she could already hear the rumbling of thunder. Lane knew her anxiety had nothing to do with the money she'd given Trudie—she'd been happy to add some of her own cash toward her sister's degree. But plenty of other feelings tugged at her spirit, feelings that caused her sorrow.

Lane rose from the bed and stood near the window. In the distance, she could see the lightning flash over the golfers like flickering florescent lights. How many people were struck each year while they were out playing golf? She couldn't remember the statistic, but she knew it was enough to make her want to throw open the window and warn them all. But she knew it would be ridiculous since people were determined to do what they pleased, no matter the consequences. No matter what.

Hmm. That thought certainly opened a cerebral can of worms. Lane crossed her arms as she thought of the one man who had indeed finished his life as he pleased and had cared little for the consequences of his actions. When she'd seen, really seen, the anguish on Trudie's face that day in the bathroom, Lane had wanted to shout at her father for his self-indulgence. But he was long gone to hear her rebuke, which was probably best, since she had some serious questions for him.

She placed her palm on the window glass, feeling its warmth. How could their father have done it—taken Trudie's money for something so frivolous? Mother would never have approved of such a scheme. Or their grandparents. And then for their father to suddenly sell the farm, pull Trudie out of school just before her senior year, and move them all to another state was needless and wounding. Grief had turned their father into a selfish man.

Lane let her head roll back and forth against the window. But until their mother's death, he'd been a fine father. How could such a good man do such a bad thing? Was it his own fault, or did he feel helpless and pushed over the edge?

And what about her own guilt? She suddenly pulled away from the glass, pondering that hard fact. If she'd been paying more attention to her sister she would have known what her father had done. Perhaps she'd even vaguely remembered him mentioning something about Trudie's artwork and how it had made the tiara what it should have been. She was never sure what he'd meant, but had she really wanted to know? She'd been too busy spinning in her new world. Scenes came back to her as she recalled entering a new high school after thinning down to a size six. To have heads turn as she walked down the hallway had been intoxicating. Maybe the sudden attention had blinded her to the needs of others.

Lane thought how unusually brooding she'd become. She'd always been lucky to have more than her fair share of the sanguine temperament, so she tended to be somewhat oblivious to the grim emotions that her sister had always suffered with. What was happening to her? She reached down and picked up a pile of clothes off the floor, amazed at how disorganized she'd gotten even in a week's time. She shook her head. Her life had become like a ball of yarn unwinding willy-nilly until it was all gone. *That's me. I've reached the end of my yarn.*

As Lane hung up a skirt and tossed a couple of blouses into the hamper, her thoughts continued to dance around the greatest of all mysteries—Mason. For a moment Lane thought she smelled his cologne on one of the dresses in her closet. She held the fabric to her face. Could she detect the faintest hint of it there? Or was the desire to have him near her so strong that she was conjuring up an illusion? The mind could be a friendly apparatus at times, and it could be quite an enemy at other times. Was the interest she'd seen in Mason's eyes really all in her imagination? Perhaps she saw hope where there was none. But what would she do if Mason never chose to ask her out again or move forward in a relationship? Would she be able to let him go?

God, please don't make me do it. Anything but that. *I love him.* What if he only needed a little more time to see that he loved her? Just a little more time. But was she being fair to Trudie? Surely the money was enough. Shame pinched at her. Had she given up some of her savings as compensation? Had she become that manipulative? Lately nothing seemed right in her heart and mind. Nothing seemed as uncomplicated as it had been before. She was out in deep water. And drowning.

Tears filled her eyes again. Lane dropped the clothes in her hands and shuffled to her bed. She crawled back under the covers where she felt safe. Was that what love had done to her—made her into a whimpering child?

She remembered the moment of the change, when her heart had softened toward Mason. The day of Trudie's birthday luncheon. She'd seen qualities in him that she'd never noticed before—qualities she deeply admired. There was no doubt that Mason was a man she could love for a lifetime, but she was beginning to wonder if her affections would ever be returned.

Chapter Thirty

....

Mason knocked on Lane's front door. He rarely went to anyone's home without an invitation, but he felt she would forgive him for the intrusion. Phone conversations and e-mails just didn't seem like the right move with something so personal and important.

He mashed the doorbell, wondering why his plan concerning Lane hadn't worked. He'd thought she'd quickly give up on him. He hadn't shown any interest in her romantically since those first dates months earlier, and he'd made her very aware of his potential career change. But he'd learned over the years that women were far from simple creatures. They were like complex roads to be navigated with a watchful eye, since there were plenty of potholes for men to fall into. Just as Mason thought of leaving, he heard the quiet sounds of someone unlocking the deadbolt.

Lane peeked around the door. "Hi, Mason."

She looked surprised to see him, but she also looked so unlike herself he paused, trying not to stare. "Lane?"

"Would you like to come in?" She opened the door.

"Sure. Thanks." Mason walked into her entry. He felt uncomfortable immediately. Should he offer an explanation? "I'm sorry I didn't call first."

Lane shook her head. "No...you never need an invitation, Mason. Why don't we sit down?" She motioned toward the living room.

Mason followed her and then eased down on one of the lush couches. Its softness almost swallowed him whole. He sat up straighter, wondering what he'd planned on saying. He should have practiced something. Maybe he should pray. A lot. Maybe he should just leave.

He rose. Then he coughed. Finally he sat back down again. There was no reason to do the upside/downside routine. Both were pretty obvious. He just needed to open his mouth.

Lane leaned forward. "Are you all right?"

He nodded, knowing he looked pretty antsy. It reminded him of the strange sensations he'd felt when he'd given blood and then tried to stand up too quickly.

"Would you like something to drink? Iced tea or Perrier?"

"No, I'm fine. But thank you."

"You're welcome." Lane smiled at him and folded her hands in her lap, looking refined and pleasant as always.

But he could also see that her eyes were red and puffy. Even though she wore a smile, underneath she seemed, well, distraught. And she'd been crying. He wondered what could be wrong, but he was afraid to ask, in case the matter was too private. Mason looked around at the furnishings, trying to figure out a way to ease into the subject he'd come to discuss. "Your couch. Is it new?"

"No."

"Oh." Mason crossed his arms and studied the floor. "Well, and the rug on this hardwood floor. It looks good."

"Thanks." A confused look crossed Lane's face. "Was there something you wanted to talk about...in particular?"

"You're right. I do...have something...that needs talking...about." *Oh, brother.* He couldn't even construct a sentence. *I'll be grunting out syllables soon.* "Well, I've been wanting to talk to you for some time. So, this is good that you're here."

"Well, I would be. It's my home." Lane grinned at him.

"Oh, yeah, right." Mason shook his head and laughed. "I'm coming off like a real idiot, aren't I?"

"Not at all. I'm just teasing you." Lane lit up then, looking more like her cheerful self. "Actually, there's something I've been wanting to say to you too."

"Really?" Mason put up his hands. "Well, ladies first." He suddenly felt like such a coward.

Lane leaned forward. "Well, we've known each other for some time."

"Yes, we have."

"And I cherish your friendship." Lane looked at him, her brown eyes almost twinkling now.

"And I yours."

"But sometimes that little bud of friendship can blossom into a flower." Lane placed her hand over her heart.

"Flowers are good." *Aren't they?* Mason wasn't totally sure what Lane was trying to say. Was she saying their friendship was in good shape, or was she saying something else? "Maybe I don't understand what you mean."

Lane took in a deep breath. "Well, I know how important it is that we tell people how we feel. I was reminded of that recently. To speak our feelings clearly and never hold back." She sighed. "Well, I'm in love with you. I am. There it is. I've said it."

Mason tried not to show his shock at her words. He hadn't considered the idea that Lane would feel so strongly. He knew she was interested in dating again, but he'd no idea she was in love with him. He smiled and tugged on his necktie. The goofy thing had him in a strangle-hold.

In the meantime, Lane seemed to be holding her breath.

Then his blasted cell phone came to life. "I'm sorry. I'll turn it off." Mason glanced at it and saw that it was his mother. Since he was concerned that the call was about his father's health, he looked back at Lane, hoping she'd understand. "My father has been ill. Do you mind?"

"No. Not at all." Lane rose. "Let me give you some privacy." She stepped into the kitchen.

Mason answered the phone. "Hi."

"Hi, son."

"Is Dad okay?"

"He's at home this time. I can't convince him to go to the hospital or to let me call 911." All the usual animation was gone from his mother's voice. She sounded so weary.

"I'll come over. Maybe I can convince him to—"

"Your father said he didn't want to spend his last moments in a hospital bed surrounded by plastic hoses and strangers."

Mason gripped the phone. "I guess I can't blame him for that. But I'm still coming."

"Do come. This may be the last..." Her voice broke, and he knew she was crying.

"I'll be on my way soon. Bye." Mason coughed, feeling a little lightheaded. He'd known such a moment was coming—when he'd be forced to say his final good-bye to his father. He'd prepared himself a hundred times, and yet the feeling was worse than he'd ever imagined.

Lane came back in the room, looking worried. "What is it? Is your father okay?"

"No." Mason rose. "I think he's dying."

Her hand covered her mouth. "I'm so sorry, Mason. I'm so very sorry." She came towards him and took him into her arms. He let her comfort him as he put his arms around her.

"I need to go." Mason gently pulled away. "I'm sorry. We'll have this conversation. It's important. But I need to go now." He went to the door, and Lane opened it for him.

"Is there anything I can do? Anything at all?" Land lifted her hands to her face, her fingers trembling.

"Pray for us all. My father is ready to go. But I'm not ready to let him go."

"I will."

Mason started walking toward his car but then broke into a run. He had no idea if he had hours left with his father or minutes, but he felt a strong tug of urgency.

Chapter Thirty-one

Trudie flipped the TV off, wondering why she'd ever bothered turning it on. All the programs looked the same, and not much of it was worth watching anyway. She headed to her studio.

The phone rang, and she caught it in the hallway before the machine picked it up. She saw that it was Mason calling. She reached for the phone and then hesitated. What should she do? For a moment, she stood in a fit of indecision. She walked away and then went back to answer it. "Hi. Trudie speaking."

He paused for a second. "Hi. This is Mason." His voice sounded raspy.

"Is everything okay?"

"It's about my father...he died."

"Oh, Mason." Trudie sat down on a chair in the hallway, clutching her heart. "I'm so sorry."

Mason was quiet for a moment.

"When is the funeral?"

"It's ten o'clock a.m. on Tuesday at Pine Forest Community Church." Mason cleared his throat. "It would mean a lot to me if you would be there."

"I will. Absolutely."

"Thanks."

It tore Trudie to pieces to think of Mason's grief. She knew he'd loved his father deeply, and so she knew his sorrow would be acute.

"You know how it is to lose a parent. You've lost both."

"Yes. I do know."

Mason paused. "It's hard to see through the fog."

"Time helps, but I've never forgotten."

"Nor would we want to."

"You're so right, Mason. We wouldn't want to."

They went quiet again, but it seemed to be a good kind of silence, like between two old friends, and a comforting moment, just knowing the other person was on the line. "Will you be okay? I'm here if you want to talk about your dad." Trudie cradled the phone in her hands, wishing she could say the right words to comfort him.

"I'm sure I'll be ready to talk on Tuesday...if you'd like to listen."

"I will. Of course."

"Thank you. I'll see you Tuesday then."

"Yes. Would you like me to call Lane? I know she would want to be there."

"That's a good idea. Thank you."

When Trudie hung up, her heart had never felt so heavy. She wondered how Mason would deal with the loss. Then she thought of his future. Would he be the new director of Wimberley Funeral Home?

* * * * *

On Tuesday Trudie thought the funeral had gone beautifully. There had been a presentation of Mr. Wimberley's life, showing special moments he'd spent with his family and his many friends within the community. Several hundred people passed by the casket afterward, and Trudie and Lane were among them. Mr. Wimberley had been a striking man with a dignified and kind face, and Trudie regretted that she'd never gotten the chance to meet him.

After the service and the burial and the luncheon were all coming to a close, Mason walked up to them once more. "If you both have the time, I'd like to show you something."

Lane tucked her clutch purse under her arm. "I would love to."

"Of course." Trudie shuffled her feet.

"I assume you've both heard of the old bridge at Black Cat Ridge," Mason said to both of them but looked at Trudie.

"Of course." Lane smiled.

"It's that old bridge that goes over the San Jacinto River." Trudie looked at him.

"Yeah." Mason nodded. "Below that bridge is where my father used to take me fishing when I was growing up. I haven't been down there in years. I don't even know what it looks like anymore. But I have a need to see it now...that is...if you both would like to go."

"It might be very therapeutic." Lane pursed her lips.

Trudie clung to her purse, not knowing what to do and wondering if she should bow out of their little excursion.

"All right then." Mason pulled a set of keys out of his pocket. "Let's go in my car."

They said their good-byes to Mrs. Wimberley and a few lingering relatives. After he opened his squeaking and slightly askew car door for his guests, he drove them out onto Loop 494 North.

Trudie decided to go along but sat in the back of the car, allowing Lane to sit in the front with Mason. She couldn't help but grin as she watched her sister taking sneaky glances around in the car. Lane must have thought, "Why would such a successful man drive such a rickety vehicle?" But to Lane's credit she said nothing about it. She did, however, squeeze the very life out of the front seat. Mason was a good driver, so she wasn't sure why Lane would be so tense, except for the fact that she loved him and was still unsure of his feelings. That made sense.

They exited Hamlen Road, drove around under the bridge, and parked. They were alone, except a stray cat or two. Trudie wondered if that was how Black Cat Ridge had gotten its name. They all got out of the car and looked around. The old ornate bridge with its two arches was still there—now in all its rusty glory. Old-fashioned lamplights had been added as well as a ramp so anyone could take a stroll across the bridge. Nice touch.

Mason pointed ahead of them to the river. "Right over there is where my father and I used to fish." He removed his black suit coat and pulled off his tie and tossed them into the car. "Are you two going to be okay with your shoes?"

"We're just fine. But are there snakes down here?" Lane asked as she surveyed the ground.

Trudie grinned at her sister. "Since when did you get so citified, Lane Abernathy? We used to play with snakes on the farm."

"Correction." Lane pointed at her. "*You* played with snakes, and I was always running from you."

Trudie chuckled. "Perhaps that's true. And I guess there could be some copperheads around here."

They all walked toward the riverbank with Lane watching her every step. Unfortunately, her sister already looked wobbly in her stilettos as she sank into the sandy ground. *Poor Lane.* To Trudie, high heels always seemed as stable as walking on pogo sticks. She glanced down at her flat pumps. They were therapeutic-looking and ugly, but at least they were comfortable.

"Here's the spot." Mason came to the edge of the bank and sat down. He looked back at the two of them. "Lane, you look like you need some help."

"I'm fine." Lane laughed him off, but she still appeared to be about to topple over. "Thank you, though."

Lane and Trudie both made it to the edge of the water and then stood on either side of Mason. The sound of the traffic above them turned into a monotonous roar, but it didn't drown out their voices.

Trudie looked down into the green murky waters of the San Jacinto River, wondering what sort of living thing stirred just beneath the surface. Probably something bulbous and slimy and glutinous. Maybe she'd paint the creature when she got back to the studio.

Mason rested his arms across his knees. "We caught some pretty good-sized fish in there. Mostly catfish. I always felt sorry for Mom, though. She usually got stuck with the cleaning." He said the words quietly as if he was speaking to no one in particular.

Lane crossed her arms. "I used to fish, but I just hated putting the worm on my hook."

"First time I hooked a worm...I was ten." Mason grinned. "I got woozy."

"Did you?" Trudie looked at him.

"I managed to keep my food down. But mostly just from the fear of being embarrassed." He chuckled. "But I got over it eventually...that queasy feeling. Somehow I felt I had to." His tone took on a pensive quality.

"So, do you still go fishing?" Lane swatted at an insect.

Mason looked up at her. "I do. I go hunting too." He seemed to wait for her reaction before he went on.

There was a lengthy pause. "So what sorts of animals do you hunt?" Lane dabbed at her face with a wad of tissues.

"Deer mostly."

Lane's expression went sour. "You don't mean Bambi, do you?"

Mason laughed.

Lane crossed her arms. "Doesn't it seem sort of barbaric?"

"Not any more so than buying hamburger at the grocery store." He grinned. "Well, if it counts for anything, whatever I kill, I have processed. Whatever I don't eat, I give to my family and friends."

Lane lowered her gaze, looking sheepish. "I'm sorry, Mason. I didn't mean to question your morals. Please don't take my silly ramblings seriously."

He didn't respond for a bit, but then said, "Sometimes our ramblings carry more weight because the words come from our heart before we have a chance to censure them."

Lane's hand flew to her mouth. "Oh, no. I guess I've offended you."

Mason laughed. "There was no offense taken."

"Okay. I'm glad." She stared at him for a moment and then pressed a tissue against her face.

Feeling herself slip into a quiet mode, Trudie eased herself down onto the riverbank.

Lane looked around in the sand and smoothed her black linen suit, but didn't sit down.

Trudie couldn't blame her for standing, since her suit looked expensive, and it certainly wasn't machine washable.

Mason watched Lane. "I'm sorry I didn't let you two stop at home to change before I brought you out here. It's not really a good place for nice clothes. Are you sure you don't want me to take you back?"

"I'm sure." Lane put on her most congenial smile.

Mason pulled a handkerchief out of his pocket and unfolded it on the ground for Lane. "It's not much, but it might help."

"Thank you." Lane clutched her purse and lowered herself onto the piece of sheer fabric. "That was very genteel of you."

"You're welcome."

Once Lane was on the ground her high heels suddenly seemed too high. She tried to find a way to get comfortable, but it appeared impossible without getting her clothes dirty.

Trudie felt sorry for her. Most of the time, Lane's shoes look ultra chic, but at the moment she just looked miserable.

Lane picked around in her purse, pulled out the program from the memorial service, and started to fan herself with it.

"There's supposed to be a Spanish treasure buried over there somewhere." Mason pointed behind him, away from the river.

Lane seemed to study him. "I suppose I heard about that legend years ago. Seems to me if it had any real merit the city would come out here with a backhoe and dig up the place. Try to find it. You know, settle the matter once and for all."

Mason breathed in deeply. "Yes, I guess that would be one way to handle it. But sometimes I think people are more interested in the great stories passed down than they are in reality. Besides, treasure would be spent, but myth holds romance forever. Well, at least for as long as the tale is told."

Lane smiled at him but said no more.

They all sat quietly for a while, listening to the katydids and the roar of the traffic above them. The air seemed to get heavier, if that were possible. Trudie was afraid to say anything to Mason. She remembered Job's friends. They didn't fare so well in helping their friend with their multitude of words. Instead they became a burden to him by not remaining quiet and just grieving.

Mason pressed his hands over his head, letting his fingers run through his hair. "I suppose my only regret is that my father didn't see his house filled with grandkids. He would have loved that. But the timing wasn't right."

Lane fidgeted on her square of cloth. "Did you have any other siblings or was it just the one brother...who passed away?"

"Just the one brother. Nate."

"Oh." Lane licked her lips.

"My mother loves kids too." Mason rolled up his sleeves. "Who knows? Maybe I can make it up to her."

Lane stopped fanning herself. "Make it up to her with children?"

"Yes." Mason turned to Lane.

"So, you really do plan to have lots of kids then? You weren't kidding?" Lane rested her palm on the ground and leaned toward him.

"No. I wasn't kidding." Mason released a chuckle. "Of course my wife would have some say in the matter. But I do like kids. Always have. Most of my friends have kids, and so I get a kick out of baby-sitting for them sometimes. It gets pretty wild and noisy, but I haven't lost my sanity yet."

Trudie liked listening to Mason talk about his life. In fact, he amazed her with every word he said.

"I had no idea." Lane shook her head slowly as if taking it all in. "I mean I've known you for a while now, but I honestly don't remember you talking about how much you loved children and your hopes for a big family. Although I guess I just never asked."

Trudie wasn't sure, but she thought Mason may have figured out the mystery of why she'd backed away from his life. And now he was allowing himself to be transparent so that Lane would have an opportunity to see inside him—perhaps parts of him that he hadn't revealed before. Seemed like wisdom. Lane might grow to love him all the more for it, but then again, she might see that they weren't quite as compatible as she'd first envisioned.

Lane loosened the hold she had on her purse, stared at it for a while, and then with some resignation in her gesture, set it on the ground. "Well, I'm afraid Trudie is the one who does well with kids. They love her at the children's hospital."

"I'm sure they do...love her." Mason turned and looked at Trudie, catching her gaze for the first time. He had a lost expression, but his eyes were also filled with what looked like yearning.

Trudie felt her eyes sting a little with tears, so she looked away.

"I know this comes off whiney," Lane said, "but I've coiled myself into a knot, and I can't seem to get up without being unladylike. I'm sorry."

Mason quickly came to Lane's rescue and helped her up. "This was my fault."

"No, I was happy to come." She released Mason but continued to look at him. "I have a question for you. Please, though, only answer if you want to."

"Ask away." He handed Lane her purse.

"What will happen to you now? Will you be taking over your family's business?"

Mason turned back to face the river but didn't say anything for a few moments. "Yes." His voice seemed resolute, but without joy.

Lane dusted off her suit. "But what will happen to *your* business?"

"I'm not totally sure yet."

Quiet settled amongst them again as they stared out at the river. Trudie watched the flow of the water as it made its way slowly but steadily to wherever it was destined to go.

"You've been through a great trauma," Lane went on to say. "Don't you think it might be wise to wait about making such a life-altering decision?"

"I've been thinking about it on and off for years." Mason slipped his hands into his pockets. "I want to honor my father's wishes."

"I think I do understand now." Lane gently shook out his handkerchief and handed it back to him. "I'm sorry, Mason. But I just can't take this heat any longer."

"I shouldn't have kept you both out here so long. Why don't we go?" Mason reached down to Trudie. He lifted her off the ground and for a moment he held her, perhaps longer than was necessary. For a second she thought he might not let go. When he released her, Trudie could see that Lane had been watching.

As they all hiked back to the car in the smoldering heat, Trudie wanted to say so many things, wanted to comfort Mason, but the right words didn't come.

They drove back to the church, making comments on the river and the bridge and the heat. Later in the parking lot, Trudie and Lane gave Mason another round of condolences and hugs, and then in his gentlemanly-like fashion, he helped them into Lane's car.

As they pulled out of the parking lot, Trudie glanced back. Mason waved at them, but his expression appeared as immeasurable as the Texas sky above them.

Trudie clutched the material on her black dress and fought back the tears. She'd never felt so lost, since her heart was no longer her own. Secretly, she'd given it away—to Mason.

Chapter Thirty-two

Trudie placed her pile of watercolor paintings neatly on the worktable. She had gone through them about fifty times, organizing them and then rearranging them so that Wiley would get the best impression of her work. She wondered what he would think of her watercolors. Were they lovely and salable or childish and boring? Now that the time had come for a viewing, she was a wreck.

The doorbell rang. *That would be Wiley.* Trudie hurried to the door and opened it. "Hi, Wiley. Hi." She tried to remain cool, but the effort was useless.

Wiley stepped back. "My goodness, Trudie. Have you been out in the sun or something?"

"No." She shook her head. "Makeup. Lots of it." *Well, and Lane's expensive outfits.*

"Well, makeup looks very good on you."

"Thanks. Come on in."

Wiley stepped inside and kissed her hand as if he'd happened upon a princess in a fairy tale. "Thank you for letting us come with such little notice."

"Did you say *us*?" Trudie wondered if she'd heard wrong. What could he mean?

"I hope you don't mind. My partner came along too. Kat."

"Kat?" Trudie's face started to tingle.

"Yes, she's—"

Before Wiley could continue his speech, a middle-aged woman dressed in black whirled inside her apartment. "You must be Ms.

Abernathy. I'm Kat Stone." She raised her chin, looking Trudie over. Kat had the body of an ironing board, the countenance of a prosecuting attorney, and the voice of a mouse. That is, if mice could talk.

"Hi." Trudie reached out and shook her hand. "Ms. Stone, it's so good to—"

"Wiley tells me you have some work for us to look at. I have a few minutes." Kat glanced at her watch. "I don't normally do this...come to someone's home. It's just not kosher. But, well, Wiley convinced me to. What can one say about Wiley?" She patted his cheek. "He's just Wiley."

Wiley smiled, rolling his eyes.

"Well, let me take you to my studio." Trudie led them into her spare bedroom, hoping the space would give the right impression. Kat didn't look like the sort of woman who would tolerate hobbies. It had to be either real work or nothing at all. Trudie held her breath as Kat and Wiley shuffled through her ultra neat pile of watercolors.

Trudie stepped away from their huddle as they made little comments and little grunting noises. She got the impression their tiny sounds back and forth were private, so she stayed away until they'd made it all the way through the pile.

Kat spun around and looked at Trudie. "How long have you been painting?"

"Well, not that long." Trudie clasped her hands together to keep them from shaking. "But I did paint and sell my work when I was a girl."

Kat glanced around the room. "There's not much natural light in this room. Does that bother you to work in a dungeon?"

"I would prefer a better place to paint, but this is all I have at present. But I hope to attend a school—"

"What are these?" Kat's forefinger pointed toward the floor.

Before Trudie could stop her, Kat reached down and pulled up a miscellaneous stack of paintings, ones that had been hidden between the worktable and the canvas cart. Apparently they weren't hidden well enough. "Those were experiments. I'm sorry to say they went—"

"Upp." Kat's arm popped up like a traffic guard to stop all chatter.

Trudie bit her lip, waiting for Kat to explode with disgust. But she didn't. She tilted her head and studied them one by one. Wiley looked over her shoulder, and together they made a new kind of grunting sound. She overheard the words "Fauvism," and "Rousseau," and "pure color." When they were finished, they both turned and faced her simultaneously.

"We have an opening soon, since the artist we were going to feature became quite ill with shingles. So, you may have her date on our calendar. We wanted to bring in something fresh, and this is it."

Trudie felt her face go hot. "But I don't feel it's my best work. It's just not what—"

"Upp." Kat raised a forefinger and looked her up and down. "So, you don't want us to feature your work?"

"No, I do. Of course. It's just that it's such a surprise. I wasn't even going to show you these pieces. I don't think they're ready to be—"

"Well, life is bursting with surprises, isn't it, Ms. Abernathy? Just when we think we know the shapes and colors of our lives, we see new ones that come from nowhere. You're an artist. You should know that. Great art doesn't just jostle us awake. It grabs us by the throat." Kat made a fist in the air. "It demands that we take another look, experience a new awareness. Great art tells us that there are still things in life that can provoke us and confound us and arouse us. If art gives us even a faraway glimpse into that dimension and ideal, then we have succeeded." Her hand floated outward as if she'd just completed a grand soliloquy on stage.

Trudie swallowed. "I don't know what to say."

Kat tilted her head, appearing stunned. "I think a thank you is considered customary. Don't you think?" she added in her little mouse voice.

"Thank you." Trudie straightened her shoulders. "Both of you."

Kat handed the watercolors to Wiley, and he returned them to their hiding place. "You'll need a few more for the show. So get busy. We'll be in touch to work out the details. There'll be an agreement to sign."

Trudie nodded. "Yes. That'll be fine."

"I was right about Ms. Abernathy." Wiley wiggled his eyebrows. "I could see it in her eyes."

"Don't start gloating, Wiley. It'll only add to your waistline. And it makes you much too loquacious to endure." Kat raised her arm in a dramatic gesture. "Shall we go?"

Wiley rolled his eyes, grinning. "We shall."

Then Wiley and the woman named Kat marched toward the front door. Trudie fell in their wake, swallowing two lumps—one of awe and one of panic.

Chapter Thirty-three

....

Lane sat in her car in front of Mason's office, feeling drained of her usual vigor. Two weeks had passed since the day of the funeral, and she hadn't seen or talked to him since then. She prayed the worst wave of grief was over for him. For herself, she only hoped that she could get through her little speech—the one she'd practiced over and over in front of the mirror. The speech Mason would need to hear. She left her car and opened the front door to Wimberley Financial Services.

"Good morning, Ms. Abernathy," Lily said from behind the front desk. She quickly set something down and wiped her mouth on a napkin.

"Hi." Lane glanced down, curious about what Lily was munching on. It was a protein bar. *Hmm. Be careful.* Sometimes those things could really pack on the calories, but she also noticed that Lily didn't have an ounce of fat on her. *Well, isn't that just lovely for Lily?* Lane breathed a quick prayer for the young woman. It was a new routine she'd just adopted—to say a prayer for anyone she'd entertained an ugly thought about. Lane noticed the habit was keeping her busy praying for people.

"Mr. Wimberley has been expecting you." Lily pursed her lips into a rosebud. "But before you go in, I wanted to ask you a question. Mr. Wimberley told me you were an image coach."

"Yes, that's correct."

"Well, you always seem so, well, graceful and put together."

"Thank you."

"I'd like...I think I could use some help. I want to do a really great job for Mr. Wimberley, and sometimes I get kind of, well, tongue-tied. So, maybe I could hire you to help me with that."

"I'd be happy to." Lane pulled a card from her purse and offered it to her.

"Perfect." Lily accepted the card, beaming, and then motioned toward Mason's door. "You may go right in."

"Thanks." If Lily was still concerned about being a good secretary for Mason, he must not have told her his news—that he was making a very profound career change. Lane stepped into Mason's office and shut the door.

He rose a bit when she came in. "Hi, Lane." He smiled and motioned toward the chair in front of his desk. "Please have a seat."

Lane sat down and looked around his office, avoiding his eyes. "I like all the plants you've added."

Mason glanced around at them. "They're from the funeral."

"Oh. I think it's nice when people bring live plants as gifts. It reminds us...you know, that your father is still alive. Just not here with us."

"It is a good reminder." Mason folded his hands in front of him. They both paused.

Mason started speaking at the same time as Lane. They chuckled. "Ladies first."

Lane sighed. "I'm afraid that line makes me nervous now. The last time you said that, I admitted something to you that has since embarrassed me. Or at least I feel requires some explaining. Which is why I made this appointment with you."

"You mean what you said in your apartment that day."

Lane felt her face color. "Yes, that would be the line I'm referring to."

"There's no need to—"

She put her hand up. "Please. Let me get this out. I've practiced it many times. Some months ago when you asked me out, I enjoyed being with you, but I wasn't sure it was wise for us to go out. I'd learned in the past that business doesn't always mix with dating. But as I got to know you better...in spite of my own warnings, I..." Her voice faded.

"You fell in love." Mason smiled. "There's no crime in loving someone. I'm deeply honored that you would feel that way."

Lane looked at him then, seeing nothing more than compassion in his eyes. "Yes, but as you know, the problem comes in when the other person doesn't feel the same way."

"To say anything but the truth wouldn't be right." Mason looked at her. "I'm fond of you, Lane. I respect and admire you. But I'm not in love with you."

She nodded. "I appreciate your openness. It makes everything clear that way."

"I can see the pain in your eyes, and I'm sorry to have put it there."

"But I'm not surprised at what you've told me." Lane fidgeted with her hands, a luxury she never allowed herself to indulge in. "You're a gentleman in every way. I suppose that was one of the reasons I...well." Lane crossed her arms to stop her twitching. "It's funny. Well, not really funny. But I'd convinced myself that you felt differently. I had forced myself to believe a falsehood." She shook her head. "How can we fool ourselves so deeply?"

"Easy. People do it all the time."

Lane leaned on the arm of the chair. "How do you mean?"

"Well, I frequently see clients who become very good at fooling themselves. They live like they're rich when they're anything but. They've told themselves the lie long enough that they start believing it."

"Yes, I guess I can see that one pretty easily. But to do it with the heart seems...I don't know...I guess *imprudent* is a good word for it." Lane gave him a smile that she knew was weak.

"You're being kind of rough on yourself. Don't you think?"

"No." She shrugged. "Maybe I am a little. But lately I've been learning all sorts of new things about myself. Things that aren't so positive. I guess it's that season of my life." Lane wondered if she were being too outspoken with Mason. Perhaps she'd gone too far baring her soul.

Mason rose and sat on the edge of his desk. "Since my father died, I've discovered a few things about myself as well."

"Oh?"

"I found out that I miss my father even more than I imagined I would. And that the transition over to the family business is not quite how I had envisioned it."

"Is it harder?"

"Yes. For me it is." He took in a deep breath. "These past two weeks have been...illuminating."

"What do you think will happen?" Lane was surprised at Mason's candor.

"I don't know. I feel at an impasse in my life. Well, more precisely, I feel like I'm standing on the edge of a cliff without any ropes." Now Mason was fidgeting with his hands.

"Is there anything I can do?"

Mason looked at her. "Pray."

"That I know how to do. I've done a lot of it lately." She cleared her throat. "The other reason I came...actually the main reason I came...was to mention that there is a woman named Trudie...who will no longer run from you." Lane smiled. She tried to make it a genuine smile even though she thought it might have come off a little propped up. "Trudie knew how I felt, and she was being kindhearted toward her younger sister. But my acceptance of her generosity caused a lot of pain. I can see it now. And for that I apologize."

"But you did it for love. Hard to be too upset about that, Lane."

She smiled again, this time feeling it all the way through her. *Time to go.* She rose to leave.

"Thank you for coming today. It must have been hard to say all that."

"It was." Lane chuckled. "And you're welcome."

Mason went over to her and gave her a brotherly hug. "So, are you and Trudie going to the high school reunion coming up?"

"I'm not sure yet. How about you?"

He opened the door for her. "Maybe next year."

Lane stepped into the front room.

"Good-bye, Ms. Abernathy." Lily waved.

Good-bye suddenly sounded so final. Lane gave her a little wave back. "See you soon."

Mason followed Lane outside and opened her car door for her.

A gentleman always. "Thanks."

He put his hands on his hips. "See you later."

Lane started the engine as she watched Mason walk back inside. Such a fine man. Mason had great taste in everything but cars. She laughed to herself as her eyes blurred with tears. So many tears came that the whole world in front of her became hazy. She hoped soon, very soon, life would be clear again.

She sat for a moment to regain her composure and to think about all that had transpired. How had it happened? She hadn't searched for it—love had somehow found her. There'd been no logical pattern to it. Love seemed to be the one thing that could not be organized into neat little bins and shelved away in the closet. Love was random and unmanageable. It was as if her heart had set its own course, and her brain and body had just been along for the ride.

And even as gentle as Mason had been, his words had been difficult to hear. There was no positive way to spin it, no self-talk to brighten the moment. Sometimes life was just hard. She clutched at her chest, aching with the loss, remembering that even Jesus wept.

After the tears had done their cleansing, she slowly began to feel better. At least she felt no more despair. Lane pulled out of the parking lot, still contemplating the nuances of love. The idea of compatibility in marriage drifted in and out of her thoughts. Would she have been compatible with Mason? She was no longer sure. But when had she ever met a man who was perfect for her? Only one man had fit that description over the years. *Hayden Montgomery.*

Lane glanced at her watch. Since she had a little more time before her morning appointment, she decided to stop by Trudie's apartment. Lately she had been in the business of making some wrongs into some rights, and so the trend seemed to continue. She would tell Trudie about her little chat with Mason. Maybe it wasn't too late for them. Maybe they could start right where they'd left off. That's what she would hope for now.

Lane parked and then freshened her makeup. After running up the walk she rang the bell. "Come on, Trudie, please be home." Then she knocked.

After a few seconds, her sister answered the door. "Lane? What a surprise."

"I have some news, Trudie." Lane smiled. "News you're going to like."

Chapter Thirty-four

....

Hayden Montgomery shifted in his chair as the hairstylist finished dusting off the back of his neck. He looked in the mirror. Not bad. He handed the hairdresser a large tip and then rose from the chair. "Take care."

"You too, Mr. Montgomery."

He walked out of the shop feeling anxious, which was an emotion he wasn't very familiar with, but the idea of going back to a high school reunion after so many years made his insides twitch. Like he'd eaten too many raw oysters. It wasn't the reunion, though, that had made him buy new cowboy boots, go back to the gym, and get a haircut. It was the woman who'd been on his mind for months—Lane Abernathy. After more failed dating experiences than he could keep track of, he was ready for a certainty in his life. And Lane, his dearest Lane, was a woman who'd cared for him long *before* he'd come into money.

Hayden slid into his Mercedes and started the engine, but instead of pulling out of the parking spot, he just sat there tapping his fingers against the steering wheel. Any time he looked back on his life with Lane, the reality of why they weren't together always surfaced. It'd been a pathetic combination of his father's influence along with the fact that he'd been a young and crazy fool. *But no more nonsense and no more waiting.* As they said in Texas, he would take the bull by the horns. Fortunately, an old high school buddy of his had been good enough to let him know that Lane was still single and that she'd probably be at the reunion. That was the best news he'd heard in a long time.

Lane probably hadn't given him one thought over the years, but something inside had spurred him on. He had to try, even if it meant rejection. But he would know soon enough what to expect. The reunion was only twenty-four hours away.

He loosened his bolo and noticed his hands were shaking. He chuckled. Lane was the only woman on earth who could do that to him—make him tremble and smile all at the same time.

Chapter Thirty-five

....

Trudie waved good-bye to Lane, shut the door, and then plopped down on a kitchen chair, dumbfounded. Lane had walked away from Mason. *Forever.* She'd given up the hope that Mason would ever fall in love with her. Trudie let the words gather round her. It was news she'd barely allowed herself to dream about—but any elation stopped cold when she remembered her sister's eyes. Lane had tried to hide the puffiness with extra makeup and smiles, but she knew. Sisters just knew. Lane had been crying.

She picked up one of Henry Bog's strawberries from the bowl and took a bite as she replayed the moment she'd finally shown Lane the art studio and told her about her upcoming exhibition. Her sister had celebrated all the good news, but then Lane promised Trudie that she'd never put her through anything like that again. The moment had become quite tender and poignant, and it seemed as though there had been a lot of those moments lately. She shook her head and took another bite of the strawberry. What a day. And it had only just begun.

Trudie looked at the wall clock. She needed to get to work, so she picked up her keys and purse and headed out to Bloomers Boutique. Driving to work did little to calm her, since there was just too much to reflect on and too much to hope for. It would be hard to stay focused at work.

Her boss chirped out a good morning when Trudie popped in the door.

"Yes, it is a good morning."

Rosalie was busy adjusting some lingerie in one of the display windows. She turned back to Trudie. "You look different. And I don't just mean all that new dazzling makeup you've been wearing and all those new clothes."

"Different?" *Oh, dear.* Rosalie was definitely fitted with emotional sensors that were set on a hypersensitive mode.

"Yes." She dropped her work and came over to Trudie, looking her up and down and narrowing her eyes. "There's something unusual in your voice. It was just the slightest bit singsongy." Rosalie's expression was full of mirth.

"Really?" Trudie decided to play innocent.

"I notice eeeverything," Rosalie said in an ominous voice.

Trudie gave her a hug. "You really do."

"It's my business." Rosalie went back to her work. "I always try to gauge what kind of mood my customers are in when they walk through that door. It helps me to help them."

"So you can help them buy more." Trudie grinned.

"Now, now. I allow them to have the desires of their hearts. I allow them to transform a mere bedroom into a boudoir." Rosalie made a theatrical gesture with her arms.

"Yes, you do." It always warmed Trudie's heart to see someone enjoy their work as much as Rosalie.

"And so what is it?"

"What was what?" Trudie put her purse under the counter.

Rosalie shook her head. "Why are you so singsongy this morning? I want some juicy juice, and I want it now."

Trudie groaned. She thought Rosalie had moved on from her sweet-hearted inquisition. "Well, I have a show scheduled at an art gallery in Houston."

Rosalie's mouth came open. "Did you say an art show? I didn't even know you could draw."

"Sorry. I just didn't think it was super important."

"Apparently it is if you have a gallery showing." Rosalie slapped the back of her hand against her palm. "I can't belieeeve you didn't tell me any of this. I could have been cheering you on. Bolstering you up. Mm, mm. And I could have taken credit for some of your fame."

Trudie laughed.

"Well, at the very least I'd better get an invitation." Rosalie cocked her head.

"Oh, you will." Trudie clutched the top of her blouse. She had now officially told someone outside her family, and having people know felt exhilarating, but scary. It meant she was committed to the life of an artist now. There was no turning back. Was she ready for an art show? She had no idea.

"So, does this mean you're going to be leaving me?" Rosalie sniffled a bit. "Honestly, I don't know what I'd do without you here."

Trudie started organizing a table full of packaged underwear. "Well, I do need to mention that I won't be able to work as many hours in the spring. I'm going to take two art classes."

"No problem. I just don't want to lose you totally."

"Oh, you won't. I'll still need to eat."

"Ahh, yes." Rosalie snapped the waistband around her tummy and grinned. "Those infernal and enchanting vittles." She walked over to Trudie. "So, was there any other reason for that lilt in your voice, sweets?"

"Maybe." Trudie rolled her eyes. "But that's all you're going to weasel out of me...for now."

Rosalie went back to her work in the display window. "You are the mysterious one. Yes, you are."

After Trudie had finished her organizing, she brought out the feather duster and her muse. When ten o'clock hit, she knew she would be watching the front door, wondering if Mason would drop in to see her. In fact, she seemed to be checking the door every half-hour. Well, maybe every five minutes. But she had so many things to talk to him about. Had he started work at the funeral home? Was the heartache feeling any lighter? She wanted to thank him again for the studio and tell him about the art show.

Then if Mason asked her out, Trudie was looking forward to seeing the surprise in his eyes when she said yes. Lane had made her promise that if Mason asked her out she would accept. And now honoring her sister's wishes would be more than easy—it would be the desire of her heart.

Trudie took her duster and cleaned off a row of feather boas, thinking how silly it felt—kind of like washing a bar of soap. Then she remembered something else Lane had said; Mason was in great turmoil about his career transition. Trudie wished she could be there to comfort him, but perhaps she just needed to exercise some patience as he had done with her. In the meantime she could get ready for her show.

The workday went by as usual, but there had been no sign of Mason. Perhaps he would call when she got home. But later at the apartment there were no messages, and the phone never rang.

After dinner Trudie shuffled off to the studio, determined to start a new watercolor. She took a large piece of paper and gingerly secured it to the table with two strips of tape. Then she flipped on the radio, since her evening program had already come on. The love song, "When a Man Loves a Woman," finished up, and the female DJ, whose voice was as smooth as chocolate syrup, came on again.

"This song is dedicated to Julianne. Stephen wants you to know that you should never forget how cherished you are. Now, ladies, isn't that lovely?" The song "You Are So Beautiful" began to play.

Hmm. Perfect for lovesick females who always spend their evenings alone. *Now, now, Trudie.* She scolded herself for sounding cynical. It was, after all, a pleasant evening of music. It just wasn't a pleasant evening for her. On that thought, she accidentally dropped a blob of watercolor paint on the paper. A big blob of cadmium yellow. *Oy! Great.*

Trudie tied her locks back with a scrunchy. Could Mason have changed his mind? Perhaps the Abernathy sisters and their perplexities had been too much for him. But that didn't sound like Mason.

Trudie shook her head, not knowing what to think. Then she grinned and smeared the yellow color around with the brush as if she were five years old and creating her very first painting. Her little work of art came out primitive, but funny, and it made her laugh. She thought for sure it would make Cyrus laugh too.

When the song "You Are So Beautiful" came to a sweet conclusion, the DJ came back on and said, "Okay, this song is just for you, Trudie. And Mason would like you to know that if you can wait for him just a little longer, rainbows are still possible."

Tears welled up in Trudie's eyes as her breath caught in her throat. Her elbows landed on the table and her paint-smudged hands cupped her face. Her cheeks were now a sunny cadmium yellow, but it couldn't compare to the glow on her face as the radio began to play "Unforgettable."

Chapter Thirty-six

....

Mason walked along the woodsy trail until he came to a pond surrounded by a meadow. He sat on the ground near the bank and looked out across the still and silvery surface of the water. An egret made a graceful landing on the other side of the pond, and for some reason the bird's delicate neck made him think of Trudie. Lately, everything reminded him of Trudie. But unfortunately, at the moment, asking her out would be difficult. The timing would be off. Even though Lane's news had brought him great hope, he also knew that hope would have to be put on hold for a bit until he could put his life in some kind of reasonable order.

He lay back on the warm ground and gazed up at the September sky. The clouds had puffed themselves up, looking angry, but he doubted there would be a storm. It was just for show. He laced his fingers behind his head. "And that's just like the promise I made to my father. Just show," he murmured.

What was he to do? Mason wanted so much to respect his father's wishes, and yet he felt that he was supposed to honor the abilities God had given him. Wimberley and Sons Funeral Home was not where he was meant to be. He could see that now. It had only taken a few days of training in the business for him to see that he wasn't meant to run a funeral home. It wasn't what he was born to do. He knew how to work with the general public concerning their finances, and yet working with people who were in the midst of grieving was very different.

He closed his eyes, hoping the weight of his thoughts would float away with the clouds. Just as he was drifting off, he breathed a prayer for direction and peace.

* * * * *

Later, he woke with a start. How long had he been asleep? The clouds had become blue-black, and the air seemed charged with the scent of rain, but he still heard no thunder. He rose, dusted off his jeans, and then tried rubbing out the crick in his neck. Why didn't he feel refreshed? And he still had no answer to his dilemma. No direction.

Mason noticed a rusty bucket full of small stones. *Skipping stones.* Darren and his wife had thought of everything when they'd created their retreat. He picked up a smooth, flat stone and skipped it on the water, but the rock skimmed the glassy surface only once. He tried it again, and the stone hit enough times on the second try that he couldn't count the bounces. Just like when he was a kid. Mason reached down to pick up another rock when he heard a faint sound.

When he heard the noise again, he could tell it was a voice—a familiar voice. He looked in both directions. To his right he saw a man walking toward him.

"Hellooo."

Mason waved to the man, who looked just like his uncle Franklin. When he came a bit closer, he realized it was indeed his uncle. Mason strode toward him, making up the distance between them.

"Greetings, dear boy," Franklin said. "Whoo. You are mighty hard to track down." He wiped his forehead with a handkerchief.

Mason reached out to shake his hand. "Good to see you."

His uncle pulled him into a hug and then slapped him on the back. "I'm really glad to see you too. So, what are you doing out here in the middle of nowhere in the middle of a workday?"

Mason stuffed his hands in the pockets of his jeans. "Thinking."

"I know." Franklin looked out toward the water. "This has been doubly hard on you. In one heartbeat you lost your father as well as your career."

"You're right." Mason paused to manage his emotions. "It's hasn't been easy."

Franklin motioned to their left. "Well, over there I see two fine chairs. And if we sit for a while I think I might have a solution to your problem."

Mason wasn't sure how his uncle could help him, but he was willing to listen. They walked over to the Adirondack chairs and sat down.

"Ahh, none of that sitting on the ground for me." Franklin rested back on the smooth wooden slats and patted the arms of the chair. "Give me a good chair like this one, and I'm a happy man."

Mason remained silent, waiting for his uncle to continue.

"Pretty little place somebody has here." His looked back and forth. "Who owns this?"

"Some friends of mine, Darren and Liza Tiller. They loan out their little cabin to friends and family and pastors when they need to get away."

Franklin sighed. "And that's what you needed...to get away." He shook his head. "I wish now I'd come to you sooner with my news. Hindsight, I guess. I wish I'd told your father before he died."

"Tell him what?" Now Mason was more than curious about what his uncle had to say.

Franklin cleared his throat. "I want to buy the funeral home, and I'm willing to give you a good price."

"Buy it?" Mason leaned forward and looked at his uncle. "But you've never mentioned that before."

"Yes, sad to say, that's true." His uncle sighed. "But it only seemed right that your father should pass it on to one of his sons, especially since the sign has always read WIMBERLEY AND SONS."

"Well, that would have been true had Nate lived. As you may remember, he was well suited for the business."

Franklin dipped his head. "Yes, he was."

Mason paused, taking in his uncle's news. "This plan of yours would certainly solve all the problems of keeping the business in the family."

"But I'm not really family...by blood, I mean." Franklin laced his fingers over his chest. "Would your father mind too much about that part, do you think?"

Mason smiled. "Yes, you *are* family. When you married Aunt Grace, my father always thought of you as his brother. He would be pleased with this arrangement. I know he would."

Franklin took out a handkerchief again and dabbed at his eyes. "Your father was always so big-hearted to feel that way. To take in an old orphan like myself. He was a good man, and I shall never stop missing him."

"Nor I." Mason leaned forward on his knees. "I know my mother would be relieved to have you run the company." He looked over at his uncle and grinned. "I think she was always afraid I'd run the business into the ground."

Franklin exploded with laughter. "Oh, your father would like that one. He always loved a good pun." He made a soft wheezing sound as he chuckled. "You don't have to worry about the money. I will make you a more than fair offer."

"I'm sure you will." Mason let out a breath of air. "Of course, all the money needs to go to my mother."

"That sounds fine, too. It's a deal."

Mason looked upward at the rays of sun streaming through the clouds. "Well, you brought some joy with you today."

His uncle slapped the arms of the chair. "My dear boy, it's great to see you smiling again."

"It does feel good." Mason rested back, feeling his shoulders relax.

Then the cloud just above them, which hung as heavily as a woman about to give birth, let go with large pelting drops. "Hmm. I think we'd better make a run for it." Mason helped his uncle out of the chair, and with brisk strides they headed toward the log cabin.

Within seconds the drops turned into a drenching rain, so they broke into a trot. Soon their clothes were soaked through, so they slowed to a walk again.

The squashing and squeaking of their shoes became so loud, it seemed to tickle Franklin into a fit of chortles. Mason soon burst out laughing too, since he'd never felt so ridiculously soggy or so wonderfully free.

Chapter Thirty-seven
....

Trudie poured herself another cup of coffee and glared at the wall clock for the thousandth time. The gallery show of her work would begin in two hours. To arrive a little early as well as compensate for any possible wrecks on the freeway, she would need to leave in fifteen minutes—give or take five minutes. She would have time to check her makeup one more time and pace the room a hundred more times before she had to leave. *I need to get a grip.*

She added cream and sugar to her coffee and stirred until the clinking of the spoon made her even more jittery. Since she was already wearing out the living room carpet, she began pacing in the kitchen. Trudie glanced in the laundry room mirror and stopped to stare at the little black dress she'd purchased just for the occasion. It seemed perfect on her. She'd tried her best to remember everything Lane had taught her about hair and makeup and dress and posture. Her sister would surely be proud of her. She'd know soon enough, since she promised to be at the gallery.

Trudie set her coffee mug down and straightened her shoulders again until her back ached. *Glide, don't stomp.* Tight buttocks. Or was it tucked? Well, at least *that* one would be easy. Every part of her was tense. But she was equally excited. Right? Yes, she was delighted about the show. Ecstatic.

On the other hand, why had she invited such panic into her life? What was the point? She suppressed the urge to rake her fingers through her hair, since her locks were all glued nicely in an up-do. She pinched her arm instead. Everything had been so pleasantly ordinary in her life before she'd stumbled back into art. She'd put the need to express herself out of her mind and out of her life. What had been so wrong with that? "Art is too illuminating," she whispered to the mirror. Too intimate— like undressing in front of the customers at Bloomers.

Trudie raised her gaze from her dress to her eyes. She could now stand to look at herself in the mirror, which was different, but she barely recognized herself. *I've changed. Who am I now?* She stepped into the laundry room, flipped on the light, and took a deeper look in the mirror. Was she just Trudie à la mode? *No.* That would have been too easy.

She picked up her mug, went over to the sink, and poured the coffee down the drain. Life had been so good. Why had she allowed change into her small world? Why couldn't the silent poet have remained silent? Now she'd gone and done it—she'd let the child outside to play and people were going to point. Guests at the gallery would either love what they saw or hate it. Or perhaps worse—they'd walk away, thinking nothing of it at all. And the media. They'd been invited too, and so her potential for humiliation would be multiplied—shame squared!

God, have You ever heard such silly rantings? Well, You're God. You've heard everything. In the end, she knew her healing and the restoration of her gifts had all been good, but at the moment, she felt as buoyant and blessed as the *Titanic*.

Trudie snapped off the coffeemaker and mashed her fist over her heart. She'd had way too much caffeine, and her heart was pounding out of control. Breathe. Maybe she could make an appearance and then disappear into the night like a stealthy and silent bat. But all her friends were going to be there. Even Mason. The idea of him coming made her even more anxious. What if he took one look at her watercolors and regretted buying her the studio?

The doorbell rang. Trudie jumped. She wasn't expecting anyone. She looked through the peephole and saw a man who looked vaguely familiar. There was no time for miscellaneous company, but she opened the door anyway. "Hi."

"Are you Trudie? Lane Abernathy's sister?"

"Yes, may I help you?" *I should know this guy. Who is he?*

The man looked down at his boots and then at Trudie. "My name is Hayden Montgomery. I don't know if you remember me, but I dated your sister in high school."

Ah, yes. "I do remember now." He was Lane's first great love, and the guy she'd spent a lot of time kissing on Moonshine Hill. Trudie grinned. How could she forget? Hayden looked older, but he was still handsome and trim. "I would invite you in, but I have somewhere I need to go in a little while."

Hayden raised his hand. "No, that's okay. I only need a minute of your time. I was looking for Lane and having a hard time finding her. She has an unlisted phone, and I didn't see her at the high school reunion."

"No, I guess she didn't go this year. Which was unusual for her." As more of the past returned, Trudie remembered that Hayden and Lane had been very serious at one point. And then she also recalled how Hayden had broken off their relationship. *Did Hayden regret his decision?* Impossible to know. But she could always play the matchmaker as her sister was so prone to do. She gave him a pleasant smile. "I know just where you can find her. I'm headed to the Flat Stone Art Gallery for an art show at seven o'clock this evening. Lane will be there."

Hayden perked up. "Is that art gallery in Houston?"

"Yes, on San Felipe. You can look it up online. I hope you'll be there."

"I have a GPS in my car. I'll be there." Hayden nodded. "Thank you so much. This means a lot to me...to find her again. I'd always been wondering." He tucked his thumbs behind his belt buckle. "Is she doing okay?"

Trudie wasn't sure what he meant. Maybe he wanted to know if she was still single. "Well, Lane never married, and she became an image consultant."

Hayden smiled, beamed actually. "Lane would be very well suited to that career. I'm happy for her."

"I'm one of her creations." Trudie lifted her arms and turned from side to side.

"And Lane did a wonderful job, if you don't mind me saying."

"I don't mind at all." Trudie reached out and shook his hand. "It's good to see you again, Hayden."

"Same here. And thank you."

"See you this evening then."

Hayden waved and hurried down the walkway. Trudie shut the door, wondering if she'd helped make a promising moment or created an embarrassing evening. Hard to tell, but it would make for a stimulating event.

After a few more minutes obsessing about everything she could think of to obsess about, she got in her car and headed out on 59 toward Houston. She turned on some jazzy music and then snapped it off. She certainly didn't want to get distracted and have an accident.

With the silence, thoughts rushed in again like floodwaters, but now they were about Mason. The one time they'd seen each other had felt more like a friendship get-together than a real date, but they'd both decided not to trample all over Lane's feelings by moving too quickly. Trudie wondered, though, how long it might be before they could all be happy. Could Hayden be heaven-sent? If Lane still cared for her first love, it would certainly solve all their problems. *Please, let it be so.* It was a selfish thought, perhaps, but it was an honest one.

With no wrecks clogging traffic on the freeway, Trudie made record time driving down the 610 loop to exit on San Felipe. After passing through a few lights and a very posh neighborhood, she suddenly recognized the gallery.

Trudie pulled into the parking lot, trying to feel nonchalant, but when she saw people already arriving in front, panic bubbled up inside her again. She cut the engine as her stomach churned.

Chapter Thirty-eight

....

Trudie pulled a peppermint out of her purse and slipped it into her mouth. Ahh. Cool and soothing. If she could just name her worst fear perhaps she could tame it. She rested her head in her hands. With little thought, Trudie knew the answer. Once again, she was anxious that people—especially Lane and Mason—would smile and nod and say all the right things, but that they might really think she'd lost her gift. She would certainly be affected by the critique of strangers, but not nearly as much as by those people she cared about the most.

She sat, staring at the front of the galley. *Trudie, you'll have to go in eventually*. Her makeup and pretty up-do weren't going to hold up in the heat and humidity. But after opening her car door, she shut it again.

Wiley Flat came striding out of the gallery and headed her way. *Oh, no*. There was no place to hide. He would find out how nervous she was.

Wiley walked right up to her window, and she let it roll down. "Hi, Wiley."

"I saw you from the foyer." He leaned down to her. "It's going to be okay."

Trudie looked at him. She could feel her cheeks quivering. And tingling. "I guess you can see I'm really energized."

"Yes, but you also look like petrified wood."

"That too."

Wiley placed his hand on her shoulder. "There's no reason to be scared. We're all going to celebrate art and have a great time."

Trudie nodded. "Okay."

Wiley opened the car door for her. "You look like pure elegance, but your elegance is going to melt into a river out here if we don't get you into some air conditioning."

Trudie chuckled. "Okay." She let him help her out of the car. "Thanks. I realize my fear makes me look ungrateful. I feel honored, Wiley, really, that my work is being shown in such a beautiful place."

"I've never doubted your gratitude for a moment, my dear." He escorted her toward the entrance.

"It must be wonderful to co-own such an incredible galley." Trudie looked at the brown stone and bronze metal façade.

"It is wonderful." Wiley opened the door for her. "But I have dreams for the future as well. Perhaps I'll tell you mine this evening, and you can tell me yours."

"I would love to hear about them." Trudie entered the well-designed and darkly lit vestibule of the gallery—the place itself a work of art. The entrance was decorated with breathtaking pieces of sculptures, paintings, and photography, all of which were nestled in imperial-looking niches and lit spectacularly with halogen lights. She'd seen the gallery once before, and yet it still took her breath away. Not only was she awed with the beauty of the place, but she was humbled with the knowledge that her work was being placed alongside such masters of their craft. "I love this place."

Wiley grinned. "It whispers something new everyday. These dreamers and creators had a lot to say."

"Yes." Trudie stopped to gaze at a bronze figure of a woman holding her child. She could feel the love between them, and the beauty of it made her heart ache.

"Yes, that's one of my favorites too." Wiley crossed his arms. "Let's go into the main hall." He led Trudie through an archway and into the largest room of the galley. She recognized her works, matted and framed and lit on black panels. Her high heels clattered on the wooden floor, which made her even more jumpy.

Wiley suddenly saw someone enter that he knew, so he rushed away in a cloud of fresh animation. She felt alone, and yet people were already gathering. She bit her lip, wondering what the evening would have in store for her.

A waiter approached Trudie with a silver tray filled with hors d'oeuvres.

"Would you like something?" The waiter lowered the tray and smiled.

"No, thank you. But it looks delicious." Trudie knew if she ate anything, there was a chance she'd throw up. Better to get dizzy from hunger than woozy from food.

A harpist started plucking her instrument not far from her. The tune sounded classical. A table of food had been set up with an ice sculpture adorning the middle. She shook her head, amazed. They had thought of everything. Trudie felt so undeserving. She just hoped two people would find it in their hearts to buy something—anything—then she wouldn't feel like a failure. And Kat and Wiley wouldn't feel as if they'd wasted their time and money on her.

Someone came up from behind her and touched her shoulder. She spun around, hoping it was Lane or Mason. "Cyrus...Kesha. You both came. I'm so glad." And it was great to see Cyrus all dressed up.

Kesha shook her head, grinning. "This is all my son has been talking about for weeks."

Cyrus looked at Trudie. "Your watercolors are good. They're like this artist I found on the Internet. Henri Matisse. Especially that one...uh, what was it? Oh, yeah. *Woman with a Hat.* Except that painting was in oil."

Trudie tilted her head and studied him. "Very good. I'm impressed. And I appreciate the compliment. Henri Matisse's work hangs in some famous galleries as well as in private collections. And his paintings are worth millions."

"Lucky dude. Well, I'm going to look around."

"Good idea."

Cyrus headed off to another room in the gallery.

His mother stared after him as he walked away. "You know, watching him grow up has been a joy, but knowing he's going to leave someday is going to be so hard."

Trudie hadn't thought much about empty nest. It seemed too distant and impossible to imagine. She hadn't even made it to the engagement-ring phase. But having several children sounded good to her. In other words, Mason's dream for a large family could easily be her dream. She looked at Cyrus from a distance. "But he will always love you. That's something, isn't it? To be loved."

Kesha nodded. "You're right. It is no small thing to be loved."

The server came over again and offered them something from the tray. Kesha took a stuffed mushroom. "This is such a nice party. And I do like your paintings. They're full of such color and life. I wish I could afford one. But being a single mom, this sort of luxury is out of my budget."

Trudie knew just what she'd be giving them for Christmas.

As Kesha strolled off toward her son, Kat strode up in an excited rush.

"Darling, it's going well." She latched onto Trudie's elbow.

"Is it?" Trudie fingered her earring.

Kat adjusted her vest and tie. "I sold three of your paintings before the show even began."

"Really?"

"I made some calls. I know my customers well, and so a few of them came for a private showing." Kat's hand took to the air. "So you've already got some little red stickers on your ID cards."

"Thank you, Ms. Stone."

"Call me Kat, please." Her shoulder swiveled forward in an elegant gesture. "Oh, and the media buzz has already been positive too."

"Well." Trudie took in a deep breath. "I'm very happy."

"You don't look it." Kat threw her head back, laughing. "It's only natural to be insecure and hesitant at first, but I can assure you that once everyone has sung your praises all evening, you'll be a real diva before the night is out." She shook her finger. "Mark my word. You'll be ordering the staff around as if they were pawns and you were the queen."

Kat traipsed off, gushing toward some new arrival, and leaving Trudie in a little tempest of panic. That was the absolute last thing she wanted to hear. She'd already lived that bright flash of notoriety with its accompanying ego, and it was dreadful. Deadly. Perhaps she should pray that the exhibition would fail. It would certainly be the safe thing to do. *I'm suffocating.* She needed some air.

Chapter Thirty-nine

....

Trudie walked toward the lobby again, hoping she'd catch Lane or Mason as they arrived. She made her way to the front door and peeked out the leaded glass doors. There in the parking lot Mason was helping Lane out of her Lexus. They'd come together? But why?

They both looked toward the gallery. Trudie backed away from the door, feeling like a guilty child. *What does this mean?*

In a haze of confusion and anxiety, Trudie trudged back into the main hall. She headed to the table of food, took a plate, and loaded it with a heaping mound of fruit, cheese, stuffed mushrooms, canapés, and pastry swans oozing with whipped cream. She nodded her approval of the feast on her plate and stuck a canapé in her mouth.

Then she turned to stare at her watercolors. The extraterrestrial flowers and the surreal landscapes and all the angled people with vibrant faces and provocative expressions seemed unfamiliar—garish, in fact—to her as if someone else had laid the brush to the paper—someone else had formed the images. Why hadn't Kat and Wiley liked her other work? Realism was more her style, wasn't it? She admired what was natural and true. No wild exaggerations. No strange interpretations. Just real art where vases looked like real vases and people were real people. Predictable people. People she could trust. *Maybe I really was born on the wrong planet.*

Trudie watched as Mason and Lane appeared through the archway together, looking like the figures on the top of a wedding cake. They looked back and forth in one unified movement. They were obviously looking for her, so Trudie moved backward into the shadows. In all fairness to them, Lane and Mason looked like no more than two friends chatting. Maybe they rode into the city together to save gas, and she was just making too many unnecessary speculations. As always.

Ten or maybe twenty new guests had appeared, but there was still no sign of Hayden. Too bad. It would have been an excellent time for his grand entrance.

And then just as quickly as Trudie's insecurity flared, Lane drifted away from Mason without even a wave or a smile. Kat approached Lane, they chatted for a moment, and then Kat walked away. *Hmm.* Lane closed her eyes. What was she doing? Did she have a headache coming on, or was she praying? Then all at once her sister's attention seemed to be pulled away to one of her paintings.

Feeling voyeuristic, Trudie searched the room for Mason. It was hard to see him, since he was now engulfed by a swarm of beautiful women. In keeping with her mood, Trudie stuck two cheese balls in her mouth—one into each cheek—knowing but not caring that she looked like a greedy little chipmunk. Then she made big cud-like chews as she felt a philosophical moment coming on. Why was it that handsome people were so prone to intermarry? She guessed they didn't like to contaminate the gene pool with plainness.

She remembered the social game in high school as well. There was always one exception to the rules—when the beautiful people made a gesture of benevolence to one ugly person. That one lucky person would have the privilege of hanging out with them—to live in the shadow of their luster. Everyone got something out of the deal. The homely person was grateful for all the unmerited attention, and the beautiful people got a human reminder of how beautiful they really were just in case they were to forget.

Trudie gnawed on a chocolate-covered strawberry. At various times, both she and Lane knew what it felt like to be the token ugly person.

ANITA HIGMAN

And it hadn't been nice. All those feelings flooded back as she watched the female sparklers firing off around Mason. Actually, it was a whole fireworks spectacular, and once again, she was merely a spectator.

Feeling hurt and a bit swinish, Trudie crammed a big round cracker in her mouth as she continued to torture herself by watching the women tease and touch Mason. There was an art to the way beautiful people moved and mingled. *Face it, Trudie. He's Everest, and you're the ant mound at the foot of his summit. And you will be forever trampled.* She knew she might look flashy at the moment, but at the end of the day after the cleverly contoured makeup was washed off and the stylish clothes were removed, she was still Trudie. Just Trudie— plain and simple.

If only I could disappear. She really wanted to escape inside one of her paintings, but that was impossible. Or maybe she could hide under the food table, but it would look far from professional. She needed to be a big girl now. Lane would say, "Straighten those shoulders, tuck in those buttocks, and glide forth with confidence!"

Trudie heard soft smacking noises next to her and turned. "Lily?"

"Hi. I didn't want to say anything. I was afraid I'd scare you, and you'd drop your plate of food. I tend to do that at parties." Lily took a nibble of her cheese.

"Thank you for coming." Trudie wished Lily weren't so nice. Then she wouldn't be forced to like her. It's just that it was hard being around yet another person who was so well-made and well-endowed, and well everything.

"Mr. Wimberley insisted that I come." Lily blew out some air, making her lips flap. "I didn't mean that in a bad way. I would have come anyway. That's why parties make me nervous. No matter how hard I try I don't know what to say."

"I'm not offended, Lily. You're doing just fine."

"It's so much easier at work. I can just repeat the same thing everyday." Lily's plate shimmied a bit.

"I'm glad you're here." Trudie smiled at her.

"Thanks." Lily stared across the room. "I see Mason is surrounded again."

"You said *again*?"

"I'm used to it. Mason attracts women. They just adore him. Who can blame them? He's the nicest man I've ever met, and he resembles that movie star...what's his name?"

"Brandon Routh?"

"Yes, but when he turns just right, he also looks a little like Hugh Jackman."

Come to think of it, maybe Mason looked a little like Hugh as well. Trudie sighed—a sigh that could have shaken the earth. "So, are you interested...in Hugh?" Once again she felt herself being catapulted into some kind of emotional garbage bin.

"Oh, no. I mean, at first I thought I was. But now I just admire Mr. Wimberley."

Well, that was at least one less female to fight off. "So, what changed your mind?"

Lily did a shy kind of shrug. "He's not the one for me. There has to be a bond that's kind of like superglue." She pressed two fingers together. "One time I accidentally superglued my fingers, and it was painful to try and get them apart. I didn't have any of that remover stuff." She chuckled. "But that's the way love should be. Like superglue. Where it feels impossible to be apart from each other. Don't you think so?"

Very astute woman, that Lily. "You may have something there." Was that the way she was already feeling about Mason? Superglued? She knew the answer even before her mind had finished the question. She was falling in love with Mason. That was why everything mattered now. And why it bothered her so much that so many other women seemed to be dipping from the same bottle of superglue.

"But I know there is the perfect man out there for me...somewhere." Lily looked at Trudie. "I can just feel it. Right here." She touched her heart.

"I'm sure you're right. There is someone waiting for you." And somehow Trudie felt that what she was saying went beyond chitchat—that Lily was right.

Wiley strolled up to them. The moment he saw Lily's face, he became dreamy-eyed with a look of total rhapsody.

It was obviously the perfect moment for introductions, especially since it had previously crossed Trudie's mind that the two of them might hit it off. "Lily, I would like you to meet Wiley Flat. He co-owns the gallery. Wiley, this is Lily Larson. She works with Mason Wimberley."

Wiley flushed as red as Trudie had ever seen him. Like fuchsia. He opened his mouth to speak. No words came out.

Lily offered her tremulous hand to Wiley.

He took her hand in his as if he were touching a priceless work of art, and then he kissed it.

A second later, Lily did the fuchsia thing.

Hmm. Fascinating.

Wiley looked like he'd started to breathe again. "Well, I see you ladies have found something to amuse the palate." He looked at Trudie's plate. "Glad to see you with such a good appetite this evening, Trudie."

"Yes." She stared down at her heaping plate, smiled, and then popped a stuffed mushroom in her mouth.

Wiley turned his gaze back to Lily. "It looks like our caterer has put out quite a scrumptious feast this evening."

"Yes, it is. It was, that is. I already ate most of mine." Lily set her plate down on a waiter's empty tray.

Wiley had not only resumed his breathing, but he'd taken so many gulps of air in the course of observing Lily's beauty, he looked fearfully close to hyperventilation.

Trudie already knew what he was thinking—that Lily was a goddess in the flesh. A living work of art. And *that* she was.

"I love your hair." Lily gave Wiley another one of her shy shrugs. "Ponytails are so manly and becoming, Well, that is, on the *right* man."

Wiley chuckled as if she'd said the wittiest thing he'd ever heard. "Lily, I would love to show you the rest of the gallery, if you'd like to see it."

"Perf," she squealed softly. "I mean I'd like that. Very much." Lily hiccupped with a gasp—a female gesture that only one woman in a million could pull off.

Wiley offered his arm, and Lily wrapped both arms around his. Tightly.

But just before taking off, Wiley leaned over to Trudie and whispered in her ear, "Thank you for bringing me my bride."

Trudie blinked. Surely he was jesting. But then one never knew with Wiley. As he left she heard him ask Lily, "Do you like protein bars?" Trudie almost burst out laughing but held it in as she watched them go off together to a secluded part of the gallery. Soon their heads were almost touching. Perhaps even superglued together. Guess Wiley found someone else to tell all his secrets to. Good for Wiley. He deserved to fall in love. Romance was apparently in the air, but Trudie felt like she was wearing an invisible gas mask.

After a brief pause of contemplation, she heard a familiar voice caress the air. "I *love* the way you paint, Trudie Abernathy." *Mason?*

Chapter Forty

....

The moment Trudie turned toward Mason, his breath caught in his throat. He barely recognized her. She had on an amazing black dress and was looking even prettier than before, if that were possible. "You look... look wonderful." *Did I just stutter? Oh, brother.* He hadn't stuttered since grade school.

Trudie tapped her shoes together like Dorothy in *The Wizard of Oz.* "Lane's work in progress again."

"I don't think so." Mason shook his head. "I'm looking at a masterpiece."

"Thank you." Trudie blushed, which made her even prettier. "I was so afraid."

Mason took a step closer to her. "And what were you afraid of?"

"Well, of pretty much everything. But one at the top of my list was that you'd regret buying me the art studio. That is, if you didn't like my work. You know, little terrors like that."

Mason leaned toward her. "No need for terrors of any kind tonight. Everything I've seen...I've loved." He caught her gaze. "But I was hoping for a private tour sometime this evening."

"I would be happy to."

He grinned as he stared down at the heap of food on Trudie's plate. "That's quite a load you have there. You're making me hungry."

Trudie rolled her eyes. "I was having an odd moment."

Mason picked up a flute of something frothy and pink and took a sip. *Not bad.* "I looked for you earlier, but then I got waylaid by some strangers over there." He motioned in the direction of the women who were still gawking at him. Women he'd found most annoying as they tried clinging to him like cobwebs. He'd known women like those over the years, starting as early as junior high. They were only concerned with the outward appearance, and after a few minutes of visiting with them, they usually turned out to be as interesting as a stack of pencils—the unsharpened kind.

Trudie stared at her shoes again. She suddenly looked so timid.

Mason took another sip of his froufrou beverage. "Your sister was good enough to drive me into the city. My car broke down on Will Clayton Parkway. She saw me and stopped. I'm afraid Old Maggie finally breathed her last."

"I'm sorry." Trudie looked up at him. "I know you loved that car." She tilted her head. "So, will you feel obligated to buy something shiny and new?"

"No. What I had was just right for me." He hoped she would get his double meaning, and he hoped she would approve.

Trudie's shoulders seemed to finally relax. "Is everything going smoothly with your uncle Franklin buying the business?"

"Very smoothly. We've all been very pleased...my mother as well."

"I'm happy for you, Mason." Trudie touched his arm. "I really am."

"I'm happy for me, too. My uncle sort of saved my life. I would have tried to run the business, but I wouldn't have been very good at it. And I'm afraid it would have suffered for it." Mason picked up another drink and offered it to Trudie. "Would you like something to drink? To wash down all that food?" He grinned.

Trudie chuckled. "Yes, thanks." She set her plate down on a small table.

He handed her the flute. It was good to see her laugh again.

"By the way, thank you for the music and the dedication on the radio. It was such a surprise. A pleasant one. And, well...unforgettable." She took a sip from the glass.

"It was my pleasure." This time he touched Trudie's arm. Then he looked out over the gallery, which was really filling up. He took note of Lane, who was standing across the room. She suddenly looked as though she were having the time of her life. "By the way, Lane went off captivated with your watercolors. But at the moment it looks like something else has captured her attention." Something Mason was happy to see.

"Oh?" Trudie stepped forward, looking across the room. "It's Hayden. He's come." Her words came out as if a great quest had just been fulfilled.

"And who might Hayden be?"

Trudie looked at Mason. "Hayden was Lane's first great love. He's come back searching for her." She smiled. "And it looks like he's finally found her."

"Oh, really." *What impeccable timing.* Mason stared at the man with benevolence. From the looks of it, their relationship was taking up right where they'd left off. Hayden removed his cowboy hat and was doing the thing that men always did when they were really interested in a woman. He was trying to be ultra charming, and Lane appeared to be doing that giggling thing that women did in return when it was working. So, Mason thought he might be watching the greatest of miracles unfolding.

Trudie turned to him, and they smiled simultaneously. Perhaps they were having simultaneous thoughts too. Just as he was about to ask her for that private tour again, a stranger walked up to them. Or perhaps barreled over was a better description.

"It's Trudie, Trudie, Trudie," the woman said.

"Rosalie, I'm so glad you came." Trudie gave the woman a hug.

"Sweets, I'm sooo proud of you. Couldn't be prouder even if you were my own daughter." The woman named Rosalie jiggled Trudie's shoulders. "Mm, mm."

"Thanks. Rosalie, I'd like you to meet Mason Wimberley. And, Mason, this is my employer, Rosalie—"

"Oh, yes, Bloomers, right?" Mason shook her outstretched hand.

"That's me." Rosalie raised a painted eyebrow and flicked at the feather in her hat. "Now you wouldn't happen to be the man that bought Trudie those pretty—"

They were interrupted by yet another woman. There were more introductions to an anomalous-looking woman named Kat, who was as thin as his laptop and had a cooing, breathy voice.

Kat turned to Trudie. "Now you must mingle. I've seen you cowering over here in the corner, stuffing yourself. But, Mason, we mustn't allow her to do that. She needs to embrace the moment. But before you do that, we have a large crowd now, so you'll need to say a few words."

"A few words?" Trudie seemed to go a little pale. "But I'm not a public speaker. I get all dizzy just thinking—"

"Upp." Kat put up her hand, stopping Trudie's objections. "You don't have to be a public speaker. Just say a few words."

"Like what?" Trudie licked her lips.

"You know, thank the people who've helped you. And the artists who've influenced you. The masters. That sort of thing." Kat linked arms with her.

Mason felt sorry for Trudie. She looked rather pasty, like she might pass out. He leaned over to her. "You'll do great. It'll be okay."

"Oh?" Trudie looked up at him. "You think so?"

Mason nodded. "I know so."

"Go get 'em, girl." Rosalie lifted the drink out of Trudie's hands.

Kat gently pulled Trudie toward the little platform in the center of the room and took the mike. "Ladies and gentleman, may I have your attention please." She waited for a moment while the people gathered and settled down from their chatter. "Welcome this evening to the Flat Stone Gallery. We're featuring a new artist whom I was fortunate enough to discover recently." Kat raised her chin and spread her arms. "Her work is fresh and vivid and it transports us from the mundane to a planet yet unknown to us. So, I invite you this evening to discover this new world through the eyes of Ms. Abernathy and the exhibition entitled 'The Electric Palette.'"

Mason noticed that Trudie had a look of astonishment. He'd be certain to ask her about that later.

"And now our artist has a few words for us. Please help me welcome Trudie Abernathy." Kat moved away from the mike as she clapped.

Applause rose and fell as Trudie stepped up to the mike, looking pale but determined.

"Good evening." The mike squealed, making Trudie step back a bit. "Oh, dear. Excuse me. Don't you just hate that?" She grinned, looking flustered. "First, I want to thank each of you for coming this evening. I am honored to be here...to have my work shown in such a stunning and prominent gallery."

Trudie smiled, looking over the crowd. "To be honest, it's a dream I didn't even have the courage to hope for. But I'm here, so that means there are people who dared to dream for me. A heart full of gratitude goes to my sister, Lane. We've been on quite a journey together, and she has proven to me over and over that she is the most generous and beautiful woman I've ever known, outside *and* inside. I'm fortunate to call her my sister and my friend. And she's also the best image coach in the city, so I hope you'll pick up one of her business cards before you leave."

Chuckles flowed through the crowd.

Mason noticed that Trudie looked right at Lane, whose face radiated love back to her sister. Lane was holding the arm of Hayden, who seemed more than happy to have her clinging to him. Mason was happy for Lane, but what had been equally comforting was that even before Hayden's appearance, Lane had assured him all was well.

Trudie then turned to look at him. "And deep appreciation goes to Mason Wimberley, who had an entire art studio delivered to my home.

He performed this act of generosity when I was still far from believing in my abilities. But he already had the faith. Thank you, Mason. Words will never fully express the gratitude I have in my heart."

Mason gave her a warm smile.

"And I'd like to extend my appreciation to so many others. Wiley Flat, who dropped into my life as a serendipity. Thank you for seeing the artist's zeal in my eyes when I'd denied it for so long. And also to Kat Stone for this wonderful exhibition and evening."

Trudie paused, but Mason noticed she no longer looked nervous. She looked contented and poised. And he'd never been happier for anyone in his life.

She took the mike from its stand and held it. "I have to say that my greatest influence didn't come from any of the great painters through history, but from a young man named Cyrus, who is with us this evening. He reminded me that art is not just about perfection. It's about fun, too. Thank you, Cyrus."

Trudie saluted an African-American boy in the crowd, and he waved back at her. "You know, I've also discovered that art has such a wonderful capacity to connect people. When words aren't enough, we can let art speak for us. It can express our grief, our joy, our triumph. It can celebrate our finest moment and share our darkest hour. It is the beauty and drama and secret yearnings of life...all unveiled in those impressions of light and color. I never knew how much I'd missed it until the love of art found me again. In my concluding words...and honestly, I didn't even think I'd have *any* words."

Laughter rose and fell again.

Trudie chuckled with them. "More than anything, I want to say that if you enjoy my work this evening and if you come to think I have any talent at all... then I want to recognize the Giver of those gifts. The Master Artist. Where all vision and design comes from." She pointed upward and smiled. "Thank you."

The stillness was replaced by a thundering applause. Trudie returned the mike to its stand and stepped off the stage. Her friends gathered around her, hugging and cheering her.

Mason stepped back, watching Trudie. It was a moment to be remembered always—one to be passed down to children and grandchildren. Now all he needed was the love of his life. Mason smiled, knowing he was looking right at her.

Chapter Forty-one

....

Hayden opened the front door of the gallery for Lane, and together they entered the warm night air. "I'm sure you're pleased for your sister. She's a fine artist."

"Yes, she is." Lane smiled at him, still trying to take him in. "Tonight was wonderful for her." *And wonderful for me, too.*

Hayden paused in the parking lot. "I've really enjoyed seeing you again."

"It's been great to see you, too." Lane looked at Hayden to make certain he hadn't vanished. He seemed like such a phantom the way he appeared just after she'd thought about him.

"Would you like some coffee?" Hayden pointed to his left. "There's a Starbucks right over there."

Lane followed his gaze and saw the coffee house nearby. "Yes, I'd really like that." She circled his arm, and they strolled across the parking lot.

"This year was my first time to go to the high school reunion." Hayden glanced over at her. "I was disappointed not to see you there."

"It's nice to be missed, but I didn't really feel up to it this year. So many people." Lane breathed in the moist air.

"Now, that doesn't sound like the Lane I always knew." Hayden grinned. "I thought you loved crowds. Thrived on them."

Lane chuckled. "Well, I still do. But this year was different. I guess you could say I was in a meditative state of mind."

"Oh, one of those." Hayden opened the door to Starbucks, and they went inside. "I know how that feels. More than you know." He removed his hat.

While Lane wondered about Hayden's remark, they were greeted with the intoxicating aroma of gourmet coffee and the happy noises of people getting exactly what they'd come for—good coffee and a pleasant place to spend an hour.

They ordered and then settled themselves in the back room. Hayden set his cowboy hat on one of the chairs. Funny how she'd never liked the cowboy look—except on Hayden. On him, it suited him well. It wasn't phony or over-the-top. It was just pure Hayden, and she loved it.

Lane took a sip of her soy latte. "So, would you like to tell me about those reflective moments you've been having?"

"Well, it was some of those moments that brought me back to you." Hayden looked at her.

"Oh, I see." Lane felt her face warm. His response was a surprise. She hadn't even known he was thinking of her.

"So, I'm a big advocate of reflection." Hayden grinned. "Should have done more of it years ago instead of all that football."

Lane leaned forward with genuine interest. "So, you never married?"

"I came close once. We were engaged. But it didn't work out."

"Oh? What happened?" She lifted her hand. "I'm sorry. That's really none of my business."

"No, it's all right. I don't mind talking about it." Hayden took a sip from his cup. "The short version of the story is that...I found out my fiancée was already married."

Lane's hand rested over her heart. "Oh, no."

"I was blind."

"I guess we've all had our turns at that."

Hayden laced his fingers on the table. "Yes, but it seems like I'm making a lifetime habit of it."

"I'm sure that can't be true."

His brows furrowed. "It sure feels that way sometimes." Hayden's expression softened. "By the way, do you happen to remember that evening we went bowling?"

"Yes, I do remember that." Flashes from the evening came back to her. "As I recall, I was terrible at it. I'm sure I was the worst bowler in history, and you, I'm sorry to say, sprained your ankle trying to impress me with your ballerina-like maneuvers."

He laughed. "Yeah, it was a pretty crazy night."

Lane finally let her body relax. "What made you think of it?"

"Well, it was the night I'd planned on proposing to you."

Hayden had definitely gotten her attention. "I never knew."

He leaned towards her.

"What changed your mind?" Lane hated to come off too pushy with her questions, but she had to know. "Were you scared?"

"No, not really." Hayden rubbed his neck. "As I'm sure you remember, I grew up pretty poor. And, well, my father made me promise I'd make something of myself. He'd wanted me to concentrate on my education and then find a career that would make a lot of money."

"And that's what you did." Lane felt her words escape more as a confirmation than a judgment. She too had made mistakes over the years and knew what it was like to not be paying attention to what was important.

"I got a degree in business, and I made the money my father always dreamed I'd make. But I pushed love aside for the making of money." He glanced away and his hands grasped the table as if in pain.

Lane felt sorry for him. Perhaps he truly regretted walking away from their relationship. All their hours of heart-sharing. Their laughter and their kisses. Memories of their joy came back to her along with the pain of losing him. When Hayden had stopped calling and she realized the relationship was truly over, she'd cried on and off for several months. Those thoughts returned now, but without the anger. Without the despair.

Hayden sighed. "The terrible irony was that the day I bought my parents a new home to replace that drafty little house they'd always lived in, my father up and died of a heart attack. Just like that. My mother lives in the house now, but my father never even got to see it."

"I'm so sorry." Lane reached out to him and touched his hand. "I had no idea that your father died." Why hadn't anyone told her?

He covered her hand with his. "It's been almost a year since he died."

"I wish I had been there for you."

Hayden squeezed her hand. "I know you would have come had you known." He paused for a moment and then said, "So, tell me about your life. I heard you didn't get married."

"No. Never did. About five years ago, though, the man I was dating did propose to me. But I couldn't marry him."

"I assume it wasn't because he was already married."

Lane chuckled. "No. I just didn't love him. And I've discovered that it takes both people participating in the whole love thing to make it work right." She grinned. "Imagine that." For a moment, Lane went quiet, wanting to enjoy the warmth and strength of his hand. His touch had not been forgotten, but it had been missed. And she hadn't realized how much until that moment.

Hayden caught her gaze. "But I also heard you've made a nice life for yourself. Being an image coach sounds like a good career choice for you."

"I do like it. I enjoy helping people make adjustments in the way they present themselves. And then when they reach a particular goal, it thrills me." Lane took another sip of her latte and realized her cup was almost empty. She hated for the evening to end. "So, did you move to Houston?"

"I did." Hayden set his cup aside. "And it's been good, but I've missed some of my old friends in Humble as well as the town. But most importantly, I've missed you."

"I've missed you, too."

"So, do you ever wonder about us? You know, what could have been?"

"Yes, I have wondered. Many times." Lane smiled.

"And what have you concluded?"

"That I don't want to spend the rest of my life without love... especially when it's so..." She wanted to say, "So close to me," but she hesitated, not wanting to be too bold. She looked into Hayden's sparkling gray eyes and saw the same qualities she'd grown to love—the same compassion and goodness that had first attracted her to him. It was all still there. Success had not changed him.

"I'm sorry I didn't stay in touch all these years. Another mistake on my part. But then after so much time went by, I thought maybe you'd gotten married. I imagined you with two children, a boy and a girl. And they would both be wonderful like their mother, and they'd both have great manners."

Lane chuckled. "That's nice."

Hayden looked at her, his expression filled with longing. "I wanted to ask you something else."

"Yes?" Lane took in a deep breath and held it.

"I was wondering if...if we could begin again."

Lane reached out to him. No more hesitation. "The answer is yes."

"Well, that is good news." Hayden's face brightened. "Very good news. So, do you think you might like to see a play downtown next weekend?"

"Yes, I would like that very much." She felt a smile coming on. He brought both of her hands to his lips and kissed them.

Lane thought she'd never felt so warm, and hope had never felt so good.

Chapter Forty-two
....

Trudie waited on the couch, dressed in her finest outfit, twiddling her fingers. She'd never been the kind of person to twiddle, but waiting for Mason to take her to his family reunion put her on edge. Even though Lane's coaching had made her more comfortable in her own skin, now that the official day had come to meet the rest of Mason's relatives, she felt that she might not only forget all the coaching, but that she might dissolve into a little puddle of panic.

The doorbell rang, making her jump. When she saw Mason standing on the welcome mat, some of her worries melted away. "Hi."

Mason grinned. "Are you ready? You look beautiful."

"I've been ready since ten this morning."

He chuckled. "Trudie, it'll be okay."

"But what if they all hate me?"

Mason pulled her into his arms. "They can't possibly. They have good taste like I do. And my mother already loves you."

"Really?"

"Really." He kissed the tip of her nose.

Mason had the most romantic way of disarming her. "All right. I surrender."

"Good. Let's go."

After locking up, Mason escorted her down the sidewalk. "Have I told you I like your car?"

He laughed. "Yeah, every time you ride in it." Mason opened the passenger door to his 1969 Corvette Stingray, and she got all snuggly in the seat.

Mason went around to the driver's side and scooted in next to her.

"It has such character." Trudie ran her hands along the seat. "Truly a classic."

"I couldn't agree more," Mason said as he looked right at her. "When I first saw it, I found it to be irresistible."

He had such an intense, romantic stare—like the one Clark Gable gave Vivian Lee in *Gone with the Wind*—Trudie could have melted right there in her little seat. But she refused to be dissolved so easily. "Yes, but sometimes there's such a thing as buyer's regret."

He shook his head. "None whatsoever. I'm holding onto this baby until I go to heaven." Mason leaned over and kissed her full on the mouth.

Okay. All right. Melting was now an option.

Chapter Forty-three
....

Mason pulled up to his mother's home and parked by the curb.

Trudie saw the house and gasped. "You grew up here?" She stared at the delicate adornments on the eaves and the dollhouse features.

"I most certainly did. What do you think?"

"I think it's amazing. I mean, who lives in a gingerbread house? Except in fairy tales." She turned to look at him. "You must have loved growing up in it."

Mason cocked his head. "Well, sometimes my brother and I got a ribbing or two on the bus from being picked up here. They used to call me Hansel."

"I hope they didn't call your brother Gretel."

"They did. But only once." Mason raised an eyebrow.

Trudie laughed.

"But I can appreciate the architecture. Especially since I no longer have to be picked up here on the school bus."

She grinned. "Did *both* your parents like the design?"

"Actually, it was Mother's idea, not my father's. After several years of marriage he told my mother that since his profession wouldn't be as easy on the family as other professions, to compensate, he wanted her to choose whatever house plan she liked."

"I wonder what made her choose something so whimsical."

"Well, you'll understand when you get to know her better." Mason slid out of the car and came around to open her door.

Trudie wondered what that comment might mean, but she didn't think negatively about it, since any woman who would choose to live in a gingerbread house had to be wonderful.

Mason helped her out, and they strolled along the curving stone path up to the round top front door. He lifted the doorknocker and gave the door a few hard raps.

Trudie half expected to see an elf or a hobbit greet them at the door.

Within seconds Mrs. Wimberly, a portly woman with a cherubic face, emerged from the house, throwing a tea towel over her shoulder and enveloping Trudie into her soft folds. "It's so lovely to see you again, Trudie. What a precious young woman you are."

"Thank you. It's good to see you again too, Mrs. Wimberley."

"Oh now, pish, posh. No formalities here. Please call me Mom. Come on in. My sisters have made enough to feed the whole town of Humble." She scurried inside, her tea towel swishing back and forth cheerfully.

As they followed her, Mason whispered to Trudie from behind. "See? She loves you already."

Trudie grinned, thinking of Mrs. Wimberley's kindness in letting her call her Mom, but not feeling altogether deserving of such an intimate gesture so soon. Mason's mother was indeed charming, though, like a loveable fairy godmother. All she lacked was the wand.

As they bustled through the house, Trudie tried to memorize every detail of the décor. The rooms were decorated with lots of overstuffed furniture and cozy-looking knickknacks. It was just what Trudie had expected from such a warm and welcoming lady. They stepped into the kitchen, which appeared to be the central hubbub of the house.

Within seconds Trudie was engulfed in relatives, mostly aunts of every shape and size, hugging her and generally loving on her.

Mason cleared his throat. "Ladies."

Everyone quieted down. "Everybody, this is Trudie Abernathy. Trudie, this is Aunt Lydia, Aunt Grace, Aunt Lorelei, and over there by the door is Aunt Beckie and Justina, who are the family's twins."

Mrs. Wimberley took hold of Trudie's arm. "I have five sisters and only two of us married, so I'm afraid our beloved Mason grew up in a world of women. Pity him, dear."

Trudie chuckled.

"No child was ever loved so much, though." Mason spread his palm over heart.

"Ahhhh," all the aunts sighed together.

Trudie smiled. Apparently Mason knew how to schmooze his aunts, and they adored him for it.

He stepped over to the big soup pot on the stove. "So, where's Uncle Franklin?"

"Oh, you know, he's always a little skittish when we all get together." Mrs. Wimberley pulled a pan of cornbread out of the oven. "I think he's hiding out somewhere. With so many hens in here, he probably thinks he'll get pecked."

Several of the aunts chuckled.

Trudie followed Mason over to the pot of soup that was bubbling on the stove. Whatever was cooking smelled heavenly. "May I help you with lunch?"

Mrs. Wimberley shooed them on. "No, dear, but thank you. I just want you to enjoy yourself."

Trudie looked into the huge pot. "Is this gumbo?"

"Gumbo Surprise," one of the twins said. "We start with a secret family recipe, but then each of us brings a surprise to put in the pot. So, the gumbo is a little different every time."

"But it's always good." Mrs. Wimberley wriggled her eyebrows. "Now, Mason, why don't you give Trudie a tour of the house while we finish up." She handed them cups of cocoa loaded with mini-marshmallows.

"Thank you." Trudie took a sip. Oh, the ladies knew how to make it right. "It's very good."

"Yes, it is." Mrs. Wimberley beamed. "But that isn't a secret family recipe. I just got it off the Internet."

Trudie laughed.

Mason turned to her and motioned to the hallway. "Shall we?"

"I'd love to see the rest of the house." Trudie circled her arm through his.

They went through a long hallway, and then Mason turned and headed into a large bedroom. "This was my room growing up."

Trudie set her cocoa down, bounced on the bed a little, and then went around to each item in the room, studying it. She pointed to the baseball trophy. "So you loved baseball?"

"I guess all boys do. What's not to love about it?"

Trudie touched the photo of Mason with his parents. They were all laughing. "I like this one."

Mason walked over to her and looked at the same photo. "That's one of my favorites."

"I can see why." She looked up at him. "I was wondering...how has your mom been since the funeral? She seems to be recovering well, but I know how people try to be strong for everyone else."

"She took it hard at first, but her sisters have stayed by her side constantly."

"I only have one sister, but I know how indispensable they can be."

Mason set his mug down on his desk. "And Dad told her he didn't want her to grieve too long. He said we'd all be together again someday, and that all would be well. And since she knows that to be true, her grief hasn't been overwhelming."

"I'm glad." Trudie gazed back at the wall. Among the family photos were some from high school. One picture in particular stood out— Mason was surrounded by a crowd of beautiful young cheerleaders. They were all either kissing his cheek or puckered up ready to do so.

Mason took the photo off the wall. "That one is my least favorite."

Another twinge of uncertainty rose in Trudie's heart. So many women. The world seemed to be full of beautiful women, and they were all in pursuit of Mason Wimberley!

"My brother put that on the wall, and I never had the heart to take it down since he was the one who put it there. It always made him chuckle." Mason slid the photo into the drawer.

Trudie touched his hand. "I would hate for you to put away a memory that's linked to your brother."

"Don't worry. I can put away this photo without putting away the memories of my brother." He shut the drawer and turned his gaze back to the wall of family photos.

Trudie wished now she'd kept her expressions in better check. Mason must have seen her twinge of pain. Perhaps he'd even seen a flash of jealousy. Someday she would need to talk to him about her concerns. But how would one say it? *You're too handsome for me?* She wasn't sure if she could spend her life watching women young and old drooling over him. Trudie knew she'd be lucky if gawking was all they were interested in doing. Some women would no doubt want more.

Like the women at the gallery. Trudie looked back at the wall of photos with Mason, but her mind continued to fret. Those women who'd surrounded Mason that evening at the gallery weren't interested in his views about art. Actually, they'd journeyed to the next level—the pawing mode. Perhaps at gatherings she would forever be shoved aside like an old shoe. Or maybe people would feel sorry for Mason for getting stuck with someone who wasn't quite up to par in the beauty department. There was indeed a pecking order when it came to attractiveness. The question was—could she deal with being substandard every day of their marriage?

Mason turned her around to face him and then lifted her chin. "You look deep in thought. And I don't think it has anything to do with family photos or baseball."

Trudie took in a deep breath and went over to sit on the bed. The time had come. "I guess we need to talk."

"Okay." Mason sat on the bed next to her.

"Well, I..." Trudie ran her hands along the soft bedcovers. "You know, I can't think straight when you sit next to me like that. You know, so close."

"I'm a good foot away from you."

"You're just too close...too gorgeous." Trudie blurted out the words before she'd filtered her comment.

Mason chuckled but didn't budge. "Thank you for the compliment, but why do you think I want to sit on the bed anyway?"

"Because your legs are tired?" Trudie knew her voice had gone weak as skim milk.

Mason shook his head. "No. It's because I want to be near you. *Very* near you. If we were married, we certainly wouldn't just be sitting on this bed."

Trudie felt her face go white-hot.

"My point is, don't you realize that whatever thoughts you've had along those lines, I've been thinking the same thing about you? I'm just as attracted to you as you are to me. Well, maybe a lot more."

Trudie puckered her brows. "Well, that thought certainly never crossed my mind."

Mason tossed his head back, laughing. "Now that *is* funny." He looked at her. "You're not laughing. But it is kind of funny that you can't see how you affect me."

She stared at her hands. "I guess I've seen some of it. Maybe. But I'm pretty faithful in not believing it."

Mason touched her wrist and then let his finger glide up to the inner curve of her arm. "Well, maybe you'd better start believing it."

Trudie tried to keep her cool, even though sirens had just gone off all over her body. She bolted off the bed and turned to look at him. "But you look like...you resemble..."

"Superman?"

She rolled her eyes. "See, even *you* knew about it."

Mason chuckled. "Not really. I've heard a few people say that over the years. I'm not sure I see what people are talking about, but even if it were true, what does it matter?"

"Those gallery women for one thing." She already sounded like a spurned woman. Not good. Trudie pulled out a desk chair and sat across from Mason. "You've already forgotten. It's because you're so used to it. But those women at the gallery...they were fondling you with their eyes."

"Fondling me with their eyes?" Mason covered his mouth, obviously trying to hide his amusement.

"With some pawing thrown in too."

"I haven't forgotten, Trudie." Mason frowned. "To be honest, one of those women invited me home with her."

"Really? Truly?" She moved her finger back and forth along the top of the chair as she thought about Mason's comment. "Wow, I wish I hadn't been so right."

"But I said no, and then I walked away." He made an open-handed gesture. "Please know that I'm not interested in any kind of short-term pleasure. I'm only interested in long-term joy."

"Okay." That certainly sounded chivalrous and exactly what a woman wanted to hear. "But what about your uncle buying the family business and all?"

"Yes?" Mason rose off the bed.

"Well, from what you told me, one of the reasons you hesitated in bringing women into your home office was because...well, you know... they couldn't quite deal with the idea of being the wife of a funeral director. That possibility is gone. You can now date any woman you want." Mist filled her eyes to think of it.

He walked over to her.

"Any woman in Humble or Houston." Trudie looked up at him.

He lifted her into his arms.

"Any woman in the whole state of Texas," Trudie added. "And maybe even—"

Mason kissed her then. And his message, though without words, was quite effective. He apparently didn't want to date any of those women. He wanted to date her.

While they kissed, Trudie could think of several more arguments, but they were all drifting away like petals in the breeze. She was helpless, and she knew it. In fact, she could feel herself falling so deeply in love that there could be no turning back.

When their kiss came to a satisfying close, Mason eased away. "You never have to worry about me not knowing what to do if women approach me inappropriately. I know how to handle women."

Trudie grinned. "Oh, you do, do you?"

Mason pursed his lips and nodded. "Yeah, pretty much." He broke out into a grin.

"Well, you did grow up in a world of women."

"It's true. And I know enough that if we don't show ourselves back in the kitchen soon, they're going to come after us." Mason handed Trudie her cup of cocoa and led her back through the hallway. When they reached the edge of the kitchen doorway, he stopped and whispered in her ear, "I thought you might need a reminder."

Trudie gave Mason a puzzled look. When she stepped into the kitchen, all the aunts were lined up facing her, and they were all wearing T-shirts, each with a big, bright rainbow splashed across the front. Sentiments of the sweetest kind swept over Trudie.

Mason's mom gave her a hug. "It is a happy day."

"It is indeed." Trudie hugged her back.

Chapter Forty-four
....

It was on a Saturday morning in early October when Trudie noticed something different about Mason. He seemed a little anxious. There'd been a quiver in his voice on the phone, and then when he'd picked her up for their outing, she'd seen a slight tremor in his hand on the steering wheel. What was going on? Nerves just weren't his style.

Since Trudie knew their plans were to play tourists all day, she felt certain there'd be plenty of time to find out what was wrong. They both walked into the visitors' center at Mercer Arboretum and Botanic Gardens, and then after signing in, they headed out into paradisiacal grounds. A cool front had passed through in the night, making the air dry and silky and creating what promised to be a spectacular autumn day.

Trudie's concerns about Mason seemed to temporarily fade as they strolled through the gardens. "I can't believe I've never seen this. Right here in Humble. Have you been here before?"

Mason didn't answer. His hands were stuffed in the pockets of his slacks, and he seemed lost in thought.

"Are you okay?" Trudie touched his sleeve.

"Sure. What do you mean?"

"Well, I asked you a question just now."

"I'm sorry." Mason looked at her.

"You seem anxious about something. Or maybe preoccupied."

"You're right. And I will tell you all about it. But first, let's enjoy this garden."

Okay, but leaving a big question mark in her head wasn't the best way for her to enjoy the day. *Give it up, Trudie.* Mason would talk about it in due time. She decided to go with the flow.

Mason took hold of her hand, and together they walked through the garden. They saw an impressive array of plants and trees, some that were exotic like the Australian bunya pine, and others that were more common like the camellias, hibiscus, and zinnias. When the morning was spent and they'd hiked the trails and enjoyed the splendor of the gardens, Mason suggested they sit on one of the wooden benches to talk.

He seems so serious. Trudie sat down next to him and looked up. The sun filtered through the trees, giving the light a dappled effect, which was both enchanting and calming. She straightened her shoulders, readying herself for what she thought might be bad news.

Mason reached out and touched her cheek. "Did you have a good morning?"

"The very best." She took his hand and kissed it. "I just want you to know that whatever is troubling you, well, I'm here for you."

Mason smiled. "There has been something on my mind. Something I've needed to talk to you about."

Trudie released her hold on his hand and waited for Mason to continue.

Instead of speaking, he looked down at the walkway where a box turtle was making its way across the path. "I used to have one of those when I was a kid."

"I did too...when we lived on the farm."

"I've always liked box turtles." Mason smiled. "They make good pets, although I discovered at an early age that they don't give hugs very well."

Trudie laughed. "True."

"You know I never understood why they were called *box* turtles.

They aren't really in the shape of a box." Mason rested his arms across the back of the bench.

"I have no idea either." Trudie enjoyed reminiscing about reptiles but wondered why Mason was avoiding what he really wanted to talk about.

"Because I certainly do know the shape of a box. You know, it's like a cube. And it usually has a lid." Mason pulled something out of his pocket. "Kind of like this one." He held the tiny box in front of her. "Only this box has a bow."

"What is this?" Trudie looked into his eyes for an answer.

"It's a cube with a lid." Mason handed the box to her. "Maybe you'd better see what's inside."

Surely it wasn't the obvious. Could it be? She lifted the lid and saw a black velvet box inside—a ring box. Maybe it was just a generic gift. She looked at Mason again, but he wasn't giving away any clues with his expression. Then she pulled out the velvet box and opened it. Her breath caught in her throat. "Is this a dinner ring?"

Mason shook his head. "No, darling." He leaned over, whispering in her ear. "It's an engagement ring."

She was almost afraid to touch it. "It's the most exquisite thing I've ever seen. Is it a pink diamond?"

He nodded. "From Tiffany's."

"You mean *the* Tiffany's?" She tried to absorb the news.

"Yes, *the* Tiffany's."

Trudie snapped the lid shut and glanced down at her jeans. She should have dressed up more, but even then, would she be worthy of such an elegant and life-changing gift? "How can I possibly accept such a luscious present?"

Mason wrapped his arm around her. "Because I love you."

She held the box tightly in her cupped hands. Life wasn't supposed to be so good—so fairy-tale like. "I have questions." Maybe instead of pelting Mason with queries, she should ask herself why she was determined to ruin such an idyllic moment. But Trudie had to ask, "Have you been acting anxiously because you were afraid of commitment?"

Mason chuckled as he raked his fingers through his hair. "No, not at all. Actually, I was afraid you'd say *no* to my proposal."

Trudie felt a smile teasing the corners of her lips. "Oh." She took in a deep breath and then let it out slowly, knowing she still had several eggs of uncertainty that needed hatching. "I have two more questions before I say yes."

"Okay. I'm ready for you."

She looked at him. "Why is it that you love me?"

Mason rubbed his chin. "Is this a test? I gotta tell you that except for math, I didn't do well on exams in school."

Trudie chuckled. "I'm sorry to torture you like this." She hugged her middle. "But I just want to know."

"Well, maybe it's dangerous to dissect love...too much."

"I don't understand."

Mason shifted in his seat. "Well, if I tell you that I love you for your art, what happens if you choose to stop painting? If I say I love you for your beautiful ivory skin, what if you go to one of those salons and get a tropical tan? Or if I love your humor and sense of wonder, then what if you lose those qualities someday? All I know is that until I met you I didn't even know I could love this much. You drew it out in me. Like a chemical bath developing a photo in a darkroom." He looked upward and cringed. "Hmm. I don't think that was the best example."

Trudie laughed. "I love your answer." She looked into his eyes. They were wonderful eyes of a golden brown hue, and they revealed honesty and tenderness and loyalty. And she would be a fool not to marry Mason.

"But I have one more question."

"I think my ego can handle one more." He grinned.

"You are a man without defects, and it scares me. It's intimidating. I have flaws. Big gaping ones that you can sail a boat through."

"Oh, yeah, like what?"

Trudie made little circles on her jeans with her finger. "Well, even though I have a history of pride, I am also full of self-esteem issues. Weird combo, huh? And sometimes it's hard for me to trust people. I tend to think the worst first, and then I gradually migrate to the positive."

"Like right now?"

Trudie nodded. "Like right now."

"Hey, you know, you're right. Those are some pretty big flaws." Mason puckered his face. "Do you think I should ask for my ring back?"

"No, I don't think you should." Trudie gave him a teasing punch. "And you didn't answer my question. I need shortcomings."

"Okay, got it." Mason took in a big breath and let it out. "You know, come to think of it, there is no downside to marrying me. I guess you're right. I *am* perfect."

Trudie chuckled.

"All right, here's one that's truly disgusting. I'm not only addicted to mac and cheese, but I eat bean burritos in bed while I watch baseball. And I won't be able to give up the habit even after we're married, in spite of the obvious romantic drawbacks."

Trudie laughed. "I can tolerate baseball just fine, and I adore bean burritos. Especially the fatty kind made with lots of lard."

"Okay, here's another one." He crossed his arms. "I'm a real oaf sometimes, which is another reason I hired your sister for some image coaching sessions."

"I've never seen you be a klutz once. Okay, well, maybe I saw you trip over the welcome mat at my apartment one time. But that was more of a lurch than a real stumble. Actually, you're the most genteel man I've ever known, so you'll have to do better than that." Trudie made a little check mark in the air. "Next."

"Hmm. Well, since the first grade I've had a fear of rats. When I was five, a rat lunged at me from the woodpile and then chased me a good two miles."

Trudie laughed.

"So throughout our married life, if we ever encounter rats, you'll have to be the macho one to deal with them." Mason shook his head as if he'd told her a dark truth from his past.

"I think I can handle that, since I had a pet mouse when I was a kid."

Mason shuddered.

"I'm still wholly unimpressed with your imperfections. Why don't you dazzle me with some real deficiencies?"

Mason looked down at his hands. "I guess you should know that even though you think I look like a superhero, I'm not, Trudie. I'm not at all." He took her hand in his. "But I *am* a man very much in love."

"And I'm a woman very much in love." Trudie scooted closer to him. "The answer is yes." She handed him the velvet box. "And I am more than ready for you to place that ring on my finger."

Mason took the ring out of the box and slipped it on her finger.

Trudie looked at the ring—a pink diamond—the color of seashells and nymphs, and blushing brides-to-be. She felt God smiling then, and the truth was, He'd always been smiling on her. He'd always loved her. The sun burst through a bank of clouds, and that sense of time passing came to her again, but the seasons no longer seemed to be rushing past her. She felt herself living inside them, falling into the rhythm of her life. Was she using the minutes and the decades wisely? With her all heart, she hoped so.

Trudie reached up and gently turned Mason's face toward hers. "And now...I think this would be a very good time for us to make some rainbows."

And Mason did just that.

Chapter Forty-five

....

Months later—on St. Valentine's Day—Trudie stood at the back of the stone chapel, ready to take her first steps as a bride. The wedding planner lifted the delicate veil over Trudie's face, smoothed her long train, and then gave her an encouraging wink. "Are you ready?"

"I am." Trudie waited for the music to signal her entrance. She glanced down at her billowy gown. She hadn't selected traditional white but the palest pink to match the engagement ring that Mason had given her from Tiffany's. And match it did, along with her cascading bouquet of peonies.

Trudie took in a deep breath. *What a day.* Drenched in the color of heaven—a hue unfamiliar to her—but she knew the angels were surely wearing it, and they too were celebrating. Yes, one could almost hear the angels singing.

The string quartet began to play Pachelbel's Canon, and the guests rose with a soft swishing thunder. Trudie's heartbeat quickened. Bits of life's happiest moments came to her then—whispers of compassion, songs of worship, the bright eyes of children, sunbursts and candlelight, and the champagne laughter of lovers. So many gifts. She looked upward, breathed a prayer of thanksgiving, and began her walk up the aisle.

Trudie continued her slow and steady steps as she noticed all the nods of joy coming from so many who wished them well. Light streamed in through the stained glass windows in glittering rays of colored light, reminding her of the kaleidoscope that she and Lane had always viewed in different ways. Perhaps in the end they had both been right. Life was a collage of pretty pictures as well as a thousand shattered moments. But

God brought marvel to it all as He took those broken pieces and, with the light of His grace shining through them, made something beautiful, something treasured.

Trudie looked toward the front of the church at her waiting groom. Mason looked so handsome—so full of love. It was a day made of all things good and all things lovely. A day made unforgettable.

POST CARD
CARTE POSTALE
Love Finds You

Want a peek into local American life—past and present?
The *Love Finds You*™ series published by Summerside Press
features real towns and combines travel, romance,
and faith in one irresistible package!

The novels in the series—uniquely titled after American towns with unusual but intriguing names—inspire romance and fun. Each fictional story draws on the compelling history or the unique character of a real place. Stories center on romances kindled in small towns, old loves lost and found again on the high plains, and new loves discovered at exciting vacation getaways. Summerside Press plans to publish at least one novel set in each of the 50 states. Be sure to catch them all!

Now Available in Stores

Love Finds You in Miracle, Kentucky by Andrea Boeshaar
ISBN: 978-1-934770-37-5

Love Finds You in Snowball, Arkansas by Sandra D. Bricker
ISBN: 978-1-934770-45-0

Love Finds You in Romeo, Colorado by Gwen Ford Faulkenberry
ISBN: 978-1-934770-46-7

Love Finds You in Valentine, Nebraska by Irene Brand
ISBN: 978-1-934770-38-2

Love Finds You in Humble, Texas by Anita Higman
ISBN: 978-1-934770-61-0

Love Finds You in Last Chance, California by Miralee Ferrell
ISBN: 978-1-934770-39-9

Love Finds You in Maiden, North Carolina by Tamela Hancock Murray
ISBN: 978-1-934770-65-8

Love Finds You in Paradise, Pennsylvania by Loree Lough
ISBN: 978-1-934770-66-5

Love Finds You in Treasure Island, Florida by Debby Mayne
ISBN: 978-1-934770-80-1

Love Finds You in Liberty, Indiana, by Melanie Dobson
ISBN: 978-1-934770-74-0

Love Finds You in Poetry, Texas by Janice Hanna
ISBN: 978-1-935416-16-6

Love Finds You in Revenge, Ohio by Lisa Harris
ISBN: 978-1-934770-81-8

COMING SOON

Love Finds You in Sisters, Oregon by Melody Carlson
ISBN: 978-1-935416-18-0

Love Finds You in Charm, Ohio by Annalisa Daughety
ISBN: 978-1-935416-17-3

Love Finds You in Bethlehem, New Hampshire by Lauralee Bliss
ISBN: 978-1-935416-20-3

Love Finds You in North Pole, Alaska by Loree Lough
ISBN: 978-1-935416-19-7

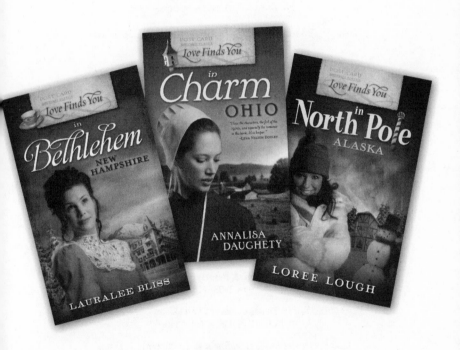

summerside
PRESS